LEAVING
WISDOM

LEAVING
WISDOM

SHARON BUTALA

Thistledown
Press

Thistledown Press Ltd.
Unit 222, 220 20th Street W
Saskatoon, SK S7M 0W9
www.thistledownpress.com

Library and Archives Canada Cataloguing in Publication

Title: Leaving wisdom : a novel / Sharon Butala.
Names: Butala, Sharon, 1940– author.
Identifiers: Canadiana 20220493596 | ISBN 9781771872362 (softcover)
Subjects: LCGFT: Novels.
Classification: LCC PS8553.U6967 L43 2023 | DDC C813/.54—dc23

Cover and book design by Tania Craan
Cover images from Stocksy and Unsplash
Author photograph by Jennifer Chipperfield
Printed and bound in Canada

Thistledown Press gratefully acknowledges the financial assistance of The Canada Council for the Arts, SK Arts, and the Government of Canada for its publishing program.

In memory of Hazel
And for
Nikki

CONTENTS

PART I
WISDOM

CHAPTER ONE

CONCUSSION

At first she heard nothing at all, only perfect silence, even while flesh-coloured orbs slowly materialized, wavy and dim, before her unblinking gaze. It took a second before they became faces, and another second or two — as she tried to rise and Adrianna tried to help her, while others, their voices fraught whispers in the frigid air, told her to lie still — before a cacophonous roaring began in her head that settled into a whistle and then began to swirl and pulse rhythmically at the same time as Adrianna said "Judith" several times — was she talking into her cellphone? — as hard, dry snowflakes struck and moved away, and the wind that surely accounted for the racket in her head got louder, and a young man fiddled with gadgets he was trying to attach to her while speaking briskly in some brand new language into his shoulder. Of the noise in her head, she thought, *It is like static on a broken television*, while her current, local brain reverted to report-writing: *Mrs. Aziz, a slightly obese, short woman of thirty-eight with four children and a good command of English*, and her shadowy larger mind that was equally herself, or was a bigger self, observed it all rather as though she were an actor in a film being watched by the omnipotent audience, only she herself was also the audience.

Without love, what is the world?

She had read that somewhere, although she had no idea where, nor did she know what it meant. But it would not leave her, and for all the next days and nights, as she ranted, babbled, remembered, forgot, saw things that weren't there, or saw two of things that were, it remained in her head as if God wanted her to know this question, to never forget it, even though what it meant was, to her, perfectly nothing.

The next thing she would remember in the years to come was the sight of two of her four daughters gazing at her from the foot of the bed she was unaccountably lying in: blonde, blue-eyed Catherine's expression quizzical, faintly annoyed; Jessica's carefully neutral, but with a touch of something she couldn't then quite identify — questioning? sympathizing? — widening her dark eyes. For an instant she puzzled over how she had produced daughters so different; then she remembered — different fathers — and it was as if something miraculous had risen into view. She would remember how she laughed out loud then, in wonder.

But she had two more daughters. Where were they? She couldn't recall their names, a fact that didn't bother her, although she suspected it should.

"We're taking you home today," Catherine said in her familiar no-nonsense tone. Judith noticed then the wheelchair by her bed, the clothes laid across the bed's foot, the nurse hovering impatiently at the door.

"Where the hell am I?" she asked, using her elbows to try to push herself upright. As the girls opened their mouths in unison to explain, she said, "Oh, never mind. This is a hospital. I can see that." The nurse stepped forward, brushing along the bed to look directly down on Judith's face. *Alice and Lucy?*

"Yes, hospital," she said, smiling professionally and reaching for Judith's wrist, which Judith irritably pulled away.

"Now let's get this straight," Judith said, as if addressing a recalcitrant client of whom she had always had far too many — especially the teenagers — then stopped mid-sentence. Get what straight?

"You don't remember?" the nurse asked. Her skin had the glow of dark honey and seemed to give off light.

"What?" Judith said, but she gazed into space, frowning, lifting one hand to the back of her head, encountering some odd-feeling thing there, and dropping it as pictures passed in front of her of which she could make little to no sense. Noise — a siren, maybe? Faces peering at her. That foul taste in her mouth.

"Gilles — is he coming?" Her daughters exchanged glances. "To take me home." But — Gilles, who is he, exactly? She tried to shake her head to clear her confusion, but pain struck with such intense precision she gasped and froze.

Jessica spoke. "Gilles was here yesterday, Mom. He came before too, as soon as Cathy called him." She came up the other side of the bed to stand opposite the nurse. "We talked about this yesterday. I guess you don't quite remember yet." She lifted her mother's other hand to hold it in both of hers, at which Judith didn't protest. "You had a fall — on the ice — on the sidewalk — on the way to your retirement lunch. Adrianna called the ambulance." Adrianna? Oh, her co-worker at the Department of Social — something — Services: short, dark, once beautiful, now a little worn looking. Who wouldn't be?

"You hit your head. Hard. You had a concussion." This was from Catherine, as usual trying to rush things along.

"Well, I don't remember that," Judith said dubiously, as if they were trying to put something past her. "I've been here a while, haven't I?"

"Two weeks," Catherine answered. At this, Judith, who had been trying to sit up, fell back against the pillows.

"Amazing," she said. "Simply amazing — that I don't remember a thing." Yet how bright everything was, such perfect edges everywhere, the colours scintillating in their purity.

"It will come back," the nurse assured her. "Or not. Either way it's not something to worry about. We just have to worry about getting you well. We think you will do better in your own home now."

"You're outta here, Mom," Jessica said, grinning, but Judith was still wrestling with . . . what?

"Alice is in Africa, right?" The daughters nodded in unison. "And Lucinda . . .?"

"In Israel," they said, both at once. "And doing very well," Jessica added.

At this, Judith saw her own hand, a distant, pale fish swimming the air nonchalantly, at the same time as she heard herself mutter, "When has Lucinda ever been doing very well." Not a question. "So, you see?" she continued, "It's coming back already. I have four daughters. My name is Judith Clemensen — no wait — I seem to remember . . ."

"You've been going by Dad's name," Catherine instructed her. "My father, I mean, Horvat. But you said when you retired you would go back to Clemensen, so we called you Mrs. Clemensen-Horvat because we weren't sure . . ." She looks embarrassed, and well she should, Judith thinks, she's a bloody lawyer, and is pleased with herself because — whatever. But what was Jess's last name? It was . . . it was . . . Stratton. Jack Stratton, Jessica Stratton. Alice Stratton. I was, first, Mrs. Stratton. This was too off-puttingly strange.

"Okay, get me outta here, whoever I am." She had meant to be funny, but there was a terrifying second when she didn't know the answer, found herself floating free in a sea of meaninglessness she had discovered just back of language. Frantic, she floundered for meaning, failed, and finally, out of sheer throat-seizing terror, seized on names: Clemensen, Stratton, Horvat. Clemensen. Judith Clemensen. This answer didn't feel right, but the panic at not knowing *who she was* dwindled and almost disappeared.

In Catherine's car, Judith began to cry. She couldn't say why, but everything — by which she seemed to mean her sore head, the strangeness of everything outside the car's windows, the sensation of being not quite inside her own self but watching herself from a nearby vantage point, the sensation of that outer person thinking the inner person's thoughts, and because of whatever it was that happened to her that must have been pretty awful but she didn't know exactly what it was, and, as they passed snowbank after snowbank, how she hated winter.

Jessica, seated beside her in the back seat, moved her body up against her mother's and put one hand against her mother's cheek, and, oddly, the pure physicality of her touch brought Judith, at least for the moment, back into her own body. Then she could feel the tires fighting the icy ruts, how they were anchored to the ground after all.

A small, neatly dressed Filipina she had never seen before stood back, smiling nervously and holding open the door, as they entered Judith's condo. She had only a second to register that her place, too, looked strange. Some of the furniture was missing, the overflowing magazine rack that stood beside the armchair was gone, the end tables were pushed back against the wall, and the coffee table was sitting against the glass door that led onto the snow-covered balcony, replaced at the sofa by a moveable, over-bed hospital table. This was all so puzzling that Judith found herself unable to object, if objecting was the appropriate response. Already discombobulated, having caught a glimpse of a face in the ornately framed mirror in the foyer, about the only thing left from her marriage to Victor, the image in it that of an old woman with ragged grey hair . . .

"This is Mrs. Salazar."

"My hair," she whispered.

Catherine whispered back, "The nurses had to cut it."

"Rosaria, please," the small stranger said, broadening her smile, creating dimples so that Judith, without considering, smiled back.

"For the surgery," Jessica said in a normal voice on Judith's other side.

"If I am to call you Rosaria, then you must call me Judith." She was surprised, as if her social self, so carefully honed over her sixty-five years, seemed now to be capable of running entirely on its own.

"If you please," Rosaria replied abruptly. She roused herself, took one step to the sofa — it was a very small condo — where she, or someone, had arranged the colourfully embroidered, if threadbare, cushions to support Judith's back.

Tentatively, she sat down on the sofa just as a roaring headache hit her. She turned sideways, put her back against the pillows, and was straining to lift her legs onto the sofa when she felt someone doing it for her. Through moving slats of light and dark she saw it was Jessica, her dark hair swaying. Pills appeared before her in a cupped hand she didn't recognize, a glass of water appeared in another. The manicure said it was Catherine's.

She was retching now. More hands helped to move her back into a sitting position; the too-large metal bowl she used to mix salads in for long-defunct family dinners rested on her lap, and she vomited into it, losing at once the much-needed pills.

The days went by, only three or so Rosaria told her, or did she say five? It seemed both longer and shorter a time to Judith, and yet, she had to admit it, with each passing day she was beginning to feel more herself — aside from the steady headaches, sometimes worse, sometimes better, and the accompanying nausea and vision blurring or doubling. The perception of watching herself from somewhere distant was also subsiding, at least part of the time, but the more worrying sense of not being herself would not go away. Sometimes it made her feel hopeful, as if at last she was getting that second chance at life everybody wants, and sometimes it frightened her.

She and Rosaria got on smoothly as long as Judith could disguise her faintly surprised annoyance at being hovered over, she who grew up in a strictly non-hovering, quit-complaining kind of family where, although there had been love — she was pretty sure, anyway — there was no outward sign of it, other than that she, her older sister, and younger brother weren't starved, locked up, turned into slave labour as practically every one of the kids she had for years worked with had been, or ever hit, not with a bare hand, a weapon, or a tool. And the screaming — what? She was that quickly chilled. She had heard *something*, something *terrible*. Had it a colour? She almost grasped it before it sank back down into the darkness as quickly as it had surfaced. Rosaria's kind attentiveness at such moments not only disconcerted her, but in an obscure way hurt her, as if she had committed a crime and her punishment was to be treated very nicely, even lovingly, by a total stranger.

'On the other hand,' or something of that sort, since the cliché that popped into her head suddenly made no sense to her, she could barely stand the racket.

"But what noise?" Rosaria asked, a frown breaking the smooth gold of her forehead. "There is no noise in here. Is quiet." The air in her condo seemed to be full of a thick, bluish dust, although it couldn't be — Rosaria was a meticulous cleaner, and outside, blindingly white snow covered everything.

"It's the traffic, it's the kids screaming on their way to school, it's the horns and the sirens; it's the people walking down the hall talking, the doors slamming; it's the fridge going off and on and the furnace and the dishwasher — the dishwasher especially. And that clock." She pointed to the wall at the opposite end of the small room. "Each tick, it's like a bomb inside my head." Already Rosaria had crossed the room, taken down the clock, turned it over, and removed the battery. The *crack crack crack crack crack* ceased.

"It is your concussion," Rosaria told her, putting the disabled clock on the floor behind the armchair. "The noise is normal. Is just noise."

"If you were raised in a remote area in the country like me, this noise would deafen you. The city noise, I mean." She would have stopped there, but remembering, went on in a different, lighter tone, "And people used to complain about how the city stunk."

"But it didn't bother you before your accident, right?"

Judith paused. "You're right. I think I was used to it in five minutes.

17

I think — all those years ago — I was only fifteen after all — I positively loved the noise." Another pause. "Because it meant there was life in the world; there were people in it, and things going on. I was so sick of nothing, nothing, nothing ever happening." But that other sound lurked behind her memories, incomplete and vague as they were. She gasped and shot to a sitting position. Rosaria began to rise, Judith's flattening gesture halting her.

"No, it's all right. I just . . ." Just what? "Just had this flash, I don't know what it was — a scream?"

"I bet you scream when you fall and hit your head. Loud!"

"It was a man's voice? I think."

"A dream," Rosaria said firmly. "From the drugs. It will go away in time."

Judith *had* had such dreams in the hospital, her screaming causing the nurses to come running. The woman in the next bed had scolded her for waking everybody up, as if Judith had done it on purpose. Judith had no memory whatsoever, except for the feel of the cold granite floor against her bare feet, the too-rough grasp of the orderly's large hand on her upper arm. Had she fought him? She put both hands up to rest them against her cheeks, gasping, trying to hold in her scattered thoughts, trying to order them.

"You will get better," Rosaria told her, putting her own gentle hands against Judith's, moving Judith's downward, arranging them in her lap for her. "I will bring you lemonade, yes?" Judith could only nod, dumbly. Maybe lemonade would help?

Catherine phoned, as she did every day, morning and evening. How good her usually brusque, efficient youngest had turned out to be.

"Gilles called. He wanted to know if you're able to have visitors yet. I told him, of course. He said to tell you he would drop by this evening." She added, "I hope that's all right."

"Yes, of course it is." Judith's heart was pattering so quickly in her throat that she had to swallow, and then again, to get it to stop. *My beau*, she told herself with a grin she hid before Rosaria saw it. Hadn't she said to him not that long ago, "Isn't it time we got married? Or at least moved in together?" For the life of her, she couldn't remember what he had replied.

Wait a minute — was this because she had finally figured out that on her retirement pension, she couldn't afford the condo fees here anymore and would have to move somewhere cheaper? Although as far as she could recall, she hadn't made any firm decisions about where. She would have to ask Catherine or Jessica. But no, Jessica had gone back to her job teaching school out in — Jess always called it East Overshoe, but it had a real name: Pocahontas? Periwinkle? Portofino? — near some larger town or other. In the glorious foothills.

"Rosaria," she said, after she had broken the connection to Catherine, hearing her voice beginning hesitantly. "I've been wondering if you shouldn't go home for a night. Tonight, maybe. I have a visitor coming who will keep an eye on me until you get back in the morning." Rosaria studied Judith, puzzled, clearly uncertain.

"But Catherine says..."

"Never mind Catherine," Judith said. "I am still in charge of my own life. I bet you haven't seen your husband or children for a week or more. I am giving you leave to go."

"Your supper," Rosaria began, but Judith laughed and waved her away.

"I can manage my own supper. You can see how much better I am." At this, Rosaria was persuaded to nod in cautious agreement. She gathered her belongings and, looking anxiously at her watch — she would try to catch a bus to her home on the other side of the city — she left.

It was the first time Judith could recall being alone since her accident, and she sat very still for a few minutes, trying to get back the feel of being in her own private space. But everything continued to look slightly off, not the way it used to be, a bit shabby, not quite polished, tidy now only because of Rosaria. Perhaps Gilles's presence would perform the last bit of magic that would turn her condo back into home.

She felt herself a mere occupant, not without rights to be here, not without having her own belongings in this place, and her history here; but no, her memories had been, at least temporarily, washed away, and she no longer fit into her condo the way the hand fits into a much-worn glove. That apparently she had already decided to move heartened her. *I will start again*, she told herself, *in a better place*. Although where that might be didn't immediately come to mind. She was counting on Gilles for that decision too.

At last the doorbell rang, and at the same moment, Gilles, having used his key, stood in the open doorway, taking a second to gaze at her before he closed the door and turned the lock, pulled off his gloves, shrugged out of his overcoat, stepped out of his boots, and walked toward where she sat on the sofa, slipper-clad feet on the floor, hair combed and makeup on, not having taken her eyes off him since he had entered.

"Judy," he said. He was not a tall man, and when he sat beside her, bringing with him the fresh, cold air from outside, and placed his arm along her back, they were almost perfectly face to face. But when she leaned into him, offered him her mouth, he merely brushed his chilly lips along her forehead and tightened his clumsy hold around her torso.

"I am glad you are doing so well," he said into her ear, releasing her. Now she realized how awful she must look with this embarrassing new scarecrow hairdo, and all these new lines in her face, not to mention the weight she had lost so that the sleeves of her favourite sweater bagged around her newly bony wrists. He disengaged himself, moved to the armchair, and sat there.

"I found the scotch," she announced. "Would you like some?" How handsome he was still, in his sixties, his dark hair grizzled and brushed back in a way that gave his face a nobility she hadn't seen before. Looking at him, she felt breathless, like her teenage self.

"I see it," he said, and got up, went to the sideboard, and poured himself a couple of fingers. "No," he told her, "of course you mustn't have a drink, what with the painkillers and one thing and another." He took his drink back to the armchair. She noticed he had left the key to her condo beside the scotch bottle.

It was dark outside, but no one had pulled the blinds or closed the curtains, and above the wide swath of darkness of the park and the elementary school across the street, the glittering lights of the city seemed to her icy and distant, as if they were on another planet. Gilles cleared his throat, a familiar sound, his voice low and rich, always with a hint of a rumble to it, and she remembered how it was making love with him. A chill prickled at her. As if he were remembering with her, he looked away, out the window beside him. From her place on the sofa, she saw the room reflected, both of them sitting motionless, their faces faintly grim. Something was starting in her chest, moving downward; the atavistic sense of something being very wrong.

Finally, Gilles spoke: "Camille has asked me to come back." His wife, mother of his grown children. When Judith had begun seeing Gilles, he said he was separated, but a year or so later he announced that he and Camille had separated, and Judith realized that during that year when she had been falling in love with him, he had remained at home with his wife, despite the — he said — constant quarrelling, and Camille's — he said — shameless infidelities. When she reminded him, he insisted that he had not said separated but estranged, and that 'separated,' this time, meant he had moved out.

"I have loved our years together — five or so?" he said now, and she said, over his voice, "More like eight," and would have gone on to say, *You SOB*, but it seemed too soon for that. Under her too-loose clothing, though, her body felt about a thousand years old, all melting, sliding, too-soft flesh.

"I thought that we would marry," she told him, her voice thin. "I thought it was time, after so many years together. Or that, at least, you would move in with me, or I with you."

"I moved back when you were . . ." He didn't look at her.

"Out of my mind in the hospital," she said, too loud.

"They were not sure, at first, that you would survive, then later, that you would ever get back your mind if you did live. Your brain was swollen, you . . ."

Judith couldn't speak. *I was that ill?* How it frightened her to know this; no one had given her even a hint that things had been this bad.

"Camille . . ."

"Saw her chance!"

"No, no, we had been talking for a while. I did miss her, you know. I always did. You were so different from her. So . . ."

"Anglo," she said, and laughed. "My DNA is Norwegian. Fundamentalist Protestant — once Lutheran." She realized this information wasn't for him; she was trying to remember things that in her injury had receded so far from her that when they bobbed up, she grabbed them, desperate to hang onto them.

"I hardly know anything," he said, and sighed. "I think it's our past, you know? We were young together; we came from the same village; we knew each other's families. We left Quebec together, after we married."

Judith was suddenly angry. "You'll never get any of that back!" He was a fool. "Was I never anything to you?"

He put down his hand and gazed at her for a long moment, searching her face, breaking his look to study the room. Outside, high, a jet whispered overhead, the sound broken, faded, dying. "You aren't even crying. What was I to you?" he finally said.

But she could see he didn't care anymore. She was no longer sure herself who was right.

"I know this is a bad time to do this. I am really sorry for that, but circumstances . . ." He shrugged, again not looking at her.

"I loved you."

"Well, sort of," he said, his face twisting into a wavering smile. "You loved something — I don't know — it wasn't me, I don't think. Your daughters, your . . . job, your — whatever it was. Our nights in bed."

All the things she might say: *Don't go, I can't live without you*, but, unfortunately, she knew all too well that she could live without him, maybe not well, maybe not without longing for him, but she would live. She found she didn't even really blame him for going back to Camille.

"I wish I had someone to go back to," she said, but this sentiment was so self-pitying she had to laugh. Jack, who had stopped loving her and left her years ago? Victor, impossible to live with, whom, finally, she had thrown out? Another silence. Then she said, staring into space, "I was lucky to have you. You made my life better." Anger returned. "But you and Camille were always the couple, weren't you? It wasn't me and you."

"Let's not do this," he told her. "I have come to say goodbye, to say thank you for what you gave me, to tell you I will miss you, but that my real life is — has always been — with Camille."

She was silenced by the truth of this. *But what*, she was thinking, *is my real life?*

At the door, he said, "She has breast cancer, Camille. She needs me." She was struck by how very old he looked when he spoke, despite being a couple of years younger than she was.

"I'm sorry" was the best she could manage.

After he was gone, without having touched her again, she managed to squeeze out a few tears, allowed herself a few seconds of a near-blinding rage — which only worsened her headache, as if someone were trying to screw off the top of her head — and tried to picture this new life without a man. It made her feel sick to her stomach. She forced herself to stop.

Gilles was right. His real life was with Camille. She suspected — no admitted — that she had known this all along.

Catherine showed up at about seven on the day that Rosaria, her contract ended, went back to her family. Looking exhausted, her navy designer suit so tightly fitted it wrinkled at the top of her legs, and seeing Judith had reclaimed the armchair, she sat on the sofa, kicked off her stilettos, let her head fall back against the cushions, and closed her eyes.

"Hard day?"

Catherine opened her eyes, straightened, and unbuttoned her too-snug jacket. "How is the memory?"

"Weird. Alice phoned, and for a minute I didn't know who she was. Oh yes, eldest and seldom-seen daughter. It's just that . . . we have a hard time thinking of anything to say. You know."

"It's been a long time since they've been home for a visit."

"I feel as if I barely know her," Judith said, but she felt she shouldn't be saying this out loud.

"And Lucinda?"

"Oh yes."

"Okay, what did she want?"

"Nothing. You know, she really does sound happy. I couldn't quite believe it."

"Really! A Jewish family? In Israel? Bizarre, as only Luce can be bizarre." Lucinda and Catherine were full sisters, both Victor Horvat's daughters, although he favoured Lucinda in a manner that upset Judith more and more as the years passed. No wonder Catherine's steady state was simmering anger. "Did she even ask how you are?"

"I think so." But Judith couldn't be sure. Communications with daughter number three always left her confused. Victor came into her mind, clutching thirteen-year-old Lucinda's upraised arm, probably to stop her from hitting him, the expression on their faces as they stared at each other — not the way fathers and daughters look at each other, but something else she thought she saw in the gaze that horrified and sickened her. It was the night Lucinda disappeared, and she had to call Victor home from a trade show downtown; then Lucy simply opened the door and was home, as if nothing had happened. Victor shouting at Judith, "Your incompetence, your slovenliness is ruining our lives!"

All the things she had yelled in reply still, this minute, seething inside her: *four kids, a full-time job, your constant rages, your demands* ... But her passion was gone now; she was worn out with defending herself to him, even if now only mentally. Lucinda was not like other kids; it was as if she had arrived by accident into their midst from another planet. Except that she was the spitting image of her dark-haired, handsome father, in her his good looks transformed to female beauty.

Outside, below her windows and balcony, a horn blasted, and tires screamed. No crash ensued, just another slowly fading wail. She placed both hands over her ears; inside her head the pain blossomed like an evil brown weed threatening to blow off the top of her skull.

After a moment, during which Catherine sat frozen, staring at her mother, Judith put down her hands and said, "I have to get out of here. The noise is unbearable, and I can't afford the condo fees here any-more. I have to go ... I don't know where."

But suddenly, behind her eyes a meadow appeared, and with it the pure scent of spring: sages, grasses, the warming earth itself, all of it fill-ing her nostrils and invading her brain, shutting out the ever-present pain.

"We only want what's best for you, Mom. Can we give it a few more weeks before we take any drastic steps?"

"Sure ..." Judith said slowly, because behind the tongue and teeth making the words, as she wiped away saliva dribbling minutely from one corner of her mouth, the pieces of an idea were flowing sweetly and perfectly together. Thinking of Gilles and his *real life*, she knew now where she would go.

Bless you, Gilles, she thought.

CHAPTER TWO

SETTLING

For days before the March morning they left for Wisdom, Judith and Jess had read weather reports and checked the highway hotlines to be sure they wouldn't get caught in a storm anywhere along the way, spring blizzards being as vicious in the area they were travelling through as they were commonplace. Jessica, who lived in the kind of community where even the teachers drove trucks, had borrowed a shiny new half-ton with a tarp for the box and had taken Friday off from her school in order to help her mother move.

"I wanted a little time to help you get adjusted. I didn't want to rush away and leave you all alone in that godforsaken place."

"Why is Wisdom godforsaken, and Pettiforge or Plantagenet or whatever it's called isn't?"

"Parmeter," Jessica said, but she was laughing. "Boy, do you ever resist the fact that I choose to live in the country. Why is it okay for you, but not okay for me?" They both knew the answer, though, and Judith kept quiet.

Jess wheeled the truck with perfect calm through the heavy Calgary traffic, using her mirrors easily, even giving the finger to a youngish male driver in a three-quarter-ton club-cab truck who seemed to feel that he had more right to Jess's place in her lane than she did. The truck driver, seeing Jessica and her finger through his side window, laughed toward her in an amiable, even flirtatious way, and blew her a kiss as he roared ahead of her into her lane. Judith could see the flush of red appearing on Jess's cheek. So, forty-something, never-married-or-even-partnered Jess wasn't immune to the male gaze. This, for some reason, pleased Judith, although she pretended she had seen none of it.

"Catherine drives with her jaw clenched, gripping the wheel as if the car might get away on her. I swear she's going to have a heart attack one of these days if she doesn't relax."

"She has a lot to be tense about," Jess said. "You know: Ian, and that job, always having to be Miss Perfect in her dress, and those shoes! Stilettos alone could ruin anybody's life." Jess was wearing a quilted parka and jeans with her usual worn hiking boots, although Judith didn't think she'd ever heard of Jess actually hiking. "Ian likes to show her off, but at the same time he expects her to keep up with him, whether she feels like it or not."

Judith had only recently been able to watch TV again and didn't like to think of her youngest as one of those abrasive, skinny women in too-tight clothing, with their manicures and absurdly inappropriate coiffures, who appeared in all the courtroom dramas. Life, in Catherine's case, imitating art rather than the other way around.

It was a dull day, and all the way east from Calgary the sky never lifted. During a particularly gloomy stretch near the Alberta–Saskatchewan border, they stopped on the outskirts of a village for gas, a bathroom break, and something to eat at a new gas station with half a dozen pumps, incongruous in the general emptiness on the nearly deserted highway, but most likely designed to catch the interprovincial traffic, which in summer could be heavy. In the empty café, they ordered hamburgers and coffee from a slow-moving, grey-haired waitress who, once she had served them, stood in silence for long periods, her back to them, gazing out the room's big windows.

"Look at the acres and acres of grain fields," Jess said. "Every bit of biodiversity stamped out. Just nothing out there but monocrops." At this time of year, though, there was nothing to be seen but a smooth blue-grey covering of snow, in this grim light looking not so much beautiful as Arctic-frigid and utterly blank. "But it would be kind of nice to live way out there in those hills." She nodded toward the horizon strung with hills that at this distance seemed so low as to barely break the sky.

"You can't imagine. Or what you imagine isn't quite right."

"What then?" Jessica's interest wasn't feigned. What was it she thought she would find there?

"Loneliness. It's the very fabric of life out there," Judith told her. "It becomes so ingrained that if you live there most of your life, or all of it, you don't even notice it. *Everybody* lives inside it. It's omnipresent, like the bloody sky."

"So why move back?"

"I have to."

"Have to? We would have helped you find a cheaper place in Calgary. Or else a village not so remote, closer to the city."

"I wasn't raised in any of them."

"So that's what's behind this choice! Not cheapness; not silence. It's about going home."

"Not . . . home . . . exactly." She was aware her voice was filled with misery and tried to change the sound. "Of course, my brother and sister hate me; everybody will gawk at me; rumours will spread: I have AIDS and have come home to die, or I'm on the lam from the mob, or all my family was killed in a car accident and . . ." But that was too close to home. Victor had died in a car accident not long after Judith threw him out. Judith suspected suicide — everybody knew that turn, it was a moonlit night, and yet he had driven straight into the concrete abutment that had been there for twenty years. And oh, the guilt. Ever since the night the police had come to the door to tell her, and in their questioning had hinted at it.

"You're right," she said finally. "Wisdom may well be too awful, even for me."

Hour by hour, once they turned south off the main highway, the roads became narrower and then narrower again, the shoulders too slim, often crumbling, and frequent potholes opened, or else asphalt frost bumps rose up, slowing them down. The landscape, too, became gloomier; there was a hint of the ominous in the silhouette of the long slopes of the hills, graceful in any other light, now stark and black against the dark-stained horizon. She had to fight not to say, "Turn back, I can't do it. I was wrong."

In late afternoon, they finally drove into Wisdom. They had little trouble finding Judith's new house, not only because the village was tiny, but because the house was easily recognizable from the online photos she and Catherine had studied when she was buying it.

"That's it." Her headache suddenly thudded at the top of her skull as if to crack it in two.

Jess pulled up in front, shut off the engine, sat for a minute peering past her mother at what little was visible behind the giant fir tree that took up one entire side of the miniscule front yard: a tiny, one-storey frame house, the white paint peeling along the wall beneath the large front window. Feeling Jess's dismay, Judith reminded her, "I paid only ten thousand dollars for the house, the furniture, the shed out back, and the lot. And I can get out any time without too much loss." Then, "Beggars can't be choosers," and good heavens, it was her own mother's voice saying it. Jessica couldn't stop an exasperated *tsk*.

In the end, unable to get the front door open, partly because of the half-melted snowbank frozen against it and partly because the lock was jammed with ice or maybe rust, they drove around to the back, up the alley, and parked in the dilapidated shed. The alley was too narrow to leave a vehicle in, and the yard couldn't be used because sagging grey pickets fenced it without a break from the shed wall on one side to the hedge on the other. Anyway, the yard was still full of crusted, partially melted snowbanks.

Separating Judith's lot from the house on each side were unkempt caragana hedges, thick enough to screen nosy neighbours as well as a barrier against too much friendliness. A sudden memory came to her of the spontaneous popping of caragana pods on hot, dry days in summer, and the heat then, often so extreme it was itself a medium through which you pushed your way. She tried, but it was growing too dark to see much of the neighbours' houses, one a wood-frame construction and one a fairly substantial pale brick. The windows of both were dark, which she hoped meant they were empty, or at least that their owners, almost certainly farmers, had gone to Texas or Arizona for the winter. She had no desire to hobnob with neighbours.

Her house's interior smelled of disinfectant and cleaning products, but as she and Jessica walked through it, the reassuring odours were overtaken, for Judith at least, by less-welcome ones: worn linoleum, aged varnish on the kitchen cupboards, the propane heater sitting in the corner of the tiny living room, shorn of its stovepipes, disused once a furnace was installed but still giving off that faint, nauseating propane smell. Mice also? Maybe. Or maybe the smell came from the faded cheap cotton curtains covering the front window, so familiar she had to look away. Now her headache, which had intensified the moment she entered the house, began to spread through her neck and, like an electric current, travel down her right arm.

Almost at once, Jessica's arm was around her shoulders; "Let's stay in the motel tonight," she said. Now everything had a blurred, murky halo around it; already she was pushing her way clumsily past Jess — in strained situations, her balance tended to go wonky too — and out the back door, where in her confusion and dismay it seemed even the snowbanks gave off a stench at once familiar and disgusting.

They had brought take-out hamburgers from the village's only café, had eaten them in the motel room, and now lay side by side in the twin beds, when Jessica said, "Mom, will you please, finally, tell me something about your childhood here?"

"I have told you!" An eighteen-wheeler roared by on the highway not far from the door, and around the curtains, as in a noir film, blue and red neon light glowed. Otherwise, there was only the unbroken,

30

faintly purring silence of a windless country night. Not any country night: a sparsely populated countryside miles from anywhere. For once, Judith's headache had retreated to a soft background murmur, and in the near darkness and the motel-room calm and anonymity, her vision had returned to normal.

"Something real," Jessica said.

Judith said, laughing, "What's real?" But she was remembering Gilles, who had said he was going back to his *real life.* "I don't know what to say. My parents are dead; my brother and my sister — your Uncle Sam and Aunt Abbie — both still live here, out on farms. I'm going to have to see them."

"Why did you leave?"

"I told you that too."

"You never really answered us. Fifteen is so young, and then you never went back, did you?"

"I was angry."

"Well, I guessed that. At what?"

"My parents' religion, I guess, mostly, the way they never stopped praying. Every time we turned around there we were, down on our knees again. *Mumble, mumble, mumble.*" But she sounded more furious than mock pious. "And the constant churchgoing. Sundays we were gone from right after morning chores to just before evening chores."

"You've said that lots of times too. And anyway, I don't believe that's the real reason. Or not the whole reason."

"You've never lived in a religious household."

"Don't need to. I can imagine."

Judith chose not to dispute this. It was just like Jess, wanting to live in the distant hills, where there was indeed peace and beauty, but for which treasures one paid a terrible price. That, Jessica couldn't imagine either.

"Once I went around the corner of the house and there was my father, hitting his head against the wall," Judith said. "His eyes were

31

closed; he didn't see me. Just *bang, bang, bang.* I got out of there as fast as I could. I forgot all about that. I was about six, I think." Jessica drew in her breath sharply. "I wanted to tell Mom, but I knew it wouldn't be safe to. We were trained in not-talking-about-it." This last comment approaching a molten bitterness, and then there it was again, that soul-rending noise coming out of some blackness both deep inside her and from some other wholly alien level of existence. She groaned and threw herself noisily on her side.

"Is your head hurting again?"

"Ever since that damn concussion, I've been remembering..."

"What?"

"I don't know, just things — that scare me. Things that I think I know, but I can't — I can't quite identify them."

"Do you mean ... um ... things from your childhood? You don't mean things from when you and my dad were together, and Alice and I were little? Before Victor and Lucy and Cathy came along?"

"Honestly, I'm not sure where they're from. I wish I did." But as she half sat, half lay in her single bed, her head now thumping again, hearing Jessica yawn, she thought that maybe Jess had hit on it. These were things from her buried childhood. After a while, knowing she shouldn't, she took a sleeping pill anyway, on top of the pain meds.

Asleep, she dreamed of Alice and Jessica as little girls, both of them barefoot and wearing their long, eyelet-trimmed nighties, and Jack Stratton, their father and her husband — for, in the dream it was ten years — angry, giving her his dismissive glance that used to make her ill with shame — doesn't see Alice take little Jess by the hand, open the door and lead her softly out into the glittering city night. Judith whirls to send Jack after them, but where he had been standing now is only an absence, one just as real, but both larger and more potent than his presence had been.

How I loved him, she thought, as Jess was gently shaking her shoulder.

"Morning, Mom, time to rise and shine."

"Oh, right away, I'm up," Judith said, trying to untangle herself from the sheets, thinking she would be late for work, Jack would be upset.

"I know you're stressed right now, Mom," Jess was saying, "but I hope you'll be careful with those drugs. You don't want to get addicted."

Coming awake and back to herself and the motel, Judith had a blinding headache and welling nausea. She was still groggy with drugs too, and couldn't have answered if she had wanted to.

After Judith had showered and dressed and taken more pain meds, Jessica, in a tone reminiscent of one Catherine might use, announced that she would not leave her mother without a car, and that they were going, right now, to the dealership in the next, bigger town, Dillon, to set things up so she could buy one immediately. Judith had sold her own battered, elderly Volvo for a couple of hundred dollars, not telling her daughters until it was done, and had been looking forward to buying her first new car. Now her head hurt too much to do anything but acquiesce.

Afterward, having had to settle for a nondescript blue, four-door Ford, driving away in Jess's truck from Dillon and back to Wisdom, having thrown up only once into the toilet at the dealership and not telling Jessica, her headache under control again, and her short period of confusion, as the car salesman explained numbers to them, or failed to, having abated, she said to Jess, "I've never bought a new car before. It's ridiculously exciting. Just think, in a couple of days I'll be driving it!" They had left the new car behind while the paperwork was being finished — bank scrutiny and so on, she wasn't sure what all; it would be delivered in a day or two. Running through her mind were the near wrecks she had bought with help from a boyfriend, or somebody else's husband, which had been her lot most of her adult life, since her husbands. "At home we never had new vehicles. Too poor for that."

"I know I forced you into it before you were ready."

"You know me. I'd be ready about two weeks after the big emergency I needed it for."

"Mom, you know that's not true," Jess protested, but what Judith knew was that it was mostly true. What she didn't quite know was why.

They had arrived at the lip of the valley where Wisdom sat. From this distance, it was just a brown smudge in the landscape of last year's matted ochre grass, mottled with patches of snow among dull grey rocks scattered down the hillsides. The effect made her think of a thousand-piece puzzle, the kind that takes years to solve.

"Mom and Dad honestly believed that doing without made you a better person and that God despised the rich, unless they gave their money to the church, of course. So it turns out you *can* buy your way into heaven." They were humming down the long hill that made up the last few kilometres into the town. "But I think being poor seeps into your blood, like the taint of criminality can do; you can never feel you're an okay, equal person. If there are lots of the well-off around you, like in the city — and believe me, in my work I saw what being poor does to people who live in the midst of the wealthy: It's bloody well soul-destroying. Worse, it's medieval."

"So, you were poor, but I knew that. What else?"

"Everything was either about the farm or the church. And Dad . . ." How lean he was, or maybe gaunt was a better word, his forehead lined, deep lines etched around his mouth. His hair was grey from the first moment she remembered him, and his eyes ice blue and frighteningly penetrating.

"Dad?" Jessica prompted. But Judith said nothing more, and now they were driving down Wisdom's main street, which was also a secondary highway — not that there was much through traffic — past a few half-tons parked in front of the café, turning down the alley, parking in her shed, then together carrying the few groceries they had bought into the clean but nonetheless shabby kitchen.

At best, she had eight hundred square feet, still marginally bigger than her condo. But now she had the shed, too, and a tiny cement basement beneath the kitchen, probably originally a dirt cellar, as their home cellar had been. Judith suddenly recalled its always dank smell, and the tiny lizards that scuttled along its dirt walls when you pulled the cord on the bare light bulb and forgot to thump your feet on the stairs.

While they were tidying, cleaning, and arranging, a wind came rushing across the prairie and through the village, whipping laundry on lines (if people here still hung their laundry on lines), scudding down the dusty streets, blowing tumbleweeds — even though it was winter — and food wrappers and children's plastic toys to hell and gone; whipping the branches of the big tree in the front yard so that they whistled — a sound sometimes thick and deep, sometimes high and thin — and thumped and scraped noisily where they hit the front wall. She stopped what she was doing, her hands in soapy water in the sink, the window before her facing the blank brick wall, a pleasant creamy yellow in daylight, and a partial view of the snow-filled back yard of the house next door, and listened.

"What are you smiling at?" Jess stood in the doorway.

She had been remembering running with her big sister, Abbie, down into the coulee in the pasture behind the house, losing her footing, and tumbling down through the dusty grass, scraping her legs on tiny rose bushes, small stones bruising her arms as she rolled, and Abbie screaming, her voice puny on the roar of the wind. And Judith herself laughing, even though she was pretty sure she had given herself a nosebleed. But she said only, "Nothing."

They were eating quietly in the dimly lit kitchen, both tired, each lost in thought, when Jessica, as though it had just occurred to her, asked, "Did you really sever all connections? Did you never hear from any of them again? Not your mom or your dad or your brother or sister?"

"No," Judith said, not looking at Jess. "I mean, yes, sort of, now and then." She sighed and pushed her plate away. Jess watched her. "After Mom died, Abigail wrote me a few ... notes."

"Saying what?"

"Oh, nothing."

"Did you answer them?"

Judith shrugged. "It's hard to remember. I suppose I must have."

In the basement, the gas furnace had begun to whirr, blowing warm air into the kitchen, and for once, instead of stiffening at the sound and being rendered nauseous by the dry blown heat, Judith found it comforting.

She woke in the night, at first not sure where she was. For a second she couldn't catch her breath, started to call out to Jess, but Jess had gone home the day after she had helped her mother buy her new car. Now she remembered she was alone here in Wisdom, and an intense inner quivering came flooding through her chest and brain: terror at the unknown, horror at what she had done, both mixed with a confused satisfaction, all the emotions or sentiments then blending into something that might be called relief or, at the very least, a momentary peaceable calm. *I have done the right thing*, she told herself; the quivering ceased, and she fell back to sleep.

Much later, she woke to the muted trill of her cellphone. Daylight streamed from the small window high in the living room wall above the sofa, through the open door and across the threadbare no-colour carpet. She threw back the quilt and padded into the front room, but the cellphone, still merrily burbling, wasn't on the coffee table or the sofa. She went on through the arch between the two rooms, the mere sight of which this morning caused her mild revulsion, and into the miniscule dining room, where the phone lay on the scratched, dark-stained, heavy table. She picked up the phone, about to turn it off, thinking that at this time of the morning it had to be a wrong number, when she saw that the call was from Lucinda.

"Mom?"

She was tempted not to speak, her right hand still tingling from her having lain on her arm, but said, "Good morning, dear," aware that her tone was resigned, if not downright annoyed, and that Lucinda would hear this at once. "This will be an expensive call!"

"No, no," Lucinda said. "I have news. Good news," but her voice faded slightly. Judith shook her hand to get rid of the unpleasant prickling.

"What news?"

"A baby! I'm going to have a baby!" Lucy's voice went a bit wonky halfway through the sentences, then righted itself.

Judith struggled to repress her dismay, resorting finally to cliché.

"Oh my dear. What wonderful news."

"Lev is overjoyed; we are all celebrating," Lucinda said, with that slight twist to her vowels that had appeared recently, as if English were her second language and Hebrew had become her first. Judith thought, *I'll never get her home now.*

"When?"

"August." In far-off Israel, Lucinda made a tiny squeal of what Judith could only think was delight. "You wouldn't come to the wedding, but now you must plan to be here for the baby's birth. Now promise me, Mother."

"I can make no such promise." Judith was abruptly furious, as quickly ashamed. "I'll try." She hesitated, searching for the necessary thing to say to her daughter, but panic was rising. "It's not too late," she ventured. "You could still . . ." As if Lucinda didn't know her options better than her mother ever had. At a certain level the troubled and, to Judith's mind, suffering Lucinda could be as transparently untruthful, even as sly, as any petty crook. Then, equally unpleasant, as abject in her shame as a Christian martyr.

"Mother!" The cry was familiar. "I would never . . ."

"Yes, yes," Judith said soothingly, her mind elsewhere. In this temporary peace, they said goodbye.

She had not said, *Leave Levi, come home,* for who in her right mind would want Lucinda back? She supposed even Thomas (whom

Lucinda had married at sunrise in the middle of a wheat field, she in a long, smock-like dress and Thomas in a Johnny-Depp-pirate-movie shirt), in the end, had been glad to be rid of her. *Such a terrible thing to think about your own daughter,* but the rebuke was routine and, as usual, did no good. *What a terrible mother I must have been,* also routine, was more painful because she knew it was largely true.

Later that morning, she went very early to buy a carton of milk at the Co-op, and there was her older sister, Abbie, her frizzy white hair pulled back from her face and knotted low at the back of her neck, exactly as their mother had, unfortunately, worn hers. Under the threadbare and faded old sweater they used to call Siwashes she was wearing — wasn't it once Dad's? — Abbie was dressed in a pinkish-yellow T-shirt that might have started out orange and a pair of men's too-large striped denim coveralls, as if she'd been shovelling grain or cleaning out the chicken shed. She was bent over the long freezer at the far wall that held packaged vegetables, frozen pizzas, and nearly chickenless chicken pot pies and, busy tossing aside one frozen package and lifting another, didn't see Judith. As struck by guilt and fear as a hooky-playing schoolchild about to be caught, Judith stepped out of view against the end of the row of shelving, pressing herself against the jars of peanut butter. She had gasped when she saw her sister and now was having trouble breathing.

Giving up on the milk, she lowered her head so as to hide her face and went as quietly and rapidly as she could out the door and, instead of heading down the cracked and uneven cement sidewalk past the privately owned grocery, the café, and the convenience store, turned down the narrow alley between the drugstore and the Co-op. Even as she rushed away, she had begun berating herself not so much for her cowardice as for the way the mere sight of her sister had reduced her to the disobedient child again, so that she had hidden from her, hoping not to be confronted with her crimes.

Only a few days after Judith had arrived, spring finally began to show a flicker of interest in the village of Wisdom, named, she had been told, after a pioneer whose full name nobody seemed to know, nor where he had come from, nor what had happened to him, and not referring to the quality of astuteness or perceptiveness. (Considering what happened to most settlers, maybe it had been a macabre joke.) Already the dust was rising, and the remnants of banks of snow, blackened and crystalline from thawing and then freezing again, sprawled exhausted in patches of shade along the north foundations of the settlers' houses or under leafless caragana hedges and against fences. She could never see those fences, paint long gone, pickets missing, without thinking, *Somebody else's dream gone to shit.* Whenever she briefly contemplated the settler-dead who had given everything they had to the project of building a new country, only to end, their bodies worn out, their herculean labour mostly unrewarded, their lives unsung, in the grave like everybody else, she had a hard time believing in the creed of the intrinsic justice of the world. Mostly she just didn't.

As she turned onto the street running perpendicular to her own, the sound of a door opening down the block and slapping shut propelled her into a quick right turn into her back lane, which she scurried down, coming into her own soggy yard through the narrow gate that had finally appeared as the snowbanks melted, without, as far as she knew (although she also knew that in villages nothing escapes the residents), being seen by anyone. She knew she was being ridiculous, but she couldn't bear the thought of dealing with the townspeople, knowing their intense curiosity about strangers, although not so as to integrate them, but only so as to *know.* She hadn't liked them when she was a child, and she knew she wouldn't like them now.

Back in her own kitchen, still trembling a little, embarrassed, and also ashamed by her flight, she thought that if Abbie had seen her — she felt sure Abbie hadn't — then soon her younger brother Sam would come pounding on her door too. As if in answer to her worst imaginings, somebody was knocking hard on the door right beside her. She nearly jumped out of her skin, froze, then cautiously cracked the door open. Abigail stood before her, taller than Judith, skinnier, and a whole lot angrier.

"It *is* you," she said, and not waiting for an invitation, stepped into the kitchen, grabbed the doorknob and with a strong pull that forced Judith to drop her own hand, slammed the door shut. "What is the matter with you, not showing up for fifty years and then one day just moving in as if nothing had ever happened! And not even to come near me — or Sam! As if we were nothing!"

She took a step toward Judith; involuntarily, Judith stepped back. "We are children of the same parents; we are sisters and brother; we . . ." Abigail turned away, throwing herself into a chair at the tiny kitchen table, and closed her eyes.

At the sight of her sister praying in her kitchen, Judith revived. "Who do you think you are to come bursting into my house like this? I didn't ask you to come. If I'd wanted to see you . . ." She took a breath, then went on in a calmer tone. "I had planned to see you as soon as I got settled. I needed some time first." She stared at her sister, whose eyes were still closed, lips still moving. "Stop that! Why the hell do you think I left in the first place?"

Abbie's eyes popped open. "Because we prayed?"

"All — the — time," Judith said. She forced herself to turn away, plug in the already filled electric kettle, reach for the teapot and tea bags. She worked noisily, banging open the cutlery drawer, smacking two mugs onto the counter, reaching into the fridge for milk, remembering there was none, and only then turning back to Abigail. For two or three minutes, neither of them spoke. At last, when the electric kettle clicked noisily off, Judith asked, "Who lives in that house?" indicating with a head jerk the brick wall she could see through the window above the sink.

"I think his name is Harris," Abigail said. "Jerry or Junior or something Harris. He used to teach school here. He left . . . I don't know why he left, but he came back a couple of years ago and moved in there."

"He's not from here?"

"Sure he was. Don't you remember the Harrises over on that farm south of town? The one with the red barn? They always kept that barn painted, even though their house hadn't seen a lick of paint in years." Judith thought, *That easily we have fallen into the local parlance.* She wanted to laugh, but pain was drumming in her forehead, streaking down her neck and into her shoulder. She poured water into the teapot, added the tea bags, and carried the pot and mugs unsteadily to the table, then sat down in the matching chair opposite Abigail.

"How did you recognize me?"

"A strange woman in town in the early morning, all alone? We knew you were back, so it had to be you. Did you know it was me?"

"You looked so much like Mom, rummaging in that freezer."

"You have Dad's eyes."

"I don't!" Judith said. "He had such piercing eyes. They scared me."

"He only smiled for Sammie."

"Not even for Mom." She could see her mother's face clearly, and the large purple bruise along her cheekbone.

"What are you looking at me like that for?" Abbie was drawing back, as if something in her sister's face frightened her.

"What? Nothing." She couldn't stop looking at Abbie and forced herself to reach toward the teapot.

"Oh Judy, how could you go away and not come back even once for fifty years? And for heaven's sake, why?"

"You know why."

"I don't know why. Sammie didn't go, I didn't go." Later, Judith would realize that the second sentence had contradicted the first, that Abbie knew perfectly well why, but refused to admit it.

"Sammie was going to inherit everything; he would have been stupid to go. And Dad loved him. He didn't love us."

"He did love us! How can you say that? You don't even know ..."

"Know what?" But Abigail, apparently tired of waiting on her sister's obviously deficient hostessing skills, was pouring the tea, clicking her tongue because it was too strong, or else not strong enough.

"You even sound like Mom. And I did come back. I came back for both their funerals!"

Abigail had set down the teapot. She was staring at Judith with surprise that slowly changed to bafflement. "What?"

"I was back for their funerals," Judith repeated, but even as she said it, she was assailed by uneasiness. "Of course I was," she said, as if Abbie had challenged her.

"Why ... why would you think that?"

"Because I was!"

Abigail was shaking her head no, her lips pressed together.

"Of course I was," she insisted, although she was realizing that she could remember nothing about either one.

Abbie set the mug down with a thump on the bare wood of the table and closed her eyes. "I don't know what to say to you. I just don't know."

"Don't you dare ask me to pray," Judith countered. "Let's just leave Jesus out of this one. Okay?"

She thought for a second that Abigail, whose eyes had popped open at this blasphemy, might slap her, and for once she wasn't afraid of her big sister, but instead drew herself up so that she was sitting straight, her chin thrust out, her eyes firm on Abbie's.

"I will have my own opinions," she told her. "Whether you like them or not. You will not foist your ideas on me." Now that she had the floor, and her sister's undivided attention, she recited the speech that she had been, she realized now, unconsciously rehearsing ever since the day she had decided to move back to Wisdom. "If you mind your own business, and I mind mine, we should be able to get along here in the same village. We should be able to present a reasonable front to the community that apparently means so much to you. And I will give Sam the same respect. But you have to respect me."

"Respect you for what?" Abbie asked, and her tone was faintly taunting, or else wry.

"For having made my own way in the world. With no help at all." She could see Abbie considering her response, was suddenly aware of how vulnerable she was in this argument, or whatever it was, having made rotten decision after stupid decision, until now, an old woman, she had arrived back where she had begun, with nothing to show for fifty years in the city, her job, her two marriages, except, she supposed, her four daughters. Ending up in a shack practically identical to the one she had run away from all those years ago. Except the old one had an upstairs where the bedrooms were. No, Mom and Dad slept downstairs.

Her head had begun screaming, her heartbeat hammering in her ears. She raised her hands and, pressing them over her ears, screwed up her face and shut her eyes, trying to force back the tidal wave of pain.

Abbie's chair scraped back on the cheap linoleum — then she was beside Judith, both arms around her, crying out, "Judy, Jude, what's wrong? What's the matter?" Judith staggered to her feet, throwing off her sister's grasp, rushed into the bathroom, where she vomited into the toilet, then vomited again. When she had finished for the second time and felt a cold wet cloth on her forehead, she realized Abigail had stayed with her.

Judith started to say, "It's nothing," but seeing the tight-lipped anger reappearing on her sister's face, she stopped. "I got a concussion the day I was to retire. I fell on ice, I hit my head on concrete, I was two weeks in the hospital, and I didn't know anybody or anything. It takes quite a while to get over a concussion that severe. That's what they tell me anyway." She made a noise close to what she knew would sound to Abigail like a self-pitying sob. "So far it's turning out to be true."

"At least it's not cancer," Abigail said. "I was afraid it was something awful like that. Maybe breast cancer like Mom." Judith chose not to answer. "So *that's* why you came back?"

"I need a quiet place to recover in. I don't have much money, and it's cheap to live here."

"So," Abigail said, as if these reasons were at best spurious, always ridiculous, at worst lies. "And you did not come to our mother's funeral. You were not there."

"Of course I did," Judith said, but a memory was returning now, a jumble of pictures and feelings, dark, blurred, some so scarily powerful she couldn't stick with them until she had sorted them out. "I had flu!" Nausea was rising again. "I started out, but it was snowing, and by the time I was a couple of hours out of the city it had turned into a full-blown blizzard . . ." Was that true? She couldn't tell exactly. She had pulled to the side of the road; now she could clearly remember fumbling for her seldom-used blinker switch; had clambered, slipping, stumbling, down into the ditch in the blowing snow, had fallen on her knees in a snowbank, sobbing and vomiting until she had nearly choked and passed out, the wind whipping away her very breath, and how — now it was coming back — recovering, she had pounded her bare fists into the crusted banks, screaming back at the wind; her throat raw for days after. A day or two later, as planned, she had gone coolly back to work, friends saying, "Sorry for your loss," and she flashing a quick smile then ignoring them.

"I . . . wanted to come," she said, even in her distress hearing a child's voice. "I tried . . . to come. After a while — afterward, I mean — I guess I started to tell myself that I did."

"She was our mother," Abigail said, with a gentle dignity so unlike her regular self.

"Don't," Judith said.

"We checked the weather; it wasn't good, but there was no blizzard reported. We didn't know what had happened to you. We just thought you didn't care."

"You had to know better than that!"

Abigail stared back equally fiercely; then, surprising Judith, lowered her eyes, turned her head away, said softly, "Yes." After a while, during which neither of them said anything, she said, "I guess I should get on home." She stood and walked to the door; after a second, Judith pushed herself upright and followed her the few steps.

"Well," Abigail said, palm on the doorknob, "Now we've had our reunion, you'll have to come for supper." As if nothing had happened. "Make it on Sunday, all right? I'll get the family together."

"Oh, please don't," Judith begged. "Not the first time. Not everybody," meaning an ancient auntie or two, third and fourth cousins and their spouses and kids. Abigail pursed her lips, irritated again, but also assessing. "All right, just Rick and me and the kids and their families." Judith couldn't bring herself to argue, even though she could see the mountain of family about to topple over onto her.

"I'm sorry," Judith said. "I wanted to be more mature or something about this. I didn't mean to be so crazy."

"You weren't crazy," Abbie said. "At least not any more than I was."

"It had to happen," they said, simultaneously, both of them echoing their mother, and meaning that they could not get to peace without first having the long-delayed war. But even as their bodies touched lightly together, Judith felt a shadow between them, and knew this was only a truce.

"Will you explain?" Abbie asked. "Someday, I mean? Please?"

Because this is where everything that matters has its beginnings. But she was far from ready to say such a thing out loud, not when she couldn't quite understand herself what she was doing here. Why she had left was both obvious and at the same time something about which she couldn't yet begin to think.

CHAPTER THREE

CATCHING UP

It was early enough that nobody would be about, especially not in the park down by the stream that ran through town. She and her friends from high school used to go there after dark, mostly town kids, but if they could sneak away and had a way of getting to town and back home again, farm kids like herself would go too. They went there to smoke and use forbidden language, to drink stolen alcohol and, some of them anyway, to have sex. Otherwise, to neck, or whatever it's called these days. There had been rumours of a gang rape: Some girl from somewhere else. Some girl who *had it coming to her*. She remembers when she first heard of it, it had frightened her so badly that for weeks she stayed out of the park. She wonders now if she was afraid that she too *had it coming to her*.

During her short walk there, she kept close to the hedges and, wherever possible, in shadow, skirting the weak penumbra thrown by the single light on each street corner. Passing a house, she heard the faint cry of a baby, saw a light go on in back, and it was as if, in this dusky world, she had moved back to an earlier time.

The sky had begun to lighten in the east, although the park remained in shadow. She became aware of a moving darkness not far from her and thought at once that it must be a deer. In her childhood the park was always full of deer at dawn and dusk, the does not above knocking you down and trampling you if you got between them and their fawns. She came to a halt near the shallows where the stream made its plashing run over stones, and stood, listening and watching the pale light creep softly along the glistening water. A voice spoke, and she turned toward it; it was so low it might have been a mere stirring of the air. But a man stood a few feet from her: short, evidently elderly, and heavy-set. The light was such that she couldn't tell exactly, but she didn't think she knew him.

"Good morning. I am Saul Richter. Don't I know you?" Had she somewhere heard this name?

"I'm Judith. I used to be a Clemensen."

"Ahh," he said. "I've heard the name. You have been here a long time. We are new here, my wife and I." Judith knew then who he was: half of the old couple who had had a swastika painted on their fence. She had seen a couple of sentences about the incident in the local newsletter she had found stuffed, free, in her grocery bag. "You are sad?" Hastily, Judith wiped her face.

Coyotes were crying softly far back across the fields; they listened. He laughed so quietly she barely heard.

"The world is sad," he said, although his voice was tinged with pleasure. "Even the animals are sad." He lifted a hand toward the mournful sound. "I come here each morning at this time, when the world is still beautiful."

"I never thought of the world as sad," Judith said, although for years she had thought nothing else, the little bits of happiness here and there nothing much in the end.

"Too much death, too much pain," he said, as if he were instructing her.

"I've sometimes thought that," she replied. "But you're right; it's easy to forget right here, right now."

"And what have you seen that is so terrible?" He had hesitated a second before asking this, even though his tone was jocular. But she wouldn't say *I saw people do terrible things to their own children, little ones, who couldn't help themselves. I helped rescue mothers from violent men. Sometimes, though, the mothers were evil, and I got contaminated by that evil; I couldn't wash it off anymore.*

When she didn't answer, brushing one foot back and forth against the damp grass, he said, "I am sorry to ask you that. It is sometimes on my mind."

"Oh," she said, deliberately casual, "I did some terrible things myself," as if she had no idea what they were but was only chit-chatting.

"So have we all," he said. "One hates to think of it."

"Like horrible little dark . . . *thingies.* I don't know, like lumps of badness that lodge inside you. And you can't get rid of them. They torment you forever."

He laughed a light, short laugh. "My, how very serious we have become, and so early in the morning!" But she had a sense that he had almost said other things.

"People aren't serious often enough, if you ask me," she said. "Not that you did."

"Do I disappoint you?" So he had had other things to say. Or he thought she knew something she didn't know.

"I don't know you well enough to answer that. I am disappointed in my life." She wanted to stop talking, wanted to leave, but such was Richter's presence that she was rooted in the moment and stayed where she was.

"Life catches hold of us. We make what we can of our lives." He was smiling at her.

"I sure haven't made much of mine."

"Ahh," he said. "Now I know you. You are the woman who ran away from here when she was a girl and never came back — until now."

"Oh my god! Is that what everybody is saying?"

"What did you expect? And I am the old Jew who has no business here."

"But why are you here?"

"My wife and I — we need to live where there are birds, trees . . . quiet." He paused. His tone changed. "I give the women credit though: they are good to my wife." It was growing lighter; Judith could see his face now, although she could not have said what colour his eyes were, and he was wearing a strange kind of cap, puffy, almost like a beret, but with a narrow beak across the front — the sort of hat she associated with old European men walking down winding cobblestone streets.

"You're the couple who had a swastika painted on your fence. I read about it. I am very sorry."

"Cowardly foolishness. I have seen worse."

"Worse?"

He was gazing out to the place in the east where the land and sky melded in transparent bands of cobalt and purple. A bar of brightening gold was beginning to thicken there, revealing the line of earth still lost in blackness below it, and above it, the deep blues and purples of the sky. The air was cool on their faces.

"I was born in Germany," he said, conversationally now. "I didn't leave until the war was over." He pushed his hands into the pockets of his windbreaker jacket. "My memories are . . . troublesome. So, I am grateful for this beauty and calm." Without speaking again, he turned slowly and began to wander away, toward the village.

Now the coyotes were closer and in full cry. Were they greeting the dawn as if it were alive and benevolent, their voices not melancholy as she and Richter had thought but grateful? Or maybe they thought they were singing the sun up from the regions of darkness so that it would again light the world. Perhaps they thought it was their sacred calling that kept the world alive. Slowly, she followed the old man out of the park.

How vast, in the long dusty silences of her tiny house, her dreaming had become, how wide and deep, frightening her, that she might lose her mind before she could escape: scenes from houses she couldn't remember living in, staircases, wine bottles, bruises, and her four daughters as babies, her husbands' angry faces turned toward her, her mother born and raised right here, her father — oh, her father. And night after night she heard that scream out of the darkness; each night the sound came closer, became less the howl of a night hag, a demon, and slowly permeated her own personal memories.

But she worried that, awake, the air smelled different, or didn't smell at all, that appearances were still, in some not-quite-definable way, different than they used to be, as if absolutely everything was new, as if she were seeing bathtubs, and table legs, and toasters for the first time. How surprised she was by their clarity, their solidity, as if she had never really seen the world before.

A couple of mornings later, she threaded her way in her new car down half-remembered country roads that grew more and more heart-stoppingly familiar, until she was at the half-kilometre-long approach road into Sam's farm — the home she had left at fifteen in the grip of emotions she could neither control nor fully understand. She pulled to the edge of the wet gravel road and shut off the motor so that she wouldn't show even running lights. Any later in the season, Sam would already be in the yard tuning up his machinery, getting ready to harrow, or maybe to seed, or cleaning grain, or even, if the weather was right, in the field seeding. But even this early in the morning, with the fields still far too wet to even dream of working in them, she could see a light on in the house and knew that her little brother was up, gripped by the farmer's annual anxiety to get the crop in the ground. Their dad had been the same way, which is how she knew Sam would be. That light near the back was surely in the kitchen. Not that she'd ever been in Sam's new house; she had never even seen it before.

She sat in the darkness, torn between a powerful craving to see Sammie and the place where she had spent her childhood, and an equally strong dread that made her want to do a gravel-spitting U-turn and race all the way back to Calgary. What she knew, though, what held her fast on the roadside, smelling the new car smell and gazing at that faint light in the back of the house, was that behind the sprawling new house, lost in the wide blacker shadow of the always overgrown (and probably by now dead) caragana hedge, the row of lilacs, and the crabapple trees her mother had planted, sat the old Clemensen house. For the first time in fifty years, she was within the actual range of *home*, and instead of being full of revulsion, she was drowning in longing, but not for the house, her childhood home, but for the mother she had been so angry with and spurned.

When another light came on in Sam's house, she started her car, drove slowly back to town, and parked in her falling-down garage. As she walked up the path to the back door, she heard a faint, burbling noise that grew louder, separating itself into the honking calls of two dozen geese pumping their way to the reservoir on the north edge of the village. She stopped, watched their silhouettes as they flew with easy power, so low overhead that she could hear their wings pushing back air, and calling steadily, voice over voice, as if in excited conversation. She could smell the damp spring air now, the fragrance of moist earth, mouldy leaves under the hedges, and for the first time in a long time, she felt a stir of hope low in her abdomen.

She had barely hung up her jacket when her cellphone rang.

"I'm doing just fine," she answered Catherine's query. "Is everything okay there?"

"I'm calling about the lawsuit." Judging by her rushed tone, she must be at work.

"What lawsuit?"

"What lawsuit? Don't you — oh, of course you don't remember. You're suing the owners of the building for monetary damages and pain and suffering from that fall you had on their steps."

"I am not!" Now why did she say that?

"You signed the documents toward the end of your hospital stay. When you'd started to sound more like yourself." Catherine, when it came to her law practice, didn't procrastinate like her mother. Maybe in reaction to her mother. "By the way, the doctor told you to come back for checkups, and it's important because we have to have an accurate, continuing record for the lawsuit."

"I am running low on meds. I should get new prescriptions." Her headaches hadn't let up much as far as intensity went, but as long as she was careful, she had a few hours free of them each day, and with the help of sleeping pills slept not too badly, most of the time. Although there were the dreams to contend with.

"The building turns out to be owned by the provincial government. I filed; now they've filed their statement of defence. I just thought you should know they've answered."

"Well, good — I guess. What am I suing them for?"

"Damages! Money!"

Judith couldn't stop herself from sighing. "Have you heard from Lucinda?"

"The pregnancy is proceeding normally, apparently. Let Lev worry about her, Mom. You've got enough on your hands. By the way, your book club wants you to come to town for the next meeting. What should I tell them?"

"Tell them I can't."

"It might be good for you. You could see the specialist at the same time."

"Yes, maybe I could, but . . . give me some time. I've hardly been here a week."

"You have to keep up your doctor visits, you know that."

"Catherine, I'm a grown-up." How many times had she said this lately? "I don't need you to look after me. And I'm where I want to be, whether you like it or not. I'm sorry, Catherine, I do love you very much." Why was she so defensive? Why was she sending such mixed messages? She sounded like Lucinda at about fifteen. "I'll call you in a few days."

Carefully, she pushed the end button on her cellphone. Was she now going to start quarrelling with another daughter? Before she knew it, she'd have run out of daughters — over the years, according to them, daughters to mistreat, annoy, embarrass, ignore, and tyrannize, or also to refuse direction or support, although it seemed to Judith, even in her current state of brain damage, that it wasn't possible to be guilty of all these crimes, or at least not at the same time. Well, admit it, she told herself, *you were a lousy mother.* As she had often told her clients, many of them sobbing, to be a parent is virtually by definition to be a failure. The clients who were the parents of recalcitrant, disappearing, drink-and-drug-addled teenagers living on the streets. Borderline personality disorders, those kids. Like Lucinda. Like herself.

What? Herself? But *she* had good reason. Nonetheless, ever since her concussion, some shapeless, undefined thing had been thumping around inside her, threatening to break its way out.

That night, despite the painkillers and a sleeping pill, she had nightmare after nightmare, awakened at five again, and finally, about seven or so, fell asleep on her sagging and faintly musty-smelling couch, which was eons old and had come with the house. Even that smell, though, didn't make her yearn for her own worn but less odoriferous Calgary sofa, which she had given away. Sometime around nine, she woke to pounding on the kitchen door.

She came to her feet in one swift movement but, dizzy and unbalanced, found herself abruptly once again seated on the couch. The pounding continued, and now a man's voice was calling, "Sis! Are you in there?"

Sis? It took her a second to recall that she was a man's sister. She stood again, this time carefully, and tightening the sash of her dressing gown and using furniture for support, went to the kitchen door, unlocked, and opened it. A man loomed before her, leaning against the doorframe with one forearm held at the level of his head and the other fist raised, about to bang again. He was surely six foot four, and not someone she recognized.

He seemed, on seeing her, also to have been stunned into silence.

They stared at each other until she thought to flick on the overhead kitchen light, both of them blinking. He took a step forward and was in the kitchen; she took an inadvertent step backward because he so towered over her.

"Sammie?" She had thought Sam would look like their father, as Abigail looked like their mother.

"Sammie?" he said, faintly disgusted. "Yeah, it's me. And you're my big sister Judy. I can't believe it. Last time I can remember seeing you, you had this long ponytail and bright blue eyes. And you were skinny as a starved chicken" — she couldn't think of a thing to say to this: *Boys told me I was cute?* — "and about as squawky."

"It was a long time ago." She couldn't catch her breath, as if she had been running.

"Invite me in," he told her, although he had subdued his voice and manner. Maybe even he realized how intimidating he could be.

"I'll make coffee, come on in." She was definitely not up for another round of yelling, and she went straight to the counter where the coffeemaker sat and started filling it with water. Without another word, Sam walked out into the dining room, and then the living room, pausing to stick his head into her bedroom and out again.

"Well," he called, "this isn't much of an improvement over the house we grew up in."

"Right," she said. "It might even be worse."

"Because Mom isn't here to fix it up."

"She wasn't much on fixing things up — I mean, doilies and bouquets and crocheted afghans." Amazingly, they both laughed. Judith flicked on the brew switch and turned to him as he bent his head to get through the door into the kitchen. Tentatively, calling on some trace childhood memories of how they had once been, they moved together for an awkward near-hug.

"Hello, Sammie," Judith said, gazing up at him. "It's really good to see you again. Honest." Was he blushing?

"You gotta meet my wife. You'll like her." *So, afraid to own up to his emotions*, the social worker in her thought.

"I heard you married an O'Connor."

"Sylvia, the youngest. You wouldn't know her. She wouldn't have been school-age yet when you left," he said. "You missed a whole lot of our lives. And we missed yours. Are you sorry? I mean not so much that you ran away, but that you never even came back once?"

"I came back for the — funerals!" she said. "I mean, Dad's anyway." She had pulled back from him and was taking the coffee mugs out of the cupboard. When he didn't reply, she looked over her shoulder, saw the half-wondering, half-baffled look on his face.

He said, slowly, "No. Not Dad's either." She was about to argue, but when she tried to remember the details of her father's funeral and her trip back for it, she came up empty-handed. She had a sinking feeling that Sammy might be right. But no! Surely not! She was just distracted by his visit.

"Let's go sit in the front room so we can talk while the coffee is brewing." The machine was making bubbling noises. She was afraid it was on the verge of breakdown and she would have to find a new one — obviously, in her current condition, harder to do than building the Great Wall of China. Well, hadn't she bought a new car? But she'd had Jessica to look after that.

"I had to get a load of grain cleaned," he said. "So when Abbie told me you were here, I made up my mind to come and see you first chance I got."

"I can't believe how big you grew up to be. You're always going to be that cute little blond kid to me." She laughed. "It probably sounds funny to you, but boy, I missed you. I adored you."

"Coulda fooled me," he said. She knew he meant that she had never said a word to him again, not by phone, not in a letter or even a scrawled postcard. He couldn't know about the few she had written to him but, for some reason she couldn't recall, never mailed. Hadn't she written letters to her mother too? Surely she had.

"What a jerk I was," she said in wonderment. "I was an awful jerk, wasn't I?"

"You musta been pretty mad at all of us. We didn't really talk about it. And of course, when I asked what had happened to you, Mom and Dad just told me to shut up. So I quit asking." He seated himself carefully, with a disconcerting groaning noise from the armchair he had chosen, at the same time as she threw herself onto the couch, bouncing, saying furiously, "Well, of course! Silence! Secrecy! And people ask me why I ran away!"

In the kitchen the coffeemaker was spitting, burbling, and whooshing. She rose and brought back the pot on a tray along with mugs, spoons, cream, and sugar. Sam helped himself, and without looking at her, as if she hadn't been out of the room the preceding few minutes, went on.

"Did you know that Dad sent money to Skye?"

For a second, Judith didn't know what he was talking about. Skye? Oh yes, the girl whose spotless, tiny apartment she had gone to when she realized that she had to escape, and fast, from the boy she'd hitched a ride with out of Wisdom that Sunday night she had gone on the run to Calgary, talking, as he was, about going to his buddies' "crib" and doing some grass and then ..., looking her up and down in a way that curdled her stomach. When he went into a corner store for cigarettes, she had raced frantically across the street and hidden in an alley until, after calling her name a few times and driving slowly up to the corner and then slowly back again without finding her, she saw, with shaky relief, his truck move down the empty street, gaining speed as it went.

Desperate, she had remembered Skye Shot in the Head, the only person in the entire city she actually knew. She and Abbie and their mom had picked berries together more than once at the edge of Skye's reserve alongside Skye and her sisters and mother, and when Judith had gone off the rails there for a bit — she could admit now she had gone off the rails — she had run into Skye around town more than once. Then Skye disappeared and Judith heard she had gone to Calgary. After Jimmy drove off in his truck, she had found Skye's number in the phone book at the convenience store, and when she dialed it, Skye, miraculously, answered. It was nearly midnight, freezing cold out, and the streets were deserted.

"What? Are you kidding me? How did he even know where I was?"

"Skye phoned Mom and said she was taking care of you."

Again, she couldn't believe it, remembering for the first time in years how Skye's boyfriend came and picked her up and took her to their home, how Skye had given her that Native-girl-studies-white-girl-look, narrow-eyed, beyond unfriendly, and then, softening (or something), had let her in, made a bed on the sofa for her, and said she had to go to school or Skye and her boyfriend, William — William who? Bear — would put her out on the street again. So eventually, she went to some special school for street kids. She had only been there a couple of months before she went back to regular high school, but she had forgotten all about it. That school. *My god.*

"Dad sent her money to take care of me? Our father? I can't believe it. I never knew."

"She was a hairdresser, wasn't she? Where would she get the money to take care of you?" Skye had gotten Judith her first part-time job too, doing cleanups at the salon where she worked.

"I was a kid; what kid thinks of things like that? I gave the little bit of money I earned at the salon to Skye, or most of it anyway. Why didn't anybody come and get me?" she asked, suddenly seeing that she could choose to be offended instead of only guilty.

"You ran away. Does that sound like Dad, to go chasing after you? Maybe he was kind of glad when you escaped. Or maybe he thought you would just run away again."

"At that, he could have been right." Silence again. "I'm sorry, Sam. I'm sorry I left you." He had been staring at the rug, but now he lifted his head to look at her.

"You did what you had to do, I think." Had he really said that? "It was all — pretty much."

There was that noise again, coming out of darkness. Both hands went up over her face. She gasped, choked, gasped again.

"What? What?" Sam asked, trying to extricate himself from the armchair.

"I just remembered," she said, lowering her hands. Instead of the ritual pounding pain in her head that had begun to spread and spread, down her neck, into her shoulder and down her arm, there was, abruptly, only a faintly sizzling white silence that frightened her, before the familiar pain began leaking in at the edges. And the noises from her childhood.

"You... didn't remember? You forgot?"

Judith nodded, speechless, then collecting herself said, "In my business — I was a social worker — we would call that repression, I guess."

"But why?"

But she just waved her hand at him in reply: no, can't talk about it. He leaned over and filled her mug with hot coffee.

"Drink," he said. She obeyed, burning her mouth on the first sip. How could she have turned away from him? How could she have forgotten him, stayed away from him, and from Abigail and their parents? But an inadvertent glance out the window behind him, even in her shame, partially answered her: The rows of small frame houses, the tiny yards, the too-bare hills rising behind and over to the west, the hardscrabble farm she had run away from. Picking rocks from the fields by hand on freezing spring or fall days when she was maybe ten years old, chasing their few cows into the corral in rain or snow or hurricane-like winds, rising before dawn to make the school bus. But still, that was every farm kid's life then.

"My life would have been so different if I had come back at least once a year, stayed for a while — I wish they had come looking for me. I wish they had." Meaning their parents. Sam made a *hah* noise, and she remembered: *You made your bed, now lie in it.* No wonder she had left, and she was angry all over again. How is a kid to know she is loved if she is never hugged, not even touched, or kissed — not even a peck on the cheek.

"Look," he said. "I have to get over to the elevator, but...you know." He had managed to pry himself out of the chair, and, not looking at her, said to the air, "We've got to talk about Dad." But that social self was again taking over.

"Thank you for not yelling at me. Abbie and I had a shouting match."

"She was mad because she got stuck with looking after Dad after Mom died." He was so plain-spoken, she was ashamed for remembering only the constant euphemisms, the ceremonial quality to the talk, consisting mostly of endless platitudes, polite lies and, even worse, all the things not said — never said. When there had also always been this streak of pure plain-spokenness, of stark truth. "And we both had to explain why you stopped being at school when all the kids asked. Mom told us to say you were going to school in the city." He laughed out loud. "Everybody knew what a brat you were." Silence. "Sorry," he said, then laughed again. "I'm glad my kids weren't like you, except maybe Scott, a bit there, kinda wild for a while." But he was talking to himself.

Then, in his well-practised, convivial way, "Well, got to go. You come out to the house when you feel up to it. We'll have supper. If you feel like it, we can tour the old house — you know." At this he turned and, frowning, studied her as if to fix her here in case she disappeared again.

"You bet," Judith said, as if all was a foregone conclusion she wouldn't dream of disputing. "And you will tell me about Dad?" He had turned to open the back door and now glanced at her over his shoulder, speculatively, not friendly, and without speaking again, left, closing the door with a firm click behind him. She could hear his boots on the cracked cement going around the house to the street where he had parked his grain truck with its load of seed wheat that needed cleaning before he could put it in the ground.

She sat down at the table, then got up and sat on the sofa in the living room, then moved again to her bed where she lay down, eventually remembering that she had meant to take her painkillers but making no move toward them. After a moment, she thought to take long, deep breaths through her nose, to exhale slowly, holding in the air as long as she could. She felt as if she were the victim of a wasting disease, as if the blood and guts inside her were fading, shrinking, slowly dying. The sounds and pictures of the worst of her childhood returned to her, simple things, but she could not shut them off; one by one they came, and her childhood self was overwhelmed until she thought to remember she wasn't a child anymore, that her parents were dead, and it was over. Sam and Abbie survived in the middle of it; they kept right on, and look at them today. She was the one who thought that by running she could escape it all, when staying was the only way to get through it.

She went into the kitchen, where she leaned against the counter at the sink and gazed at the blank brick wall of the house on the other side of the still-bare caragana hedge. At work she saw such things routinely — worse things, terrible things — and yet she had been unable to look at her own "worse things." Did she think in some bizarre way that by seeing the afflictions of others she could recover from her own? But thinking back, it seemed to her that her motivation had been simply to save children from suffering. Nothing wrong with that; she forgave herself that. She turned away from the sink and the brick wall that obscured her view of the town and went back into the living room, where she sat on the sofa again.

Their mother had come into the kitchen some mornings with bruises on her face or on her chest, which the children would see when she bent over them to pour their milk and her dressing gown would fall open at her throat. Dad did that. Dad shouted terribly in the night. Sometimes there would be a cry of such unalterable, rock bottom, unfixable anguish that Judith would put her pillow over her head, press it against her ears until she had to move it before she suffocated. It was the cry that still haunted her; he thumped around, there were crashes sometimes so loud her child-self had thought the house was truly coming down. Sammie would crawl into bed with her or Abbie in the room they shared; Mom could be heard talking to Dad, her voice muffled, steady, soothing. Then everything would quiet down. Sometimes she would make a noise, a strange noise. Was he hurting her? He never once laid a hand on any of the kids; he was gentle to Mom all the time in the daytime. Judith had never seen him so much as touch her, and he didn't say mean things to her or call her names or anything like that. It was only in the night. The things that happened in the night.

I was a social worker, Judith thought now. *I know what that kind of thing does to kids.*

A new thought: *Why couldn't the kids ask what happened when they saw the bruises? Why could they never ask what the matter was with Dad? Why didn't anybody ever tell them one single thing?* They lived in the middle of a horror show and never knew why, or what it was, what had happened to them. That was the crime, worse than anything. That was the horror. It was the silence; the sense that they must not ever, not once, even so much as mention it. Didn't she and Abbie shush Sammie when he was little until he learned to be silent too, like them?

Why did their father get so violent in the night? What did he dream about? What had happened to him?

Was that why they were so religious? Did they think God would save them from whatever demon pursued him? Did they think if they lived the perfect, religious life of piety and ritual they would be released from their hell? Did they think of the kids at all? Nobody ever hurt them; they never woke up with bruises. Maybe that's why they slept in the downstairs bedroom, so their dad couldn't easily go into their rooms when he was still asleep, or wherever he was when he lashed out like that. When he went crazy.

She realized she had risen and had been pacing up and down the room, and stopped. Her head wasn't aching! It felt instead, once again, very light, and she went to the chair Sam had sat in and dropped into it with a thud, realizing that if she didn't sit, she would faint and might again crack her head and that would be the end of her. She began deep breathing once more, but it was a creaky, rebellious business, and she soon gave it up.

Still, examining herself, she realized she was growing calmer, she would soon be all right again. Herself again. No, she would not ever be herself again. She had no self. She was here to make a self out of all the pieces she had tried to throw away.

She thought, then, *How could it be so simple?* She'd thought it was a thundering volcano hissing out smoke and steam, threatening to spew its guts out all over the entire world and kill them all. She'd never thought it was just her own little childhood trauma. It was that combination: the horror, and on the other side, the implacable, vibrating silence, the praying to a God she never saw hide nor hair of. *I am such an idiot.*

At this, she laughed out loud, then rushed to the bathroom, where, for the umpteenth time since her crack on the head, she threw up and threw up more until all she could do was retch, and had to force herself to stop.

Then she showered and dressed with some care and, after some effort, managed to find Lucinda's number in Israel and phone her. But, of course, Lucinda was not in, so she left an answer to the Hebrew greeting on the phone, though never having met Levi — although she had spoken with him on the phone a couple of times when he and Lucinda were courting in New York — and not entirely sure of his voice, she wasn't sure if she had even reached the right phone number.

Nonetheless, when the beep came, she said, "How are you doing? How is the baby coming along? Are you managing all right? Phone me when you get in. Love you, Lucy dear." And as an afterthought, cheerily, "This is your mom!"

CHAPTER FOUR

HOME PLACE

"Started seeding?" Rick asked his son Blake.

"Mostly still too wet."

Blake's wife, Anne Marie, a cute, small blonde, remarked to nobody, "He's driving me crazy. I hope he can start soon."

"You didn't start yet, did you, Dad?"

"Still moving equipment around."

It was as if she had never left, Judith thought: the immense, boredom-inducing banalities . . . She stopped herself. Her headache was making her blink; it was all she could do not to put up her hand to shade her eyes.

Sylvia, Sam's wife, said suddenly, loudly, "Sam is talking about tearing down the old house." She didn't look at anybody when she said it, but she was clearly informing Abbie and Judith, the most affected, although it was the home place to all at the table except Anne Marie and Debbie's spouse, Fred, each of whom had their own revered home farms somewhere in the community.

Sam said, also not looking at anybody, "It's falling down. And it looks like hell. I can use that space for some new bins." Everybody looked from Abbie to Judith and back again, but mostly at Abbie, as if it hadn't much to do with Judith. Pain seared across Judith's forehead so that, inadvertently, she lifted her hand and pushed her palm against it, then, realizing what she was doing, lowered it.

Only a day earlier she had walked through the house she grew up in, carefully, room by room, slowly, putting her feet down softly so as not to jar any sleeping demons. How small it was. Yet, standing in it for the first time in fifty years, she remembered its smell, not just food cooking, not just the farm smells — boots not quite cleaned of barn manure, the pail of foamy milk at the door ready for the separator, the hanging coveralls smelling of hay and horses, the old coffee can full of wheat kernels her father would bring in after the first round on the combine so that the whole family could see it, smell it, weigh it in the hand, even chew it — no, just the too-familiar welcome and assaulting odours of her childhood.

She had walked out of the kitchen, stopped in the living room, moved on into the room behind it where their parents had slept, then upstairs to the dormer rooms, one she had shared with Abbie, and the other that had been Sam's. The roof had been leaking in the corner where Abbie's bed used to be; brown stains now patterned the walls, and, in places, layers of ancient wallpaper had melted back to reveal crumbling plaster. In each room, the windows were cracked and too cobwebbed and fly-speckled to see through, although she could hear songbirds twittering in the big poplar outside Sam's window. Why did it seem to her that even their house favoured her brother? Now he wanted to get rid of it? *Fine by me*, she thought, and then felt confused.

Abbie said into the taut silence, "I don't know what to say."

Fred, trying to help, asked, "Could it be moved? I could find room for it on our place."

"Wouldn't make it outta the yard," Sam said. "It's rotted right through in places. Roof's gone."

"You could have fixed that roof years ago," Abbie said.

"What are you so damn keen on keeping it for anyway?" Sam asked, ignoring the shushing he got from the women for swearing in front of the grandchildren. Raising his voice, "Was anybody happy in that house?"

"That doesn't matter," Abbie cried, a sound so unusual coming from her that every head turned. "Not while Dad —" She stopped abruptly, looking around the table. Dad what? Abbie had recovered herself. Her lips pursed, she shoved back her chair, startling everyone, walked out of the room, and returned with an envelope, out of which she extracted a yellowed piece of paper folded in quarters. "Sam and I thought you should see this."

She thrust the piece of paper in front of Judith. Hesitating, gazing at Abbie's flushed face, everyone staring at her, she accepted the paper and unfolded it carefully. It was fragile; in places the folds had worn right through. She studied it, the air around the table filled with tension. The print was faded, but she finally figured out that it was a certificate of release from the United States Army, dated January 1946, for Henry Clemensen of Sage, Alberta, Canada.

"Where did you get this?" It was all she could think to ask.

"It was in Mom's papers. We found it when she died."

"But — I didn't know he was in the army! I mean, that he fought in World War II."

"The United States Infantry," Sam said, a hint of a son's pride in his tone. Their father had always favoured him, and their mother had favoured him, too; maybe that was why Judith was so mad at her.

Concentrating, she asked, "But the U.S. Army?"

Sam said, "He wasn't the only border kid who joined the other country's army. Remember Albert Wrigley, south of Wisdom?" Border families usually had come from the United States in the first place — Iowa, the Dakotas, Montana — often had close relatives a few miles away across the line, and frequently went back and forth. Come to think of it, maybe they all had dual citizenship."

"How could we not know this?" she asked, looking around the table. Debbie and Fred's two children, girls eight and six, stared back at her, mouths open.

"If you'd stayed, you'd have known it too," Sam said. Sylvia elbowed him.

"Or come to Mom's funeral," Abbie muttered.

Judith deserved this, but she kept her head bent, refusing to look at anyone. Blake shifted nervously, clearing his throat. After a few more seconds, knives and forks began again to clink against plates. She refolded the paper and passed it back to Abbie.

"Pardon?"

Her brother-in-law Rick repeated in a friendly tone, "What brings you back after all these years?"

She wanted to say that the real question that few asked — assuming abuse or maybe a teenager's craziness — was: why did you *leave*? Even as a social worker's warning bells went off — violence, brutality, slave labour, incest, constantly flattened ambition, emptiness, desire — she could not rest in this familiar array of possibilities. But she answered Rick crisply. "It's cheap to live here. My pension isn't big enough to stay in Calgary, condo fees are too high, because . . ." She stopped, and laughed.

"I guess everybody asks you that," Rick said. "Sorry."

"Good reasons," Fred said, and Debbie said, "It's so peaceful out here. City life is so crazy."

"Did you miss us, Auntie Judy?" their daughter, Keira, inquired.

"But I didn't even know you," Judith said, noticing a faint resemblance to Jessica at the same age, so that she smiled at the little girl. "You have such a pretty name," she told her, and Keira smiled with such sweetness Judith nearly wept.

"She's not the only one who came back who started out here," Blake put in. "You know, the Harris guy, and — I think I heard of another, but I forget her name. In the old Grant house."

Judith said, "Do you know Saul Richter and his wife?"

"Don't know him," Sam said. "Him and his wife came to live here a few months ago, I think. Nobody says anything about them." *Now what did that mean?*

"What is it you want to know?" Abbie asked, her forehead wrinkling. "They're strangers."

"I had a chat with him; I was walking in the park, and so was he. He seemed nice; he seemed — educated." Somebody snorted, although she couldn't identify who and understood the snort to refer to the "educated" part of her comment, which here was a mark of disfavour, not favour.

Sylvia asked, "You heard about the swastika?"

Abbie said, "Foolishness. Kids. Pass the potatoes there to Fred, would you?"

Keira's smaller sister Becky was holding her fork upright, tapping its butt rhythmically on the table. Her hand seemed enormous, or were Judith's perceptual disturbances returning? Her head had been pounding since Abbie handed her their father's certificate of release; she was beginning to feel she might faint.

"How about you kids go play in the other room. We'll call you when the dessert is ready." Anne Marie rose. "I'll just start cutting the pies. Okay, Abbie?" She didn't wait for an answer.

"Somebody needs to put the coffee on," Debbie said, rising too.

"Use the flowered dessert plates," Abbie called to Anne Marie, who had begun opening cupboard doors. Sylvia was gathering the soiled dinner plates and cutlery. Rick, Fred, Blake, and Sam began talking crops across the table. Behind the bustle of the women, the apparently easy conversation among the men and the chatter of the kids in the other room, the air was full of a high pitched, singing tension. Or was she, Judith, the only one who felt it?

She woke around three in the morning when it was still pitch dark outside, with the sensation of a heavy weight on her that prevented her from moving. The awareness of immense pain hit her; it was in her head, and simultaneously slicing through her neck, burning down her right arm, and spreading across her back to lodge, a red-hot ball, between her shoulder blades. She was frightened, trying to sit up, to reach for the light, but the escalating pain sucked her back to the pillow each time she tried. She had broken out in sweat, could hear herself making a sound: *Uh, uh, uhhh.* Such scalding intensity, like nothing she could recall ever having experienced before. She had had four babies, she knew pain, yet . . .

Just thinking about something else — her babies — seemed to have helped. Cautiously, she lifted herself onto her elbows, then persevered, rolling onto her side; finally reached the lamp and turned it on. Still using her left arm, although the right was beside the bedtable, she rattled the table's drawer, forcing it crookedly open, and fumbled for the bottle of painkillers. No good. To open the bottle, she would have to sit up. For a split second she despaired, and tears poured out of her eyes, rolling down her cheeks to drip onto the sheets; nausea hit her, the urgency of this last overriding the paralysis caused by the pain, as she pulled herself out of bed and upright, staggered into the bathroom, where she threw up into the toilet, then leaned, gasping, coughing at the sink while she splashed cold water onto her face and into her mouth with shaking fingers and spat it out again, fighting not to faint, so terrified was she of once again hitting her head, this time on the bathtub or the sink.

As soon as it opened, she went without an appointment to Wisdom's one-doctor medical clinic. When the nurse saw her, she disappeared into the doctor's office at once, and despite the three elderly farm folk already waiting, three pairs of eyes following her every move, led Judith directly into the examining room. Immediately, the young woman doctor came in, introduced herself as Dr. Chan, and began asking her questions, looking into her eyes with a light, taking her blood pressure and pulse, listening to her heart and her lungs.

"I had a severe concussion about four months ago," Judith told her, showing her the bottle of pills she had brought with her.

"That's for severe migraines," the doctor said. "How much have you taken?"

"Just one this morning, and then I vomited it up." She shrugged. She should have known there would be this grilling.

"Any others?"

"Just extra-strength Tylenol." Not quite true. There was also diazepam and, besides Gravol, some other antinausea drug whose name she couldn't recall.

"How many Tylenol have you taken?"

"Only two," Judith said.

"Two this morning? How many last night?" She seemed if not exactly alarmed, a little too intense.

"I don't know," Judith told her, although she suspected she had taken at least two. She could tell the doctor was reserving judgement as to the truth of her replies.

"Before I prescribe anything more, or try to make a management plan, I'll need to see your records, maybe talk with your physicians in Calgary." Judith was seeing two of her. She blinked, rubbed her eyes, and the two melded into one thin, pretty woman.

"You have to do something," she said. "I don't think I can stand this." She had begun shaking; water poured down her face that she recognized as tears. The doctor helped her lie down on the examining table, apologizing because she had only a sheet of thin paper to cover her, and stuffed a couple of tissues into her hand.

"I'm going to try to get your specialist on the phone. You stay here. You're going to be fine now." Judith was beginning to feel embarrassed that she had let things get so far, although this sentiment baffled her because, after all, it was not her fault she had fallen on ice months ago and hit her head, so what was she embarrassed about? In the silence and stillness of the tiny examining room, the water had stopped running from her eyes, her pain lessened; she was growing sleepy. The door opened, and at once the doctor was leaning over her.

"Do you remember going to a traumatic brain injury clinic?" Judith was sitting up now, swivelling on her bottom to face the doctor.

"I think more than once, although my memory for that period isn't very clear."

"What about a neuropsychologist, or a therapist for, say, PTSD?"

"A lot of people asked me a lot of questions. Probably, but I don't specifically remember."

"I'm going to give you a referral to a traumatic brain injury clinic in Medicine Hat. Time for a re-evaluation, I think. How is the pain now?"

"Quite a bit better," Judith admitted.

"Part of your problem may be that you're overmedicating, but I think the clinic will be able to evaluate that and help you set up a plan to manage the pain." Then she was gone. And yet, miraculously, Judith's pain had dropped to almost nothing. Pills kicking in, she told herself, although she was also thinking, in jocular mode, *Cavalry to the rescue, swelling orchestral background . . .*

She woke in the night having had the dream again: She, in her nightgown, the one with the lace trim that has pulled away at the shoulder, her feet bare, running down the stairs after Jack, who is still wearing his overcoat and carrying a hastily packed sports bag. He stops in the kitchen, turning to her one last time, Judith reaches for him, Jack pulls away, steps back from her, hurries out of the house without saying goodbye.

She lay blinking into the darkness, as fully desolate as if it had happened only last night instead of so many years ago.

"I can't do this anymore," he had said when she woke at the sound of him opening the closet. The current of emotion emanating from him was so darkly powerful that had it been from any other male she would have been afraid. "I am leaving," he said, opening a drawer, taking out his underwear and socks and throwing them into his gym bag. "I'll take care of you, and I want to see Alice and Jessica as much as possible, but —," he turned to look at her, "this is over." This last sentence spoken gently, surprising her. "You know it's over." She knew no such thing; she was his wife; she loved him; he was everything to her; he was her life. She had asked, "But where will you go?" He said, turning again to open another drawer, "Patricia." It was the first she knew of this too.

She was so thirsty that her lips were sticking together, and having drained the water glass by her bed, she padded into the kitchen to get more. She was surprised to see that a light was on in the brick house next door, not that there was a window on her side, but apparently the house had an outside light on the far wall that revealed a cone of backyard, including a short stretch of narrow sidewalk leading, she supposed, to the alley. Then a shadow, stumbling as if drunk or hurt, came around the end of the house and went down the sidewalk into the darkness. Judith hadn't put a light on in the kitchen, so the person staggering down the sidewalk didn't know he or she was being watched. There was a crash, cursing — a woman, then — followed by the creaking of the gate onto the alley opening and slamming shut. Now, silence reigned, the outside light blinked off, and that was that.

She remembered then that when she had first moved in, late one night she was sure she could hear the thump of rock music coming from somewhere and wondered now if it had been from this neighbour's house. But otherwise, there was no sign of life in it that she had ever noticed. Of course, she rarely used her own front door but chose to go out the back way, and the neighbouring house's garage was attached at the front rather than the back, so if vehicles went in or out, she didn't see them.

She was studying a map of southern Saskatchewan and Alberta she had found in one of the boxes of household goods she'd brought with her, a cup of coffee at her elbow, when her sister-in-law Sylvia dropped in. They chatted for a while about seeding, the weather, the state of the house Judith had bought, about which Sylvia was unexpectedly kind.

"What year did you and Sam marry?" Judith asked, trying to move their halting conversation along.

"Seventy-seven, in November, same year your mom died in February. Your dad wasn't doing so well out there on his own, but I think with your mom gone, Sam needed to make his own family. Abbie was at Rick's family's place then, but she was the one who looked after your dad. Sam couldn't go near him then." She moved her coffee mug back and forth, thoughtfully. "It was okay with me. We lived on the old place — my family's, I mean — for the first few years we were married." They should have moved onto Sam's old family place, not her family's. Why didn't they? Sylvia answered her unasked question. "My dad needed Sam's help. A family of girls, you know, and your dad, he . . ."

"What?"

"He was still farming his own place, where you grew up. He wasn't that old, sixty or so. And I found him to be . . ."

"Tough to get along with? We all found him tough to get along with," Judith said. "Does Sam ever say much about Dad?"

"Oh sure, Dad this and Dad that, about farming mostly."

"But did Sam ever tell you anything about him? Like, why he came alone and why here and how he met Mom?"

"Not that I can remember," Sylvia said. "Don't you know?"

"No. Just the name of the village nearest where he was born: Sage. When we were kids, he never talked about anything about his life before he married Mom. And then he died. I'm not sure when that was exactly." Now that she thought of it, how was it she could not remember such an important thing as the year of her father's death?

"You know, my cousin tracked down our grandfather's records, no problem at all. Everything is online these days. Where is — Sage, did you say?"

"All I know is that it was along the American border on the Canadian side, way west of here but before the mountains, I think. It's probably gone now too."

"I'd for sure try the internet."

"Have you ever met my daughters?" Judith asked, thinking that once they were adults, they made no effort to keep their mother informed of their comings and goings, and all of them had been curious about their mother's family, often asking Judith questions until she had refused to answer anymore. If they had wanted to meet their aunt and uncle and grandparents, all they had to do was come here on their own. "Jessica, or maybe Alice?" Her suspicion that one or other of them had was confirmed when Sylvia said, "I remember meeting Jessica once — dark hair, dark eyes? A lovely girl, but no, I never met Alice, although Abbie did describe her to me."

"What about Lucinda? She's my third daughter."

"I don't remember meeting anybody by that name."

Without noticing she had, Judith dropped her chin and held her head in her hands, then began massaging her shoulder that always tensed against a headache, increasing the pain radiating through her skull and down her neck.

"Have you seen a specialist? You know — had a thorough exam since the accident?"

"Oh sure, but it's mostly soft tissue damage now, and there isn't much to be done about that. The headaches are just the residue of the concussion, they say. Post-concussion syndrome, they call it."

"They're lasting long enough," Sylvia said. "What has it been — about three months or so?"

"A little longer," Judith said, keeping her tone neutral, although the pain was rising, that red-hot-poker thing was happening again, and she could tell she would soon be in for another bout of nausea. She hadn't told anyone, although probably her daughters knew, that she would have to endure months more of this, a year at least. Sometimes she didn't think she would make it. Or maybe there wouldn't be — hadn't one of the doctors she'd seen said that there was no reason why it didn't go away? What did he know anyway?

Sylvia said, rising, "I have to go — hair appointment in a few minutes." For the first time Judith noticed that Sylvia's hair was dyed blonde, and also that she was not only attractive, but had a sort of chic that Judith in her entire life couldn't imagine having. Wait, hadn't the O'Connor girls gone to college? A fairly rare thing in her generation.

Sam had done well for himself, and Judith was pleased for him. And yet, their kids were grown up and gone from home, and she hadn't even met them, knew only that Scott was taller than his giant father and the oldest daughter, Kaylene, was working on a doctorate in one of the sciences at some American university. She couldn't even remember the middle girl's name.

When Sylvia left, she thought, *I guess I came back to recover my family.* But with her mother and father both dead, what was there to recover? Sam and Abbie had lived their lives; she hadn't been a part of that. Did she honestly care about the intervening years she had missed? No, not really. Just the same old, same old, she told herself. She had her friends: Adrianna and a few others from work, her neighbour June in her building. And her girls.

Her birthright? What the hell was that anyway? Poverty. Ignorance. Parents who, like downtrodden old-country peasants, clasped a god to their bosoms, filled their mouths with Him, He who cared nothing at all for them or they wouldn't have been so poor and so strange. But even as she fumed, it occurred to her that her birthright had also been a life lived in the heart of the natural world, in the midst of the constant fragrances: of grassy, flower-studded meadows, of fields of mowed hay, of wheat ripening in the sun, wild roses, cinquefoil, saskatoons, and chokecherries in bloom, of sages, of the smell of water coloured amber as it ran over wet clay soil and burbled over small dark stones, and the startling, near-miraculous beauty and purity of winter, the loss of all of it a steady, at last recognized pain.

PART II

SAGE

CHAPTER FIVE

HARES

She could no longer stop the dreams that came night after night, drenched in her own bruised affect, or the ambience of the petty hell inside which she sometimes thought she had spent her entire life. But now, at last, instead of refusing them doggedly, or running from them, she sought to extract herself from the too-intense feelings, to shake free the meaning of each painful image and scene, or fragment of a scene, from her life, to see each one for what it was if she could suppress all the accompanying fear, disgust, shame, guilt, longings.

"You're not her lover, for god's sake," she had said to Victor, gritting her teeth, trying to hang onto her rational professional's voice when once again Victor had swept in, lifted Lucinda out of her current tantrum onto his lap, hugged and kissed her, murmuring to her. "You're her father. Love her like a father." She had been trembling all over with rage — was she jealous? No: daddy's little girl, how ugly a stereotype that was. She had worked with troubled children for many years; she knew what that was about.

Then that image again: Victor and Lucinda, barely a teenager, locking eyes, he grasping her upraised arm; how many times had she dreamt it over the years? How she had then realized that the child was drunk. She had wanted to fall down on the floor and laugh until she cried. It was all so predictable, so absurd, so much like Judith herself at that age, although she had always managed to either sneak up to her room without anybody noticing or she wouldn't come home until she could hide her condition. The memory of her own defiance had, for the moment, drained away her anger.

But later, after Victor had slammed his way out of the house, she heard Lucinda throwing up in the bathroom. She didn't go near her, sat stubbornly in the living room with the television on and listened to her every cough, retch, and gag, refusing to go up to her, a failure or a cruelty that she had never stopped regretting, especially later, remembering herself, the thirteen-year-old throwing up in the bathroom and neither parent coming near her. Nor Abbie, nor Sam, neither being allowed to. And Judith's own enraged shame.

And through all of this, there was Catherine, watching from a distance with wary, un-childlike eyes, a look Judith had seen too often in the eyes of other children not her own.

At this she thought, *Enough*, then checked to see if her head was aching, having — amazingly — forgotten her physical pain in her absorption in the tormenting memories. But she found, instead of pain, a high-pitched buzzing noise that swirled with each thud of her too-fast heartbeat. It was as if a strong wind, a tornado spun wildly but rhythmically in her head, so that she thought, between the pressure and the noise, her brain might explode. She turned onto her back and pulled up the pillows so she could half sit while she breathed deeply, trying to slow her heart rate and to stop the swelling, pulsing buzz in her ears.

The night Jack woke her as he threw his clothes into his open suitcase, he had said, over his shoulder, "I can't do this anymore," and she had asked, in her confusion, trying to fend off the truth, only, "But where will you go?" as if she were his mother. "Patricia," he'd said. Now she thought, *I knew there was someone; I knew it very well; I just couldn't accept it; I pretended it wasn't true.* She must have made a noise, because he came close to the bed to look into her face. His expression was sympathetic, as if she were a mugging victim he had come across on the sidewalk, blood trickling down her face. He put out a hand to soothe her; she struck it away.

Wasn't it time to stop loving Jack? Wasn't it time to end the grieving for him? The idea startled her. *Huh!* she heard herself say, and she almost laughed. Her heart had slowed now, the noise in her head diminishing, and she took a deep breath of relief.

She had picked the wrong men; she should have stayed with her family until she could have left in the usual way — to go to college or to get some training. What else? She should have taken Lucinda to a psychologist, but she worried that such visits would brand her daughter in the minds of her teachers and peers and — much worse — in Lucinda's own mind as having a problem, as being a problem. Working with troubled teenagers, she thought, had maybe complicated her best mother's instincts. She should have gotten a job that didn't take her out of the house to rescue children at three and four in the morning when she had her own little ones to look after.

But the babies she had rescued, who had been left alone for days in near-empty houses without a crumb of food or anyone to change their diapers, much less comfort them, the toddlers found alone on empty city streets at midnight — what was that? What about the anguish of the drunken, drug-addicted parents who, in the horror that their own lives were, had terrorized, then abandoned their own babies? Or the mothers, bone thin, with too many small children, knowing only violence in their lives, the soul knocked right out of them, their despair so deep, their helplessness so profound, that sitting across her desk from them it was all she could do not to weep.

Maybe in those days she too readily called things evil when really they were only human. And her four children had never been struck, although their home had been tumultuous. But, thinking back, she recalled the stillness in the house in the evenings, homework being done, first Jack, then Victor reading the paper or watching television, she working in the kitchen, or ironing, or making school lunches. She sometimes thought those were the only times in her life when she had been happy. But this was too much, she had things to do, she had to make an appointment at that clinic in Medicine Hat, she had to . . . what? Get groceries, call Catherine, check in on Jessica, start trying to have a life, and she was up and in the bathroom before she realized she had gotten out of bed.

The following morning, she woke early to much-lessened pain, and hearing through the thin walls of her house the calling of the great flocks of ducks and geese on their spring migration north, she was stirred enough to rise at once, dress, put on her now too-warm parka, her boots, and her gloves and walk down to the park by the stream, thinking that she would watch the sun rise.

But Saul Richter was already there. He greeted her, "Good morning," not as he had before, in that light, half-teasing way, but somberly, his voice coming from somewhere deep in his chest. Judith faltered, having taken a step toward him, thinking that she might hug him gently. "Or is it more properly still night?"

"That period when it is neither, I think," she answered. "A moment of magic. A good time for rituals." She was being whimsical, false, and knew it. Already the first rays of light were blurring the line of the eastern hills.

"I think not," he said.

"But why not?"

"In the night, something happened." The muted but musical trickle of water a few feet from them halted, the breeze that had come with the dawn died away. A hush had come into the air, as if they were circled by attentive listeners. She heard herself breathe out delicately. "Yes," he went on. "Such a thing. I wept."

"What?" She stepped closer to him. "What happened?"

"Someone came into our yard. There are old elms that should perhaps be cut because they are decaying. In a big wind they could blow onto the house. Yes? Break the roof, maybe. Destroy our deck."

"Yes?"

"Someone shot hares and hung them from our trees by their necks." The wild hares that populated the fields and hills around Wisdom were often as big as small dogs, Judith knew. "They slit their bellies, they pulled out their entrails to hang down . . ." He drew in a deep, slow breath as if to steady himself. "My wife got up in the night — we leave on the light outside the back door. She went into the kitchen." He paused. "I heard her fall."

Judith made a sound.

"I cannot run fast anymore," he said, brushing a hand past his thigh, "but I went as fast as I could to her, there, lying on the floor." He turned away from Judith.

It was easier to ask "Is she all right?" than to deal with what he had told her.

"A lump on the head. It will go away."

Here she knew she must say how sorry she was; how shameful this action was; how unforgiveable. But for the life of her, thinking of the old woman's revulsion, maybe even horror, mixed with instantly remembered terror, possibly even the thought that what she had long ago escaped from had begun again, here, Judith couldn't get out a sound. He had turned back to her, and she stood there looking at him — the light coming up now enough that they could see each other's faces — while water pooled in her eyes, making her ashamed.

"The world is too hard," she said, finally.

"So," he said. "You think if you make your way to the ends of the earth, there you will at last find peace."

"Not if there are human beings there," Judith said, too quickly. But they laughed together harshly, once.

In the ensuing silence, the old man seemed to have regained some vitality, or was it a return of his courage?

"They will find who did it," she told him. "*Here* there will be justice," pointing downward, toward the earth. He looked long into her face, his own unreadable.

"No," he said, although his voice was mild. "I do not think so."

He walked away, back toward the town. After a minute, she followed his shadow, but some distance behind him. They went out of the park, at the road each turning in a different direction to go back to their homes.

Later in the day, Abbie dropped in.

"I've come to tell you that the pastor has called a prayer meeting tonight about the . . . Richters. Do you want to come?"

"The Richters?"

"I mean, about what happened to them."

Judith wanted to ask if she was referring to the Holocaust, but decided not to pick a fight, things being precarious enough between them.

Abbie, seeing Judith knew about the hares, went on, "It was a cruel thing to do, frightening a couple of harmless old people. I can tell you that everybody is agreed about that."

"Does anybody know who did it?"

"Well, somebody probably knows who it was, but I don't, and nobody I talked to today when I was phoning around about the meeting knew either. Or they said they didn't. But then, they are all good church people. It wouldn't be one of them."

Judith had a picture of a couple of oafish, stoned teenage boys sniggering as they did it, but no, she thought: Too much effort was involved for kids like that to be bothered; it was too calculated an assault. And you can't shoot a hare when you're drunk or wasted. Who did that leave? She had no idea.

"Are you sure you don't know who did it?"

Abbie said nothing, but she looked away, her lips tight.

"But you do think it was because they are Jews, right?"

"No! It was probably a stupid joke!"

"They had a swastika painted on their fence! Was that a stupid joke?"

84

"It could have been, just a prank by kids, probably." Abbie was keeping her voice even. "You haven't been here for fifty years. What do you know about it? And anyway, such things happen everywhere. Don't tell me it never happened in Calgary when you lived there."

"Not gutted, strung-up animals," Judith said through her teeth. But she was being childish. "Yes, of course. You're right about that. And I didn't do a thing, because I didn't know any of the people it happened to. I've never been in a synagogue in my life. Come to think of it, I never went to school with a single Jewish kid — that I knew of, anyway. There just weren't any around in the Saskatchewan country-side, not out on the land, when we were kids. They were in the towns and cities."

"I heard that in the early days there was a farm settlement of just Jews, nobody else, way east of us. Didn't last long, I guess."

"Most people didn't last long in those early days," Judith said.

Wait a minute — she could remember hearing somebody using the expression "jewing" somebody down, referring to bargaining over the price of an object, and she had wondered what it meant, but when she'd asked, nobody would tell her. So even if there weren't Jews around, anti-Semitism persisted. People must have brought it with them from the old country. And she was struck by the phrase *old country*, and how when she was a child everyone used it the same way they used *homestead* and *dirty thirties*, and *quarter*, referring to land. And the old vocabulary of the countryside, the way of talking, the concerns and the shared history implicit in the vernacular seemed touching, even heartbreaking.

Abbie said, in a dreamy voice, remembering, "People said the Lepinskis were Jewish. When they were in the old country, I mean. Remember them?" The name Lepinski rang no bells. "I went to school with Joel, and I think Pearl was your age."

"Pearl?" Yes, there had been a Pearl in her class for a year when she was small, a nice girl, pretty, with long dark hair, very smart, sang beautifully in an era when singing in school was a daily event and being a good singer was a source of much envy. She had liked Pearl a lot, had been her friend and played with her and went eagerly to her birthday party. Almost nobody else from school had showed up, though, although nothing was said about that and she didn't think she had even noticed because she and Pearl were having so much fun, and yet she had puzzled why nobody else wanted to be Pearl's friend. She'd loved that kid, she thought now, the way little kids can love each other, and what an idiot she was. At least whatever else they might have been, her parents weren't anti-Semites. *Strange*, she thought, and was puzzled because she could see no reason why her parents should, on this matter, think any differently than the community did.

But she said only, "I might have dealt with a foster kid or two with that last name."

"What kind of a social worker were you?"

Judith was pretty sure she had told Abbie this at least once. So they were done talking about the Richters?

"Child protection. But wait a minute, I'm kind of surprised," she said, gesturing between the two of them, "that we can talk as easily as if we'd been together all along." Remembering that things hadn't been easy at all the morning Abbie had burst into her kitchen.

Abbie sighed. "If it were two years, or five years, or maybe even ten years, it wouldn't have been easy. But fifty years? When it comes right down to it, what's left to say? You abandoned us when you were fifteen and you didn't come back, not even when our mother died. We thought you were ... maybe a little bit ... unbalanced."

Judith said, softly, looking away, "Maybe I was." Outside, rain squalls hit the window above the sink, each one seeming louder than the last.

"Did you miss us?" Abbie asked. "I always wondered that."

"Terribly," Judith said, surprising herself. "Year after year after year. But I had made a life, bit by bit, in the city. I was afraid to get trapped again, afraid to lose what I had built that suited the person I wanted to be. Once I left this madness."

"Madness?" Abbie said, clearly taken aback.

"Couldn't you feel it? You couldn't sneeze without praying, or get out of bed, or go to the bathroom, or cook the damn dinner. And bible camp every blasted summer with those feeble-brained . . . And Dad, wound as tight as a spring no matter how much he made us pray. Just silent, jaw clamped shut. What was he hiding? That's what I want to know. We did not have a happy home."

"We had everything we needed," Abbie said. "No one was hurting us — no beatings like the Caswell kids, no starvation, no . . ." Judith was thinking of the Schlapp family. Nothing could be proved. Old Schlapp had never gone to jail, although finally his wife had moved out, taking all six kids with her. Even the oldest, a boy nearly twenty, wouldn't stay with him on the farm. The worst of them all, but he wasn't on Abbie's list. Maybe she didn't remember Schlapp. On the other hand, her sister had always been in a position where she didn't have to think about such things if she didn't want to. "Yes," Abbie said. "There was madness, but not the kind you think."

She got up, crossed the room to lean with her back against the counter where the sink was. Rain pattered against the window behind her and trickled down the glass. She was pulling a loose thread at the hem of her shirt, twisting it around her fingers, breaking it off.

"In his last years on the farm, Dad began to have rages," she said. "After Mom was dead. He would . . . have rages. They were terrible, Judy. He really scared me. He smashed things, he screamed. He shoved anybody who got in his way. He would . . . advance on you with his eyes . . . they positively shot out rays, just rays of — I don't know what, but they were just so scary. And the pastor couldn't do a thing. Dad forbade the pastor to ever set foot on the place again. Can you imagine that? The neighbours were scared of him — I thought I might have to call the Mounties — and the doctor tried, but he couldn't help." All of this coming at once as though she had been saving it up for years to tell someone. "Living all alone out there after Mom died. Something went wrong in him."

"Maybe Dad discovered God wasn't going to fix things after all," Judith said. Abbie lifted her head quickly. None of this surprised Judith now — there was inevitability to it — but it wasn't fair, what she had just said.

"Don't you believe in God?" Abbie said quietly, the very notion stunning her into whispering.

"I don't know if I do or I don't. But for sure not the one you believe in. I think a real god couldn't possibly need worshipping, or would pay attention to every single little person, or every meanness or snide remark on earth." *Or the Holocaust.* Oh god, had she thought that? She too had things to say that she had been hoarding for years, but that now embarrassed her with their banality. "I'd like to know more about where Dad came from."

"What on earth for? Everybody is dead on that side. The farm is long gone. Even the town is gone."

Judith stared at her in puzzlement. Surely everybody wanted to know where their parents came from.

"Rain's stopped," Abbie said. "I have to get going. I said I'd help get the church ready for tonight. I take it you won't be there." She didn't wait for a reply and was still pulling on her jacket as she went out the door.

What the hell good would a prayer meeting do besides make those in attendance feel good about themselves, Judith thought after her sister was gone. Was there anybody crying out to find out who had done this thing? Had anybody gone to the police? She had no doubt at all that it had been done because the Richters were Jews. Jews in a Christian town. If nobody would name the act for what it was, it would just keep happening. But she shrank at the thought of going to the police herself: surely the town council would be in regular communication with the Mounties, gathering statistics, that sort of thing; surely the serious people in town would call the police — maybe the Richters themselves had. Strangers in small towns had to mind their own business or they might end up with dead hares hanging in their trees too.

In the mail, besides a cryptic postcard from Lucinda, a chatty letter from Alice had arrived. Among the usual banalities, she remarked that her father had recently brought his latest wife to visit them. That Jack had been there in Tanzania, knew his grandchildren as she did not, struck her in the heart. She thought of Jacob, Alice's oldest, who had been born in Calgary, a fact Alice seemed to have forgotten. How Judith had cried when she and Dwight, a doctor by then, had taken him away, so far away that Judith had known she would never know her first grandchild.

Children had a right to grandparents; she, Judith, felt she had never had any herself, because her mother's people had been as reclusive as Judith's own parents, and had died young anyway. And Dad? He said they were dead a long time ago. He had said that when Judith and her siblings were little kids. What kind of a family — except during wartime and catastrophes of one kind or another — has no grandparents?

She would find out what had happened to her own. And then, for what seemed like the first time ever, she thought of the duty to her own parents, in which she had so clearly failed.

CHAPTER SIX

NO MAN'S LAND

From the time she left Medicine Hat, where she had spent the previous day at the brain injury clinic, she had been steadily climbing. She had sailed right past the junction leading to the legal crossing into the U.S., hardly noticing, so enticing was the view of the Rockies ahead of her, their peaks, slopes, and granite chasms smoothed by haze to a flat lilac cut-out against the even azure of the sky. Now she was sure she had gone too far west. She would have given up, made a U-turn, and headed back east, but as she came over another rise, the dark grey outlines of at least one building popped up, and she passed a sign telling her that this was not Sage but Whiskey Gap. She was heartened, having been told by Abbie, who said she had been told by Sam, that Sage was "over by Whiskey Gap," and that Whiskey Gap would be a marker, where surely Sage no longer would. "If you decide to try to find Sage — although heaven knows why you would — better find Whiskey Gap first."

Whiskey Gap: Judith couldn't remember the last time she had heard the name of the infamous village; probably when she was in school and learning about the southern prairie's history of cross-border smuggling — mostly alcohol. It was somewhere along the U.S.–Canada border south of, maybe, Cardston; she wasn't sure.

"But I thought Dad was from another patch of too-dry farming country. You're talking about the foothills. That's grazing land, I think."

90

Abbie said, unhelpfully, "What decent person would even live in a town called Whiskey Gap?"

She pulled over and stopped, but after a minute, waiting for her body to adjust to the sudden silence with no wind rushing past her car, she realized that it was past noon and she was starving and needed to eat her sandwich, drink some water, and find a bathroom. Not a soul was around anywhere, not a vehicle; she had the whole vast world to herself, so she got out of the car, stretched hard, then crouched in the ditch to relieve herself. Finished, she pulled up her jeans and strolled toward the remains of the buildings: a false-fronted store, and two more smaller wooden buildings that appeared also to have once been places of business, but no homes.

To her right, on a slight rise, she spotted a neat stone cairn, a painted metal plaque fixed to it. My god, she thought, reading the sign: the smuggling of whiskey from the U.S. into Canada had begun as far back as 1870! It went from Montana up to Fort Whoop-Up, one of the lawless forts the Mounties came west to subdue, only to find it deserted. She thought this piece of Canadian history amusing: no bloody battle, no circling of wagons, no war cries or scalpings, just some nicely brought up, if exhausted, red-coated eastern or British Isles lads with aged rifles riding worn-out horses, quietly securing the empty fort. The whiskey trade, though, had boomed once again during Prohibition in the United States, although then the flow of alcohol had gone in the opposite direction. Although the sign didn't say so, she knew that the great fortunes now enjoyed by certain Canadian families had their beginnings in this very rum-running.

There was more, but she noticed that the sky above the mountains was beginning to shade to a deeper blue, and while those innocent-seeming white clouds might sail on by and dissipate, she was afraid the mountains would soon be churning out thunderclouds and flinging them to where she stood alone in the gentle wind, about a yard from no man's land. And she still hadn't found Sage.

As she hurried back to her car, uncertainty nagged at her that this was a fool's errand, quite pointless, and would avail her nothing. But she turned the car around and drove back east, now munching on the sandwich she had bought in Lethbridge, watching carefully for any indications that there had once been a hamlet along the roadside. Soon she was back at the highway leading to the major border crossing into the U.S., but having found no deserted village or even the remains of one, instead of continuing along the east–west route she had come by, she debated an instant, then turned south as if she planned to cross into the United States.

Mere yards from the border services buildings, she came to a road that was, just as she thought it should be, two gravel tire tracks barely discernable in the wild grass, heading east on a line parallel to the border. She looked over once as she made the turn, knowing she would look suspicious, half expecting sirens, the border police chasing her for running drugs — this wasn't even a proper road, and seeing the sky hadn't changed much since Whiskey Gap, she slowed, crossed all fingers against flat tires, and kept driving. Soon, barely poking its head above the weeds and tall grass, she saw the remains of a village: a falling-down frame building, windows broken or missing and shingles torn away by weather, leaving gaping holes. She could make out bleached words painted below the building's eaves: *Sage*, and below that, in flaking once-green paint, *M.D. Single Tree*, "M.D." meaning Municipal District.

"Well, that's wrong. I see two trees," she muttered — they were side by side some distance from the building, as if there had once been a row of them — and a few crows or ravens watching her from them cawed in derisive acknowledgement. Or, it occurred to her, perhaps "single tree" was supposed to be one word, *singletree*, and referred to part of the equipment used to hitch up a team of workhorses? No, that was properly *swingletree*, not that she'd ever heard anybody say that, or *whippletree* or *whiffletree* or something, an American version of the same thing. She was gratified to think that in the dark recesses of the past, this information could only have come from her father.

She got out of the car, intending to go up the few steps leading into the building, but saw they were too cracked and splintered to hold her weight. Instead, as if history had merely retreated to the back, she waded through the stiff crested wheatgrass around the building, only to discover that its back half had calved off like a chunk of iceberg and was now a pile of rubble. Within a few miles of this decayed remnant, though, her father had been born and had lived out his youth until he had gone overseas to war. She wanted to feel some connection to him now that she was here, but a cloud scudding between her and the sun cast her in shadow, and the breeze was becoming a wind. That suddenly, she was chilled and upset, invaded by a pervasive sense of things being out of kilter, stained and rotting. Her head had begun to pound, and, as if to blot out the village of Sage, her headache caused her vision to blur; she blinked repeatedly to clear it, and when a few spatters of rain hit her face, she looked again toward the mountains.

Grey clouds had obliterated them, and fat, low clouds were sailing across the sky toward her. An instinct from her childhood in such country kicked in, and, glancing at the ground, she knew that, wet, it would turn to gumbo and she without a four-wheel drive, and alone. Nobody here to rescue her if she slid off the road, and if she used her phone, heaven knows how long it would be before help arrived. She hurried back to the car and with some difficulty on the narrow trail managed to turn around and start back toward the pavement she had driven off at the border crossing some time before — a half hour? Ten minutes?

She turned north on the main highway but, not paying close attention, turned again at the first paved road heading east. She realized quickly it was the wrong one, and here she was, after about ten kilometres, driving into a hamlet of the kind that once dotted the prairies: a two-block-long street with a handful of businesses tucked into the worn, settler-era frame buildings, a half-dozen tiny houses separated by empty lots now overgrown with weeds where there had once been other houses. An abandoned-looking curling rink and ancient community centre sat side by side, but the grass in front of them had been mowed, and ruts ran around both buildings where recently cars and trucks must have parked. She thought she would get herself a cold drink; if nothing else she could hold it to her neck or forehead to deaden the pain that had come down on her at Sage.

She chose what she thought was a café. Inside, immediately picking up a faint musty smell, seeing no counter or booths, she was about to back out again, but as her eyes adjusted to the dimmer light, she saw a few men sitting around what she recognized as a card table. Behind them were another four or five unoccupied tables, arranged more or less equidistant from each other, with the same flowered tablecloths spread over them. She couldn't see any women about, and thought, reflexively, *They'll be in the kitchen.* The men slowly revealed themselves as elderly farmers, of the kind she had once known as a boring but ever-present part of the adult scenery, and who were patiently, if glumly, passing the time jawing, drinking coffee, and occasionally playing cards, while back home their too-eager sons now did the farming.

"You lost?" the man seated nearest to her inquired over his shoulder in a not-unfriendly way, and the other three laughed companionably at his witticism.

"I guess I am," she said. "I was looking to buy a cold drink. I thought this was a café." A slim woman, her thin white hair neatly curled, wearing a flowered dress with a checked apron over it, opened the door from the kitchen at the far end of the room, then went back inside, leaving the door propped open.

"This here is the Seniors' Centre," the man across the table from her said. He was wearing a clean blue ball cap whose brim cast his face in shadow, and she saw how massive his hands were, how thick his fingers, the result of years of working with machinery and probably animals as well. "Sit down and we'll get you a drink. May!"

94

"What is it? You don't have to yell."

The woman was already coming from the kitchen carrying a glass with something dark in it, probably a soda or iced tea. It had occurred to Judith during this exchange that somebody here might be able to tell her about her grandparents, so, ignoring her inclination, which was to get out of there as fast as possible, she pulled out a chair and sat down with the men. She could feel the small shock that went round the table as she did this. To her surprise, May, after setting the drink in front of Judith, did the same, Judith gradually realizing that one of the men was probably her husband.

Pleasantries were exchanged, between which Judith gulped down most of the soda, polite questions coming out of nothing but sheer curiosity and boredom on the part of the men, while she asked them no questions — that would be unexpected and would make them nervous. She told them why she had come to this out-of-the-way spot, all by herself and in the middle of the week.

"I just thought I'd have a look at the country while I was here," she ended, shrugging, keeping her eyes on the table where a pack of playing cards sat in the centre. Now she looked up and noticed framed black-and-white photos hanging evenly spaced in long rows on all the walls. In the pictures nearby, she could make out men standing in a harvested field in front of a giant threshing machine, families grouped in front of a log house or a frame one set up on blocks, or people — mostly men — on horseback. Pioneer pictures, ubiquitous on the prairies, as if nothing mattered as much as the past, always treated as heroic.

Noticing her gaze, one of the men, tall and very thin, remarked, "We got them pictures from people around here. Most of us are related to them folks in them." Judith nodded, trying to think of something to say, waiting for one of them to start in with the stories: *My old man came here in 1910, took a quarter along the border* ... and so on and so on. But nobody did, although all of them had their eyes fixed on the row of photos that surely they had each seen a million times.

"My old man used to talk about how he made some money helping them rum-runners cross the border, showing them the way when they came by at night." All the men chuckled, the sound carrying that ritual quality; they had all heard this story before. "He could see their lights circling around out there in the dark, knew they was lost. He'd ride out and show them the way. Make himself a silver dollar for his trouble."

It wasn't just Whiskey Gap. Even Wisdom had a rum-running past, Judith knew. In those beloved early days, wherever few people lived and there was a gap in the hills or a place where burnouts and dry coulees didn't slow passage across the border, such places became prime country for sneaking contraband in one direction or the other.

The man wearing the blue ball cap, looking to be the oldest at the table, said, "I used to trap coyotes, weasels, even beaver, skin them, strap them on my back, ski across the border, sell them there. Wait for a full moon. Made my own skis. Before the war." His hand shook as he lifted his cup and drank. He set it down and asked her, "You said your father came from here?"

"Yes," she told them. "Henry Clemensen. He came from near Sage."

"I remember that name," he said, "but I don't recall just where their land was." He had lifted his head to speak to her, and she saw that he was missing half his lower lip, a surgical scar, probably a cancer from holding a cigarette there for too many years. "Bullards bought out just about everybody around there back in the sixties. But then when old man Bullard died — he didn't have no boys — the old Clemensen place went to . . . can't remember their names."

"It got all split up," another man said. "I got no idea which was the Clemensens'." These men were all maybe ten or fifteen years younger than Judith's father would be if he were alive; they weren't even born when her grandparents arrived from Norway in the early 1900s.

"Better go into Haley and check the records there," the tall man told her. "They'll have the land descriptions . . ."

"Naw," the second man said. "You gotta have the land descriptions to start with, that's how they're filed."

"Used to be that way," the third, who had asked her if she was lost, said. "Now it's by names."

"I don't know why my father left," she told them. "The land he went to in southern Saskatchewan doesn't look a bit different than here." Again the men chuckled.

"Lotta them returned soldiers got kinda lost," the oldest man said, the one Judith surmised was married to May. He didn't look at Judith, and his tone was mild, as if he didn't want to upset her. "Could be that was what did it — when he got back, I mean."

"He knows," May said to her, her small eyes bright as a bird's in the gloomy room. "He was there too. Second World War." So it was common knowledge, at least among the old-timers, that a Clemensen boy who would have to be her father, so many years ago, had gone off to war.

"But it seems that *you* didn't get lost," Judith said, studying the oldest man, seeing that he might be ill: that papery skin, the slight tremble to his fingers around his cup, May's very solicitousness. The others were silent, gazing at the pictures or out the big front window that had made Judith think this was a café. Maybe it once had been.

"Oh yeah, I hit the bottle pretty hard there for a while." Again the men chuckled. They were like a chorus from an ancient Greek play. *Mighty Agamemnon slain by . . .*

"What saved you?"

He shrugged slowly, and it was a full minute before he spoke, during which the others kept silent and motionless, as if they would venerate his answer.

"I wasn't old enough to enlist until '43. Wasn't in more than a couple of skirmishes, didn't open no . . . camps, like some of 'em did. Wounded in late '44, spent the end of the war in a hospital in England." He paused, drew in a deep breath. "And I had a good woman to go home to." Everybody at the table nodded sagely, not lifting their eyes, and May's aura, hard and crisp to that moment, softened. "She put up with me until I figured out a few things." There was a silence, during which Judith finished her drink, and May patted her husband's arm, then left her hand there.

"Our women's club did a book on the area," she told Judith. "If we couldn't find the families to write their own history, we wrote letters all over the place to find out who settled where and what happened to them all. You could buy a copy." She was already up and moving to the back of the room, where a low table Judith hadn't noticed sat, books and magazines spread out on it. She brought back a heavy book bound with a red imitation-leather cover.

"Might be some Clemensens in here. You never know. Seventy-five dollars please." She held the big book tight against her chest as if Judith might try to wrest it away. "It costs that much because we don't sell enough copies to pay for making it. Not enough old families left around. Nobody else is interested, and it took more than twenty of us three years to put it together." Judith had seen Wisdom's book, not that she had read it, not even to find out what it had to say about her own family. She supposed Abbie would have written their family story, but then she thought, *No, I bet Sam wrote it. Probably spiffed their story up as much as he thought he could get away with.* She dug out seventy-five dollars from her purse and, not without reluctance, which she hid, exchanged it for the book.

She thanked them all, especially May for the drink, and in an impulse she didn't quite understand, said to her, "Thank you for taking good care of this soldier," adding that she would read the book carefully, and went out into the spring afternoon. She had forgotten to take her cellphone in with her, and as she dropped the heavy book onto the back seat, it began to ring. She opened the door and sat sideways in the driver's seat, her feet on the ground.

Catherine said, "I think we'll probably wind up in mediation. I've finally got the building's owners and the snow removal company and the individual caretaker on that day and all their insurers —"

"Can we do this another time? My head is killing me." She leaned sideways to rest her forehead against the top of the steering wheel. She thought, *"A few skirmishes" indeed. Probably full-out battles with plenty of dead. Otherwise, why would he have started hard drinking?*

Catherine said, "Did you know your friend Mrs. DeSantis took photos with her phone of you spread-eagled on the sidewalk?" Judith didn't reply. "It was a good thing she did. You're clearly unconscious. There's something beside you that might be blood. And also of the ambulance attendants kneeling next to you looking pretty intent."

"For heaven's sake, Catherine, don't tell me this stuff!" She shoved the car door open farther in case she had to throw up.

"You better get to that clinic," Catherine said, her mind clearly on whatever came next on her busy agenda and not on her mother's misery or, apparently, her schedule either. "I have to go; I might have some more papers for you to sign. I'll call." *Click.*

For a second, Judith thought that she would call Catherine back to tell her that you don't hang up on your own mother no matter how busy you are, but she suddenly remembered that she had hung up on her own mother a couple of times, a thousand years ago, when she was fifteen and sixteen. She hadn't thought about those conversations in years. Not that either of them ever said anything of import, and her mother had never once asked her to come home, although now that she thought of it, maybe Sammie had, when Abbie had put him on the phone. She had talked to him; he had been too young to remember now that they'd talked.

When she reached seventeen and was moved to a group home she hated, she was spurred by it to find a better part-time job, and because she was still faithfully going to school, Social Services had placed her in her own tiny apartment. Besides her wages, she acquired a roommate, another screwed-up girl like herself, and with Social Services' pittance, together they managed to pay the rent. It was her social worker who had encouraged her and shown her how to apply for loans so she could go on to university. It amazed her, knowing what she knew now about runaway kids, how close she had been to winding up on the street, a sex worker, an addict, a dealer, like dozens of girls she worked with in later years. It amazed her, too, that even when she knew nothing about it, her family had been keeping an eye on her. It crossed her mind, though, that probably she did know it, but had buried the idea because it was too confusing for her to deal with when she was still a kid, her anger still so overpowering, and her shame just as great. She would have laughed out loud, but now her shoulder was aching too, and her right arm tingling all the way down to her wrist. Did she dare take two more extra-strength Tylenol? She decided in favour, then started her car and drove east, turning north at the next crossroads, then east again on a paved highway, and before a full eternity had passed, went by Medicine Hat, resisted the temptation to stop at the first motel, kept heading further east, and finally, hours later, exhausted and aching, drove into Wisdom.

It was late evening by the time she parked her car in the garage. She carried her bag and the thick book into the house, set her bag by her bed and the book with careful deliberation on the coffee table, then went to the kitchen, put a frozen dinner in the microwave, and poured herself a glass of wine. When the microwave beeped, she put the dinner and the wine on a tray and carried it back to the living room, sat down, centred the book in front of her, opened it, and began reading all the introductory pages, one after the other, carefully, as if there would be a test later, while absently munching on the dinner and sipping her wine. It took her a few minutes to figure out that the names of Sage's pioneer families were not in alphabetical order but had been arranged by school district. Having no knowledge of the school districts around Sage, this left her no choice but to leaf through the over two hundred pages, scanning them until she found her family name.

When at last, more than halfway through the book, she spotted "Clemensen" in heavy type at the top of a page along with three blurry black-and-white photos — again, men lined up in front of a threshing machine, one of a long field of stooks of wheat or barley or maybe rye, and last, two boys in their late teens wearing baggy coveralls with dark turtleneck sweaters under them, their .22s leaning against their hips, standing in snow, each proudly holding up a dead animal, one a wolf or coyote, and the other what looked like a fox. She leaned closer, trying to see the faces, since one of them might be her dad, but they were hazy beyond recognition, although in that close examination, she saw that they were holding up hides, heads still on, not the animals themselves. Below the photos a couple of paragraphs described her family.

Her palms were sweating, her heart tapping quickly at the base of her throat. She got up, went into the kitchen, poured water into her coffee machine, put ground coffee into it, then leaned with her back to the counter and stared straight ahead while she waited for the coffee to finish. Occasionally, she rotated her right shoulder, or lifted her right arm and gingerly stretched it. Her mind, curiously, had gone blank.

Faintly, the thump and screech of rock music came to her, along with the low howl of a male voice. That kind of rock was called grunge or punk or something. It was dark out, and when she caught the glow of light coming through the window above the sink, she turned and gazed out to the blank wall and the part of the yard next door, which was all she could see of her neighbour's property. She could see two people, by the way they were moving probably teenage girls, coming giggling up the walk toward the back of the brick house, and in a couple of seconds a third, this one a boy, rushing to catch up with them. Then they went past the end of the house, out of Judith's view. She thought, *Hmmm*, puzzled, faintly unsettled, wondering if something was going on, and if so, what was it? *Paranoia*, she told herself; *too many years as a child protection worker*. The outside light next door flicked off, the music stopped, and the night fell into silence.

But the coffee was ready, she had found the page she wanted in the history book, and now couldn't wait to get back to it, and the young people coming from the back lane to go into the house next door slid easily from her thoughts. On the sofa again, she pulled the book toward her. Oddly, she was having trouble reading the three short paragraphs; not that she couldn't read the words, but that she couldn't quite make sense of them. She read them all a second time, and then a third, before she slammed the book shut, bent over, and lifted her hands to grip her head as if she might be able to lift it off and set it aside.

In the kitchen, the phone rang. Around the fourth ring, she got up and answered it.

"What did the specialist say?"

"Nothing new, Abbie," Judith told her. "I just need more time to heal."

Her hours at the traumatic brain injury clinic had been so undramatic as to be boring, and all day, through the imaging, examination, consultations, and discussions, she kept having flashbacks to similar occasions, none of which she had remembered at all. It was disconcerting and, in a way, mildly funny, as if, for a while at the clinic in Calgary, she had been a zombie. No brain, just a body mutely following directions and otherwise working on habit and reflex. But in Medicine Hat, during the consultation at the end of the day, she had felt the neurologist was looking at her in a speculative although not unkindly way. It alarmed Judith, made her wonder fleetingly if she had an inoperable tumour or something even worse, like maybe . . . what? She had no idea.

"I hope he gave you some different medications."

"The doctor was a woman. No, no new meds."

"Maybe you should go back to Calgary, see your doctor there."

"Maybe," Judith said. It had taken her a while to realize that the doctor simply didn't know what was causing so much pain, or how, sometimes at its worst, it seemed to spread even to the air that surrounded her. By then, though, the doctor had shifted her discussion to new territory, talking about neural pathways, about the brain feeling the pain, not the body, and eventually actually initiating it — she thought that was what the doctor had said — after Judith had failed to stop it or limit it herself. Was she depressed? No — yes — sometimes.

All of which meant that the medical profession could find no physical cause for her pain. There would be no new, magical prescriptions, no cure other than one she would have to find or create herself.

"You were gone a long time."

"How do you know how long I was gone?"

"Tillie, across the street. I asked her to call me when you got back. We were starting to get worried about you."

"Oh for heaven's sake," Judith said. "I managed without you for a good fifty years, I can . . ." But she stopped herself. "Sorry." She couldn't decide whether to tell Abbie where she had gone after the clinic. "I have a bad headache. I overdid it today, I guess." There was a silence. After a minute, during which Judith nearly hung up, Abbie suddenly spoke.

"Did you — you didn't — you didn't try to find Sage, did you?"

"Yes," Judith said. "Yes, I did. I left Medicine Hat for Sage early this morning. That's why I didn't get back until about an hour ago. It's a long drive there and back."

"Well?"

"It looks exactly like here," Judith told her. "Hardly worth the trip." Someone she had never heard of had written their history in the book. She had read his name three times, without it exactly registering. The paragraphs were strictly about their father's parents' arrival and early days on the land, and the births of their children, and if it was known, what had become of them. A line came into her mind: *and were buried in the cemetery at Haley.* Abbie, Judith, and Sam's paternal grandparents.

"I could have told you that," Abbie said, then, changing her tone, "Well, no news here. You get some sleep. We can talk in the morning."

Judith suddenly remembered the hares hanging in the Richters' trees and wanted to ask Abbie if she had heard any news about that, and how the prayer meeting had gone, but Abbie had already hung up. And come to think of it, had anybody called the Mounties? And further, now that she thought of it, why had the daily newsletter that she kept finding in her grocery bag never once mentioned anything about the disembowelled hares hanging in the trees of a pair of inoffensive local elders? Odd, when she thought about it, and a chill crept down her back, making her shiver.

Now she knew without looking again what the three paragraphs said. The picture of a normal homesteading family had emerged, and she couldn't quite identify the oddness of her confusion, when she had realized that her father's history wasn't a myth at all, that he had been real, with real parents and real problems just like everybody else she had been raised with. The account, signed by someone named August Jespersen, gave the full names of her father's parents: Helga Christine Solheim and Lunt Henry Clemensen, that they had come from a village in Norway, and that her father, Henry John Clemensen, the youngest child of five, was born March 3, 1923. Two girls had died of unnamed illnesses as young children; a third had moved to the United States when she reached adulthood, her whereabouts now unknown; a son had left to find work in Vancouver just before the Second World War. The last was her father, who had enlisted in the American infantry and gone to war.

Beside the family name at the top was the land description of the Clemensen homestead quarter. Which meant she could probably locate their neighbours or their descendants, pick up a few more details about her own family, find out something about her father's upbringing and early life, where he had gone to school, if he had gone back home after he had been released from the army, or if he had never returned home, and if not, why not.

Usually, settler families wanted to know every single thing possible about their ancestors; Sam and Abbie's lack of interest baffled her. Why, in all the years since their father's death, hadn't they tried to do this? It angered her too, and she vowed that if nothing else, she would try to find the man who had written the piece on her family, and who might have actually known their grandparents. Was it possible he would have known their father when he was a child?

Her brain was zapping now as if the electrical impulses it ran on had begun to fire randomly, at too-rapid speed, creating a million pinpoints of pain, so that she cupped both hands around her skull, trying to contain and smother it. Fix her pain herself? She had no idea how.

CHAPTER SEVEN

FORGETTING

"It's good you look sort of pale and weary," Catherine said, studying Judith's face as she opened the door to her and Ian's Calgary condo. Judith, taken aback by the remark, gave her daughter a slightly uncomfortable hug and smiled brightly at Ian, who stood back in the shiny white kitchen, waiting for her to fully enter before he greeted her. The condo was open concept and all white except for the gleaming pale birch floor, a few bright accent pillows, and expensive knick-knacks, including a carved jade box Judith had always secretly coveted on the glass coffee table. The lucent white stone, or whatever the kitchen countertops were made of, dazzled in the evening sunlight washing through the nearly two-storey windows facing west to a looming view of the still snow-capped, steel grey and purple–blue Rocky Mountains. She could barely look at them, they were so overwhelming.

She rubbed the back of her neck as Catherine backed away, pulling Judith's suitcase to the bottom of the stairs, while Ian came forward to kiss her on each cheek.

"For heaven's sake, Cathy, why is it good that I look pale and weary?" She was exhausted from the drive, and now cranky as well, an effect Ian and Catherine's condo always had on her.

"Keats," Ian answered for Catherine. " 'O what can ail thee, knight-at-arms, Alone and palely loitering'? Something, something..."

Catherine chimed in, "So haggard and so woe-begone . . . ," her voice mocking. She grinned at Ian, Judith seeing in the grin that every defence was absent from her daughter's gaze.

"It's a long drive, and I have a headache," she intervened, too brusquely, not liking something she saw in Ian's grin in response to Catherine's.

"I'm sorry, Mom. I just meant because of the hearing tomorrow. It would make things harder if you looked to be bursting with vitality. We want a settlement, don't we?"

"I'm not faking it," Judith said. "I wish I were." After a second, she added, "But now that you mention it, I'm starving."

"Good thing, Judith," Ian said. He had a special way of saying her name; therein lay his charm, she thought, because whenever he said it that way, and despite his being thirty years younger, and her daughter's husband, and the fact that otherwise she found him hard to like, she always felt an inadvertent shiver that embarrassed and slightly scared her. "We've prepared dinner ourselves!" This meant only that they usually ate out, or had food brought in, or, judging by their skinniness, more likely didn't eat at all: a stalk of asparagus, a shred of chicken, two lettuce leaves, and for dessert, a raspberry.

Catherine said, "Don't mention your appetite to the mediator, okay?"

"Anybody can see I'm not thin," Judith pointed out. "Although I was told that I did lose something like twenty pounds during my un-fun hospital stay, of which I cannot remember one second."

"You were darn lucky," Catherine told her as she and Ian began to bring the food from the kitchen to the glass dining table, where they sat on the matching clear plastic and mostly uncomfortable chairs. "I did some research, and I can tell you that with a blow that hard, that put you out of your mind for two weeks, well, sometimes people don't come back. They have to be institutionalized. Sometimes they get a kind of incurable dementia eventually, or else ..."

"Whoa," Ian said, and put out his hand to cover Catherine's.

Catherine changed tones. "But look at you! You look — you are — just fine. Sort of, except for being pale and tired," reminding herself of the next day's hearing. They ate their salad and fish with desultory conversation, how Judith simply had to stop at Jess's on the way home — Judith hadn't told them of her new plans to go to Haley, much less why — how Lucinda hadn't gone on the run yet from Israel, and it would soon be close to two years, and how about that?

"Now, about tomorrow." Ian had taken their plates and was gone to get the dessert and to make some decaf coffee. Judith was still hungry, but decided it was probably better to say nothing.

"I've written a statement for you. You don't have to read it verbatim, unless you think you can't remember without an aid."

"How does this go?" Judith asked. "Are we going to appear before a judge? Or what?"

"No judge. Both sides agreed to appear before a professional mediator. He's coming down from Edmonton. Gerry Erlich is his name. We've all had business with him, and we agree that he is a smart, impartial broker. We're going to split his cost."

"How binding is all this?"

"Binding, binding, binding," Catherine told her. "Absolutely. The minute you sign the agreement, there is no going back." Ian had set down the dessert, a light cream-coloured mousse with a few strawberries and some chocolate curls on top, and had gone back to get the coffee. She would bet there wasn't a gram of fat in the whole thing, and she would also bet it came from a gourmet caterer's shop. "It costs way too much to litigate. And this is Canada — we don't do bazillion-dollar settlements here." Ian was filling the coffee cups and handing them around. "We've got it down to maybe twenty thousand dollars, but that's what the mediation is all about. The insurance companies agree a settlement is appropriate, it's just the amount we're haggling over. My feeling is maybe . . . ten thousand."

"Wow!" Judith said, delighted. "Wow!"

"It's a joke!" Catherine said, "Considering what you went through. What we all went through. And now you've got this residual pain that you can't control or get rid of. That sidewalk was a mess, and even in that blowing snow somebody should have been looking after it. You were really hurt, Mom." And she looked at Judith, to the latter's amazement, with a flash of real tenderness, gone as fast as it had arrived. "I have statements from people who use that sidewalk every day and they all say that it wasn't properly cleaned, and others have fallen there, although nobody has gotten as badly hurt as you did. And on the very day you were to begin your retirement. That could pluck a heartstring or two."

"See," Ian, also a lawyer, though working in some obscure job in the oil patch where it appeared he made a great deal of money, chimed in, "this daughter of yours knows what she's doing. She's like a dog with a bone when she gets her teeth into something." This, it would seem, was praise.

Later, sitting with Catherine on one of the white leather sofas, Ian gone to his study to work, they began to go over the statement Catherine had written.

"You were fine before it happened, you weren't gimpy, you weren't wearing six-inch heels, you weren't drunk or on drugs."

"The specialists can't find any continuing injuries in the imaging," Judith said, a bit tentative.

"That's our weakness; that's what keeps us from asking for a bigger settlement. But the clinic didn't kick you to the curb; they believe you, and besides..."

"I was in a hurry," Judith pointed out. "Everybody from the office was waiting for us. It was my celebration–farewell lunch. So maybe if I'd gone slower..."

"You could very well have fallen anyway. Leave that part out. That's for the defence to say, not you. You were walking at a normal pace." On and on it went, Judith's head pounding with pain, the light so bright in the room that she kept blinking and had to stop herself from shading her eyes with her hand. Nausea was once again rising, and she remembered, or thought she did, that it had been hours since she had taken any pills.

"Could we finish this in the morning before we go to the hearing?" she asked. Catherine, absorbed in her task, was saying, "The insurance companies' lawyers will say . . ." but then, seeing the expression on her mother's face, she stopped talking and quickly agreed that there would be time in the morning. Judith was already up and rushing to the bathroom, her hand cupped over her mouth.

In the car the next morning, Catherine asked, "Are you still thinking of going to Israel?"

"If we get a settlement that is big enough to pay for it, I think I don't have a choice; I have to go. I'm her mother."

Catherine said, "God, Mother, she's nearly forty."

"It worries me. She's old to be having a first baby — thirty-eight, actually. I was nineteen. When I had you, I was in my early thirties."

"You've been without a husband a long time," Catherine said, as if this was the first time she had noticed it. "That must have been hard, being alone?"

Judith had suffered a lot about it when she was younger, relieved by the occasional short-lived boyfriend, but she said, "I got used to it. It stopped seeming like some terrible punishment that I'd done nothing to deserve. It started to be sort of — I can't believe I'm saying this — enjoyable. Then Gilles came along. That was so lovely." A long silence. "I wonder how Camille is doing. His wife, I mean, the one with cancer."

Suspicion dawned: Was it Ian? Was that why she was asking what it was like to be alone?

Catherine was signalling to merge into the steady stream of traffic heading to the city centre. Something about the set of her mouth disturbed Judith, but in seconds it passed as Catherine kept her eyes on the cars ahead of her. The morning sun had emerged from clouds and its rays glinted off windshields and shiny metal finishes, so that Judith, in order not to be sick, had to put down her visor and keep her eyes on her knees.

"I wish you didn't live in that awful shack, Mom. You should be here, back in Calgary."

"I'm where I need to be right now," she told Catherine, her voice firm. "I actually hate it, you know." They both laughed at this inadvertent admission, Catherine in surprise, Judith in something closer to chagrin.

She thought, as she was introduced and everyone took their places and the hearing proceeded, that whatever else might happen, after all, she could consider this event as an interesting experience, with herself at its centre. Although actually, the lawyers were the centre, or the mediator was the centre, or the process, anybody, anything but her, Judith, with her bonked head and her headaches, shoulder and arm pain, and sometimes back pain, and nearly constant nausea, not to mention frequent bouts of dizziness and poor balance accompanying one or any of the other symptoms. When she saw, not for the first time, the photos Adrianna had taken of her unconscious on the sidewalk, a dark, ominous-looking halo around her head, but this time with anything superfluous photoshopped out, her photo-image head bigger than her real head, she was struck with dizziness and then with the nausea that she once again fought down.

When she heard the insurance companies' representatives claiming that she hadn't been incapacitated other than for the two weeks after her fall, and appeared to have made a good recovery and therefore the settlement should be much smaller, she realized, also for the first time, just how incapacitated she actually had become. Catherine even made the argument that she had moved back to her hometown and "lived in greatly reduced circumstances" because she couldn't manage in the noise, traffic, and superstimuli of the city. Judith would never tell them the real reason she had gone back to the tiny prairie town she had come from over fifty years earlier — she hardly knew it herself. All the reasons she had been giving people — Abbie, her daughters one by one — fluttered by; she could practically wave at them as they passed. She realized abruptly that the people of Wisdom thought she had returned out of nostalgia; all right, but mostly she was in Wisdom because she was broke. Her cheeks were suddenly warm.

After, she and Catherine went to a restaurant for lunch.

"You were great," Catherine told her. "I was so surprised by you: You didn't get mad, you didn't rush through it; you didn't forget a thing; and above all, you didn't pretend it was all nothing, just a great big nuisance I was putting you through."

"I'm sorry, Cathy," Judith said. She had to put a hand over her eyes until she got control of the tears that were threatening. "I felt that this lawsuit was one thing more than I could manage." She put her hand down. "But you were absolutely right, and I thank you so much for doing this." Catherine, wanting still to be angry, managed to force a smile. Now Judith grinned at her daughter. "But I was play-acting, at least some of the time." Catherine lifted her eyes to her mother's, surprised, then returned the grin, and for a split second something close to an accord arose between them.

When they were finished, Catherine offered to get Judith a cab so she could go back to the condo and spend the afternoon resting.

"I'll probably be late. There are some ready-to-eat dinners in the freezer. Just help yourself. And have a glass of wine. Congratulate yourself on doing a very good hearing."

"I didn't think this day would ever come," Judith said, "and now it's over, and I can hardly believe it even happened." Catherine was giving her a token hug, her mind already in her office. Judith muttered, "My whole life has been like that." But Catherine was already gone down the sidewalk and didn't hear her.

Judith was sitting with a magazine on one of the living room sofas when Catherine let herself in. It was nearly eight, she had heated a frozen dinner for her supper as Catherine had suggested. Now, sitting in the cavernous room with its interior reflected in odd angles and slanted sheets of shining glass, she thought, *It's like spending the night in a deserted shopping mall*, and was very glad that Catherine was home.

"Ian's not back yet," she said as Catherine hung her coat in the closet and stepped out of her high heels, leaving them where they were. She looked drained.

"He works late a lot," Catherine answered. "I'm going to make a sandwich." She smoothed down her hair, not looking at her mother. For an instant, Judith had felt a frisson of something coming off her daughter, a mixture of anger and maybe . . . sadness? It brought her to her feet to follow Catherine into the kitchen.

"Let me make it for you," she said. "Sit. Can I make you tea or coffee?" Catherine didn't argue, collapsing onto one of the high white leather chairs that lined the counter.

"Wine," she said. "White. Have one with me, Mom." When the wine was poured and the sandwich made from sliced packaged ham was sitting in front of Catherine, Judith sat on the opposite side of the island facing her daughter.

"Is everything all right here?"

"Of course!" Catherine flared at once. "Ian just works late a lot. It takes a lot of hours at work to maintain all this." She waved her hand to indicate the high-end appliances, the big window with the view of the mountains. Judith kept silent. "Let's go sit in the living room." But once seated there, Catherine seemed disinclined to talk, and Judith's careful efforts were fruitless.

After a while, Catherine asked, "What time are you leaving tomorrow?"

"If you don't mind, I thought I'd stick around for another day. Adrianna and I are going to have lunch tomorrow."

Catherine was looking at her now, her mouth open as if to speak, but after a second she turned her head to look at the glass wall, alive with fragments of the interior interspersed with patches of gleaming dark sprinkled with lights. In that glance, Judith knew: something was definitely wrong here.

She would meet Adrianna for lunch downtown at the building where she had been working on the day her so-called career ended, where she had fallen and been in limbo ever since. But, although there was still a wind and a nip in the air, all the snow was gone, there was no danger of ice on the streets, and the young trees carefully planted in large pots that lined the sidewalk in front of the building were beginning to show tips of green. People rushed in and out, pattering up the high cement steps to the swinging glass doors, or down to the sidewalk, where they hurried off in various directions. Cars and trucks whistled by or waited in long, humming lines for the lights up ahead to change, horns honked, and somewhere nearby a dozen carpenters were pounding with giant hammers, and enormous power tools whirred and whined. For once, wincing at the noise, Judith had no doubt about the wisdom of her move to the country.

At last, Adrianna, wearing a tan-coloured, wrinkled trench coat that pulled a bit over her stomach, came down the stairs and stopped where Judith leaned against the concrete railing. They hugged, and Judith felt tears come to her eyes when she saw her. Adrianna was crying openly, her professional's habitual defensively ironic stance for the moment dissolved.

They went off to the very café where Judith's party was to have been held the day she fell and was concussed and never since had seen any of the partygoers, at least that she could remember. Adrianna had apologized, tried to suggest going somewhere else, but Judith wouldn't hear of it. A part of her wanted to see if she could pick up fragments of the party-that-never-was still loitering in the corners. But once inside and ordering her salad, she felt nothing and said so.

"Maybe it's a good thing," she said. "A way to ameliorate any remnants of the PTSD." She laughed, and tears sprang to her eyes again. But she couldn't bear to see the patch of sidewalk where she had fallen on the way to the restaurant. Everything else was confusion: the hard pellets of windblown snow stinging as they hit her face; the fierce pain, so strong that for moments she had dissociated so as to let somebody else feel it; the senseless, roaring racket in her head; how cold she felt in her too-light coat; and then — nothing. Adrianna, short and dark-skinned, with the loveliest coal black hair pulled back from her face, now with an elegant swipe of white down one side, stretched her hand across the table to hold Judith's.

"My friend," she said. "How I've missed you. How glad I am to see that you have recovered."

"More or less," Judith said.

"Holy Mother of God, I thought you were dead." She snapped her menu briskly. "It's too bad you didn't let us know you were coming in sooner. We could have planned a book club meeting so you could come, or at least a book club lunch."

"I like it better this way. Just the two of us. How's work?"

They went on in this vein for some time, finally progressing from Adrianna's prickly, often unreasonable new boss to shared news about their children, and finally Adrianna's husband, Santiago, who was a poorly paid math teacher at a private school. "He has so much dignity," Adrianna said. "He is so Latin-proud. He tries to get rid of it, but he can't. Maybe he will change jobs. I hope."

Judith thought, *Everyone has such trouble*, this new less hope-filled angle wiping out the alternative one she had always held, that happiness was constantly just around the corner.

As the waitress brought their salads and they pecked away at them, talking, talking, talking, Judith began to remember her work life, something about which she had not thought since the day she'd smacked her head on the sidewalk and lost her mind. Not really. It was impossible to understand.

"I forgot everything. I forgot I'd ever worked." But that was not true, she realized, because every single day she had remembered children for whom she had been responsible. Remembered them as people, not as cases, not as the object of the government's thousand protocols and its ephemeral largesse. Little Damien, who had died in the hospital, only two, his skull fractured by a blow from his drunken mother, still drunk or maybe just stoned or catatonic with grief at his graveside despite her handcuffs, and all of them wondering how she had pulled off even being there. Eleven-year-old Tamara, covered in bruises given to her by her church-drunk father, who, it would turn out, had been raping her since she was eight. The three preschoolers she had found all alone in a pigsty of a house, even the packages of chips long eaten, not a single other item of food left, little piles of excrement from the bare-bottomed youngest everywhere on the floors, which judging by their state said that these babies had been all alone for at least a week and were indeed starving, and the oldest, at five, Melissa was her name, staring up at her with the biggest, most knowing dark eyes she would ever in her life see in so young a child. Sometimes she felt the wound in her heart would never heal from that child's bottomless gaze. There was, she thought now, no understanding what people could do to one another. None at all.

Taken them all into care, she had, except for Damien, who was dead, or Alexander, twelve, also dead, having hanged himself; not at all sure they were, the rest of them, so much better off. How gladly she now suddenly discovered that she was to never have to go back there again. It occurred to her to wonder why she hadn't felt that at the time, had just rushed off to the farewell lunch, files still waiting on her desk for the afternoon, when at five p.m., she would have been gone forever and somebody else would worry about her cases. She felt herself frowning, put a hand to the back of her neck, and then down again. Adrianna was watching her closely.

"Tell me how the mediation went," she asked, so Judith, blinking, happy to back out of her thoughts, told her how very well her law-

·yer-daughter thought it had gone, and how grateful they both were for Adrianna's quick thinking in taking pictures and in waiting for the ambulance to remove Judith so she could take pictures of the icy patch itself, and for the sworn report she had written about what had happened that day.

"She thinks you have won the case for us," she told her friend, a slight exaggeration, to which Adrianna only shrugged, but looked down at her empty plate, pleased.

Back at the government building, they hugged. Adrianna said, "Don't forget book club!"

It seemed to her now that the smack on the head, the two weeks in never-never land, marked a boundary: the end of her old life; a trip far down into the underworld and back up again whether she had wanted to come or not; then the new strange and anchorless world she had, for months now, been staggering through. Quizzically, as she watched Adrianna hurry up the stairs, slip through the door, and disappear, she thought of how the world had spun a little faster there for a few minutes, and a lot of things had flown off it into space, and, she saw now, wouldn't ever be coming back.

CHAPTER EIGHT

PICKING ROCK

A smart new tan-coloured brick building presented itself to Judith on her right, a sign printed in stern letters above its windows: *Town of Haley: Municipal District of Single Tree.* She parked, shut off the engine, put down the visor, and studied her hair in the mirror: now grown out from the fright wig she'd come out of the hospital with, medium-length, mixed shades of grey, in need of a shampoo, cut, and styling, and some hairdressing chemicals to smooth it, because right now loose hairs sprang out untidily. She couldn't go in looking like a crazed woman. She gave her hair a quick brush, covered some of the new brown spots on her face with foundation, and put on a little pink lipstick. Not great, but better. How many times over the years had she tried to hammer this home to the bedraggled, purple-haired, nose-ringed skinny girls it was her job to rescue? "If you want to get a job," she would say, "stop blaring to the world that there is no way on earth you're going to co-operate." "Be the good self that lives inside you," and so on. *Hah*, she thought, and this when her daughter Lucinda had sprouted a tattoo, and Judith usually had no idea where she was either. Was some other social worker saying the same things to Judith's own child?

And one of those kids, in that last year she had worked, Jasmine Something-or-other, had come to her with cigarette burns all over her face, her skin otherwise so white it was heartbreaking just to look at her. And then, like so many of the waifs of the world bearing the burden of all that was evil, she had vanished again, and soon news arrived that her body had been found in a dumpster on the bad side of town. Blood alcohol level — well, higher than she knew it was possible to have and still live. It wasn't just that when she'd heard, for a second she thought by the pain in her chest that her heart was cracking, but that the news also frightened her, and she knew it was because of Lucinda. Or was it because of how close she had come herself to being that girl?

The glass door of the municipal building swung open, and a middle-aged man in work-soiled jeans and a denim shirt, the omnipresent ball cap on his head, rushed out. He carried some official-looking papers in his hand, and she thought, *He's a farmer, taxes paid, rushing back to seeding, or maybe he'll stop at the café or the elevator first and have a cup of the slop they call coffee and a chat with the boys before he heads back to the farm. But it's a good day for field work; he probably doesn't want to waste any of it.*

The sight of him triggered a memory: rock picking in the days before mechanical rock pickers. And even now, she knew, rock pickers didn't get every single rock; you still had to pick some by hand. She and her mother and her sister, out in the field with the old work truck that wasn't safe to take on the roads anymore, inching along the summerfallow field and stopping a few yards ahead while the driver got out too, all of them stooping to pick up each rock they saw lying in the furrows, some the size of a fist, and throwing them in the truck box. Later, Sam and their father in the tractor with a bucket mounted on it would pick up those that were too big to lift by hand. For the first time in years, she remembered her sullen rage when she finally noticed that the females of the family didn't get to ride in the tractor. But then, Sammie had picked rocks by hand too.

One cold, windblown fall day, with occasional splatters of icy rain adding to their discomfort, her mother had looked up at the lightless sky, then collapsed against the driver's side of the truck, her head tucked low so they couldn't see her face. She and Abbie both knew she was crying, but they said nothing, because in their family you didn't say anything; you tried not to know. In a minute, she had straightened — they couldn't look at her face — and they had all gone back to picking rocks until it was time to go in and cook supper. Afterwards, when the dishes were done and put away and the kitchen cleaned, they would go back to the field and stand on the rocks in the truck box, their father helping them, and throw them into a pile in a corner of the field, the pile growing higher and higher with each trip, until their father said it was time to start a new pile over in the next corner. Every year the same thing; there was even a mythology of rocks, how they rose with the frost, so that no field was ever finished; every year it would have to be gone over again.

She got out of the car and went into the building, where a nicely dressed middle-aged woman with severely coiffed hair stood behind the counter, flipping through a file. She looked up when Judith entered and smiled at her in an open way.

"Do you keep the records here of landowners, going back to, say, before the Second World War? My father came from a farm near what was once Sage, and I thought I'd like to go see the place."

"Do you have the land description?"

Judith handed her the slip of paper with the description she had gotten from the red-covered history book printed on it, adding, "His surname was Clemensen."

The clerk sat down at her desk and clicked at her computer for several minutes: "Lunt Henry?"

"That's it! That's my grandfather." Over to one side of her a printer began to hum, and a page crept out. The clerk took the page off its tray and handed it to her. A quick glance told Judith the page summarized the history of her grandfather's claim: date of homestead claim, date of proving up, notations of dates of communication with the government about the claim.

"Now you need a township map."

She must have been through this a hundred times, Judith thought. *All us modern landless waifs looking for our pasts, for something to anchor us to the earth.*

The clerk reached below the counter and produced a hand-drawn map copied in black and white. Judith accepted both papers with a grin that she couldn't wipe away, and thanking the woman profusely, was about to leave, then remembered to ask, "Do you know anybody around who was a soldier in World War II? I know they are all old men, but I'm kind of hoping you know somebody." The woman pursed her lips, and the startlingly red fingernails of her left hand tapped rhythmically on the countertop.

"The only ones I can think of are dead. But wait a minute - old August Jespersen, he's a veteran."

"American or Canadian forces?" Wait a minute — wasn't that the name of the man who wrote the entry about their family in the local history book?

"Gosh, I don't know, I think American. He was so close to the border." She leaned toward Judith, rested her arms on the counter, and confided, as if they were friends, "His wife is dead, but he still lives out there on the place all by himself. His sons and grandsons do the farming for him. Are you thinking of going out to see him?" Judith nodded; this was all happening so fast. But, she thought, why not? "Well, take it easy. He's a bit . . ." she hesitated, "odd, I guess you could say. But he's right in the head still, as far as I know."

"How do I find him?"

"Let's see the map." Judith put it back down on the counter. Pointing with her index finger, the clerk said, "This, here," picking up a pen and putting an X on a spot, "is the original farmhouse where August still lives." Judith studied the map. "Go out that road there, head south for about fifteen kilometres, then go west for five and a bit, and you'll see an approach into a falling-down old house with some dead trees around it. South side of the road." She folded the map and handed it to Judith, who grabbed it and, dismissing ceremony, headed for the door. The woman called to her back, "There's a half-dead caragana hedge around it too."

She drove slowly down the hardtop road, watching the odometer in order not to miss the turnoff, where, her tires crackling now on the gravel, she slowed even more. Trying to calm herself, she rolled down her window in order to fill her tightening throat and chest with fresh prairie air.

There it was. A decrepit old house, its paint-stripped shingles warped by wind where they weren't missing completely, thrust itself above the promised dead caragana hedge, and, beyond that and on each side, she could make out a row of equally dead poplars reaching their leafless prong-like branches toward the sky. She braked, coming to a slow stop in the middle of the narrow passage leading into the Jespersen yard. *Why am I doing this?* she asked herself, frightened and for one second genuinely not knowing.

To find out why my father screamed in the night.

For a second, her headache came on her like a black weight, as if to say *Turn back*, before it lifted again. She drove the rest of the way through the break in the hedge and up to a hard-packed dirt rectangle in front of the house, stopping beside the aged, beat-up half-ton parked there. For a second, she sat listening to crows cawing from the dead trees on either side of the house. Weren't there any bloody songbirds in this country? How sick she was of ravens and crows and magpies swooping around and squawking in their derisive, angry way. What the hell did those birds think they knew anyway?

She got out and slammed the door hard, which threw the birds out of the trees, ragged balls of black dancing in the air, screeching indignantly at her, and walked unsteadily to the steps up to the rickety-looking open porch tacked across the front of the house, where she knocked on the door. Timidly at first, and when no one answered, louder, and when still no one answered, all her years of tracking down recalcitrant kids and/or their frightened parents who turned their terror into a steady, sometimes dangerous hostility, she turned the knob and opened the door a couple of inches.

"Is anybody home?"

"I said come in."

"I'm sorry; I didn't hear you."

He sat in an armchair much like the one she had in her own house in Wisdom, this one cracked and peeling brown leather, looking across the room at her, his eyes shining darkly. She stepped in farther, shutting the door behind her, into the odours of dirt, unwashed dishes, tobacco, liniment, mould, and who knew what else. She introduced herself; he said nothing, although she didn't seem to have interrupted him in anything. Cigarette smoke emerged from a curled hand.

"Are you August Jespersen? Mr. Jespersen?" Still he said nothing. She crossed the room to him and put out a tentative hand. He lifted his hand slowly — how thick it was, the fingers twisted and lumpy with arthritis. He barely touched hers, then dropped his, as if he couldn't be bothered. "May I sit down?"

Once again from out of her working past, she didn't wait for an answer and chose the end of the sofa nearest him, too close to be ignored but not so close as to be threatening. She could make him out now, an old man, shrunken, perhaps never big, wearing old canvas work pants stained with oil or grease, pants which had clearly been washed often but this had succeeded only in fading the stains, an equally faded khaki work shirt, the sleeves buttoned at the wrist, worn fabric slippers over thick wool socks. And then she took in his face.

The strength and clean lines of his bones startled her, even with his age's wrinkled skin and sagging flesh. His thin white hair was long around his ears and the back of his neck. And his eyes, she saw now, were full of intelligence. She could not tell what she felt, but relying on her long-ago training and years of experience, she forged ahead.

"I've come a long way," she said cheerfully. He didn't move or look at her. She started again, changing her tone. "I am trying to find out about my father." When he still didn't speak, she went on. "Henry Clemensen. You wrote about his family in the Sage local history."

"Daughter-in-law June wrote it," he said. "I just told her."

Knowing already that cajoling wouldn't work here, nor Sam's overly friendly bluster, nor even Abbie's cool tact, she said, "When I was a child, my father used to scream in the night. No one would tell us kids why. A bad dream, Mother would say. And now that he has been dead a long time, I have found out he was in the U.S. Army in the Second World War. I am told you were there too."

He drew briefly on his cigarette and straightened himself in the chair as if his back were aching, which made Judith realize that her head and neck had stopped hurting, and that an unexpected patience had seeped into her, a calm that she could not explain, unless it wafted to her from him, or was resident in the house itself.

"Not with Henry. Different unit," he said. "I knew him growing up. It was a fellow named Anders Andreasen who fought with him. He's long dead too. War killed him, I'd say. Though it was years and years later." She waited, breathing in the stuffy air, no longer minding it. "Haven't seen Henry since maybe 1942. We were pals in those days. Tomcatted around when we could get a few hours free of work." She couldn't imagine her father tomcatting, not ever, not anywhere. Later, this image would stick with her, softening her thoughts about him every time she remembered it. Chasing women? After the war, settling finally for her poor, drab, pathetically religious mother?

She asked, "Are you American?"

"The old man was. Came here when he was about fifteen, got married. I was born here. You want to know about the war."

"I want to know what happened to my father."

"Too bad Anders is dead. He's the one could tell you. Same unit as Henry. Thunderbirds, they called it."

"Did Anders tell you their story?"

"You know anything about that war?"

"Not really. At school, when I was young after the war was over, I think they thought we shouldn't know. Or else they couldn't figure out how to talk about it. Treaties, heroes, battles, lines, that was all."

"You go read about it," he said, and began to cough, leaning forward in his chair, his upper body seizing with each deep hack and rumble. Finally, he choked out, "Get me some water."

She rose, went in the direction he gestured, which turned out to be the kitchen where the bad smell was stronger, and she recognized it as garbage that needed to be taken out. She found a glass that looked fairly clean in the cupboard above the crusted, rusty sink, ran some water into it, and brought the glass back to him.

"My other daughter-in-law, Dinah, used to clean for me, till I chased her away. Couldn't stand her; she couldn't stand me, only she wouldn't admit it." He laughed, coughed a bit more, shallower now, and drank some water while she returned to her seat.

"I am sorry I'm so ignorant about World War II. I will read about it when I get back home."

"Probably won't do no good," he said.

Again she waited, while he turned his head to look out the dirty front window, with its long crack running from the upper right corner unevenly down to the lower left. In winter, she thought, it must let in a gale. Behind him sat a wood-burning pot-bellied stove that reminded her of the one in their farmhouse when she was a child: getting up on a winter morning to frost on the inside walls, sometimes frost on her and Abbie's quilts. When he turned his head, she saw his strong, straight nose, slightly bulbous now with age, broken veins that could be from booze, but in a flash she saw him as a young man; it was a sort of vision, she knew, one in which they were both complicit. She knew where his mind was going, felt her unnatural, surprising patience to wait for more, and knew how strong he must once have been, as such pioneering men were. And beautiful, she guessed, and shivered. He seemed to recognize that, and dropped his head to stare at the rag rug that covered the worn linoleum between them.

"They came up through Italy," he said. "Sicily first. I fought in France. Neither one was fun, but Sicily . . ." He stopped again. "Anders, well, he told me the story, told me about Henry in it too. I don't know it first-hand."

"Anything," she said. "Please."

"You heard of Dachau?" He looked directly at her.

"Yes."

"Anders, him and Henry, they were there. April 29, 1945."

"When they opened it?"

"Liberated it," he said, and laughed, a humourless sound, and twisted his head as if his neck had begun to hurt. "A week before the official big German surrender, the day before Hitler killed himself. But the war was pretty much over then. Or it was supposed to be.

"Now listen," he went on, his voice cleared. "I ain't never told this story, and I ain't going to tell it again." He put one thickened, gnarled hand up against the back of his neck, put it down, and said, "This here is what happened as Anders told me, and Henry — your father — he was there by Anders's side through the whole thing, all the way up from Sicily by boat, up to France on the Mediterranean side, and then back down through Germany — fought at Aschaffenburg — when the war was pretty much over, and down toward Munich."

Judith imagined him hanging on, year after year, waiting for the right person, the right moment, to tell this story. In the intensity of her listening, she was hardly breathing, and the air, how peculiar, was scintillating, as if the finest electric current were running through it. She could feel it in her temples and against the now-wrinkled skin of her chest below her collarbones and on the palms of her hands.

"They came across Dachau — some say they didn't even know it was there, some say they did and were sent there to liberate it. A few miles out of Munich it was. You read the books. Read the whole thing."

"I will." Humbly.

"Can't you feel it?"

"What?" But she *could* feel it, some ominous, dark thing spreading through the room, and Judith suppressed the sudden urge to get up and run out of there and drive back to Wisdom as fast as she could go. But if he would risk it, whatever it was, to tell her, she would sit here and listen.

He said, "The dead don't like you telling their stories, the bad ones anyway." He raised one hand that had been resting on the wooden armrest of his chair and made a slow gesture she could not interpret, as if he were talking to the air. Dismissal? Refusal? "But sometimes they want you to. It's time," he said, to the air.

"According to old Anders, his and your dad's company didn't go in the main gates, because they thought the Germans might have boobytrapped them. They went around to one side, where there was a railroad track running up through the countryside and on in through some gates into the camp." He paused, glanced at her, and went on. "Thousands and thousands of men in that camp, Anders said. Mostly POWs — Poles, Ukrainians, French, Italians, whoever. And a special section blocked off from the rest of the camp. For the Jews. Couple thousand of them at least."

It was odd how he was telling the story as if he were reciting it or reading it from an invisible book in front of him, his voice gone steady.

"What they saw when they got to them railroad tracks was a bunch of boxcars, their doors wide open — thirty-seven, I think he said, or was it thirty-nine of them? — and in them boxcars bodies were piled up, naked bodies, hundreds of them, maybe a couple of thousand, I don't know, don't remember what Anders said. A lot of them. Bodies of Jews," he told her. "Prisoners dead from starvation or torture or murder, and nobody got around to burying them or burning them.

"Well, them boys, they'd fought all the way up from Italy, that crew, hardest fighting some of it, in the war, hand to hand, it was murderous. It was hell. That company, altogether, fighting all the way up to France and into the last battle in Germany, they lost every single man, either killed or wounded out. Maybe four hundred. Had to keep bringing in fresh troops so they could keep on fighting. Two weeks for one hill, everybody dead, but Anders and Henry the only ones left, more than once."

He put one heavy, trembling hand in the front of his face. When he put it down, she saw thin old-man's tears glinting in the crevasses of his cheeks.

"These boys were eighteen, nineteen, twenty years old, come out of farms and ranches and small towns all over the U.S. Never seen nothing like it. Anders said to me, when he was dying in the hospital and told me this story for the only time — never told nobody else, but he was dying, you see — said when he was dead he wouldn't need to go to hell because he'd already been there, he said, and Henry Clemensen, your old man, he was right beside him.

"Bodies — human beings — just flung in there, waist high, like so much garbage. Well, a lot of them, the soldiers I mean, just went crazy. Anders said he couldn't even stand up, dropped to his knees, vomited, and all around him men were crying and screaming curses, and some, a few even banging their heads on the ground. Some just ran. Their commander there, he tried to stop them, but he couldn't keep them all back. Some got away and ran into the camp where some camp guards were and shot them dead."

His hand was up over his eyes again, for a just a second, and when he dropped it, his face had hardened.

"And them prisoners, some Jews, some others — I don't know who, and Anders is dead, he ain't going to tell you — whoever had been beaten and starved and castrated and all the rest of it, they went after some of them guards and killed them with their bare hands or whatever lay to hand. And nobody stopped them." He paused again as she listened, one hand on her chest. "'That there's a war crime, that,' Anders whispered to me. You see? That's why nobody was talking about it. You can only kill enemy soldiers in combat. You can't hunt them down and kill them like that. You can go to prison for a long time for that. Remember the My Lai massacre? The Vietnam War?"

She did remember My Lai, the place where American soldiers had massacred a whole village. Not quite the same thing, though surely it was a war crime to kill unarmed noncombatants? She thought that nobody had been jailed for that, or maybe their commander had been, but nobody else. *Not quite the same thing,* her critical self thought. *Or was it?*

"I never heard such a thing," she said, referring to Dachau.

"Some soldier was supposed to watch a bunch of German camp guards and soldiers the army had rounded up, and he lost it and fired and killed — I don't know — all of 'em, or most of 'em. Anders said the commander raced back and yelled at the gunner to stop firing." He drew in a slow breath. "Anders said the gunner didn't want to stop."

She was about to speak, although she didn't know what it was she would say, but Jespersen kept on talking. "Then they went on into the part of the camp where they kept them Jews. Two, three thousand. And what they saw there that Anders told me —," he looked straight at her again, "I can't even say it. But you're educated, ain't you? You must have heard about that part. You musta seen pictures." She nodded slowly. "And your dad, same age as me, twenty years old, that's what he saw. He saw all that."

She couldn't move for a long second, while Jespersen lit a hand-rolled cigarette, his hands trembling finely, and then sat, gazing out the cracked window at the empty fields beyond the thin hedge that stretched out to the sky. She felt he had been sitting that way for years.

"Do you think it's true?"

"It's true." Not looking at her.

"But how did nobody know about it? How did it stay a secret?"

"Didn't," he said. "Old soldiers started talking about it some years back, I guess. But at the time, Anders said, the army just buried it.

Didn't want nobody to know. And to tell the truth, I think the army didn't blame them soldiers. Didn't want their lives ruined because they went crazy after what they saw. After what they had been through already? Everybody around them dead, legs and arms and heads shot off, chunks of flesh landing on them, drowning in craters, bayonetted, the hellish racket of bombs and shells, machine guns, fighter planes diving, exploding over them . . . I think they weren't in their right minds. I was in France. I remember."

The smell of garbage was suddenly overpowering, and Judith's nausea quickly rose. She got to her feet and went outside into the air, hazy now, and cold as if winter were coming on instead of summer. Even the seasons had lost track. The crows had gone from the tops of the bare trees, and only the country silence of her childhood remained, when she had felt as if she were the only person in the world, and she had longed with every cell to go where there was light and crowds, colour and excitement. Maybe that was even the same reason why, all those years ago, her father had enlisted and gone to war. It was the first time in her life that she could remember when she felt affinity with him, brief as it was. Astonishing as it was. But she felt as if she were trapped inside an enormous, translucent bubble, and all feelings were on the other side of it, and she could see them but couldn't reach them.

She went back inside and sat again at the end of his sofa, closest to Jespersen. The air in the house was thinner now, the smells less oppressive.

"Okay now?" he asked.

"I only wanted to know why my father screamed at night," she said, her voice tremulous, "when we were children, and why he would never say why. Not even what it was he dreamt about." She paused, thinking. "Or why he was so silent, why he never touched us..."

"He didn't dare," the old man interrupted, fierce now. "He didn't dare let out a word of it, or any real feelings, or he would have gone crazy. That's what he was afraid of. All them years, all them boys, trying to forget what they saw, what they did themselves. He couldn't talk about it."

After a moment, she said, her voice steady again, "You had your own war."

"I told Anders that night in the hospital about my war. Don't need to tell it again. It just eats away at your guts, that stuff. I don't do no marching; I don't do no celebrating." Another long pause. "What can you say," he asked her, "when you been through hell and seen your friends blown apart, and you stuck a bayonet in the guts of a man or two? You don't know what to do with that. You think maybe marching around with your medals on your chest will do it, will help, and I guess for some it does. But I ain't never been able to do that. You ever notice how them old soldiers just sit there in their wheelchairs, and some of them cry?"

As she drove slowly down the road toward Haley, she began to relax, although every once in a while she had to wipe her eyes with the back of a hand. After a while, a rare tenderness began to creep through her body. It felt like the sweet flow of warm creek water in summer, and as it flowed, it loosened a hard knot in her solar plexus she hadn't known she was carrying, going back to the time before she had left home. Her father, that terrifying patriarch who never spoke, except in the night when he fell into darkness, had once been a normal man.

How would she tell Abbie and Sam what she now knew? Remembering Jespersen's admonition to find out, should she go to a city library and read about the details? Should she start trying to use the internet to find out the complete, the official story? If there was one. As she drove, she began to remember her father more clearly, his face, his eyes so penetrating without ever seeming exactly to see you, the tightness of his mouth and the deep lines around it, and she thought — how could she not — *How he must have suffered.*

But he was only one soldier, one prairie boy who went off to war and saw a depravity for which no words could ever be sufficient to describe: the enormity of it, by which she did not mean the six million, although that was true too, but the enormity of the darkness out

SHARON BUTALA

of which the horrors had come. And he, that prairie boy who became her father, was lost forever. Tried to save himself, left his home, got married, had children, took to God with every fibre, and in the end, still couldn't.

She sat in her idling car on the highway shoulder outside Haley, gazing through her windshield but seeing nothing. She didn't feel ready simply to drive to Wisdom and her provisional home there, not even noticing she had thought of it as provisional, and couldn't bear the thought of another night in Catherine and Ian's condo in Calgary. She would go to Jessica's.

CHAPTER NINE

JESSICA

Judith was sitting in the front yard at the rough picnic table, her back to the log house, when Jessica drove her beat-up SUV slowly into the yard. In fact, she had come down the last couple of kilometres of narrow, gravelled trail so slowly that Judith hadn't noticed her vehicle until it poked its nose through the row of great pine trees into the yard and stopped beside Judith's car. Jessica got out and came the few yards toward her mother. Her dark brown hair hung thick, wavy, and slightly unkempt around her shoulders, and the threadbare lumberjack shirt she wore as a jacket over her white blouse should have been thrown out ages ago. She had tucked her jeans into her boots, which made a crunching sound as they hit the gravel of the parking area. She was smiling nervously at Judith.

"Mom, this is a terrific surprise. Are you okay? Is everybody okay?"

"Everything's fine," Judith assured her. "I just needed to see you."

Jessica sat down across the picnic table from her. Judith sat, resting her hands on the table while a couple of tears she hardly noticed emerged to roll down her cheeks. Jess watched her for a moment, then leaned across the narrow table, lifted her mother's hands, and held them against her own face, then lowered them to cup them with her own hands. They sat that way for a long moment, not speaking. Of all her daughters, why was it that only Jessica radiated love so freely? Alice, whenever she did come back to Canada, gave off a mild unease, as if she didn't know what to do with this woman who was her mother, an unease she tried to hide with excessive hugs, kisses, and declarations about missing her, all of which served only to tell Judith that she had lost her firstborn.

Judith would gaze at the photos of Alice and Dwight's children and would admire her grandsons, and ask questions about them, and then there would be nothing much to say to each other before Alice would scurry away, back to Tanzania. And nearly every visit with Lucinda, no matter how it began, ended with tears, screaming, and door slamming, while with Catherine, Judith felt that she was the child and Catherine the mother. She knew it was her fault, but had no idea what to do about any of it.

The passenger door of the SUV opened, shut quietly, and someone small came slowly around the hood, pressing her body against it, her left arm trailing across it as she came toward them. Judith pulled her hands away and quickly swiped away her tears. The girl was perhaps ten years old, excessively thin, freckles across her nose and cheeks, and a glint of russet, even in this light, glowing in her short, raggedly cut hair.

"This is my friend Carly," Jess said. "She's staying with me for a few days. Right, Carly?" She caressed the girl's hair while the child leaned her weight against Jess's body, at first tentatively, then, unrepulsed, as it seemed she half-expected to be, and with Jess's arm going around her waist, with more confidence. Was she trembling? In the failing light, Judith couldn't be sure.

"Yeah," the child said, in a simulated mature voice, sighing patiently as an adult would, but with a faint quaver. "Sometimes I just have to get away."

Judith said, "I can understand that. Sometimes getting away is the only thing to do." She and Jess laughed at the irony of that, but quickly, so as not to offend the girl. "I can see that you are wise already," Judith said.

Carly turned her head, smiling, and after a second said to Jess, "I could make some sandwiches? Or I could make some hamburger hash for us." Yes, she was trembling — a familiar sinking feeling came over Judith, knowing what she knew about children in trouble.

"You don't have to, sweetie, you could just stay here and talk with us."

Carly smiled over her shoulder, as if another adult stood there in the growing shadows, although no one was there. "I could make us supper," she said firmly, as if somebody, maybe Jess, had told her she had the right to speak as if she knew what she was talking about.

"We would love that, Carly," Jess told her. "You're a lifesaver, but homework first?"

Carly shrugged, turned, picking up her backpack on the way, and hop-skipped through the thin grass toward the house, pausing in the open doorway to call "I can do both at the same time!" then letting the door slam behind her.

Jess said, "I'm an official emergency shelter for school-age kids in temporary trouble. Although it turns out, it's never temporary. They tend to go from me to foster care permanently, hardly ever back to their families until they turn eighteen and can do what they want. Or they escape to live on the streets. Or they run away from their foster homes, some of them time and again, to go back to the very families that mistreated them. It's a total mystery."

"That I know," Judith agreed. It was indeed a mystery no one could solve or fully explain, that no matter how awful their homes were, kids nearly all the time preferred being with their own mothers and fathers — although mostly it was just mothers and their siblings — to living with even the kindest of strangers. What was it that grown-ups refused to acknowledge?

"She is alive with potential, that one," Jessie said. "I would adopt her if I could — if things don't work out with those idiot parents of hers. They aren't even poor or addicted people; they're just selfish and narcissistic. Sometimes cruel. Always erratic."

All Judith could think of was the trouble Carly would bring Jess as she matured physically, the heartache.

"She is always afraid around people she doesn't know," Jessie said. "I am so afraid for her. I would like to watch over her and protect her. Is that a good reason to adopt a child?"

Judith hesitated, then shrugged, all her years working with such children descending like a cloud around her. "It isn't a bad reason," she said finally. "Jess, you can't imagine how much trouble such a child will bring you…" She wanted to say more but couldn't find the words. "Kids as damaged as Carly probably is — it is so hard to set them right again. I don't want to discourage you, and it's clear she needs love and security, but…" She was also wondering if the parents would let the child go. Or would they have no alternative? It would never work if the parents could come and go in Carly's life as they chose.

"I think, if it were easy, what point would there be in doing it? The whole point is how hard it will be. I mean, if she weren't so damaged, she wouldn't need new parents, a new life — do you see what I mean?"

But Judith could think only of Dachau, wanting to tell her daughter what she had just found out about it, about the bodies, about the unspeakable sufferings of at the very least the Jewish prisoners in that camp alone, never mind the thousands of Jews murdered there. She found that, for the moment anyway, she couldn't seem to separate Carly's trembling from the heaps of bodies, and now the hares, half-gutted and left to hang in the trees of the yard of the only Jews in the town of Wisdom, came back to her. A joke, people said, no doubt done by some uncomprehending moron or morons, or Jew-haters — Jew-hater in this modern world, knowing what we know now, it was beyond belief. But she had to stop this: they were three different things. Weren't they?

They began to walk toward the house, Jessica murmuring, "She's the oldest of five kids and gets left, I can't tell you how often, to look after all of them. She has taught herself to cook." They sat down at the table and chatted while Carly worked at the stove with a kind of grim determination mingled with something that might have been pride, until she had readied the hamburger hash and served it.

"How can you tell what is the right amount of salt?" she asked, swallowing visibly before daring to address Judith, her smile pleading.

"You taste it, I guess. That's how I always did it. But I was never a good cook."

"She was a *terrible* cook," Jess said to Carly, laughing and glancing sideways at her mother. And later, to Judith, "I want her to see that it is possible to say things like that among people who love each other, and are truthful, and that don't make for the end of the known world, as such a thing does in her household, because her parents *want* it that way." It was the first time Judith had heard anger in her voice. It made her think of Ian and Catherine.

"How . . . happy . . . are they? Do you know?"

Carly was in bed by the time Judith asked this question, and they were sitting on the sofa bed in the living room while a fire glowed yellow and orange in the small fireplace. A previous owner of this cabin, which was surrounded by huge pines and spruces, had added this room with its glass wall facing the mountains and thinned the trees in this direction in order to draw in every bit of light there was. Jess ate her meals here, and judging by the desk in the corner, worked here too, making lesson plans and marking papers — no, little ones didn't write papers. Making fiddly paper things for the children in her class. If you wanted morning sun, you had to sit on the front porch.

After a pause, Jessica said, "I'm thinking that the Catherine–Ian thing is just about over."

"It was so strained there," Judith said. "I felt so sorry for her. Ian — I only saw him once the whole time."

"Oh, he's got a woman somewhere, maybe a couple of them," Jess said. "As soon as Cathy figures that out, maybe gets a man of her own, she'll leave him. Then they'll spend five years in court sorting out their money."

"Who is paying for that place?" Judith asked. "It must have cost a million at least, or maybe even more. And the furniture — super chic, super expensive!"

"Ian really does make a pile of money," Jessie assured her. "You know how much money there is in oil; it's mind-boggling, but the minute oil prices fall, it will all go. And oil prices always fall. I hope she has some money squirrelled away, although I suppose it all comes out in a divorce. Anyway, I told her to come and stay with me for a while — once Carly has moved on, of course. If Carly moves on."

"There is no man in your life?"

Jess laughed at this, an inward-turning girlish laugh. It was heartening, but despite this, Judith's headache was lurking again.

"I'm not gay, Mom," she said. "Yes, I see a man. He teaches grade six. His name is Ethan. We talk about living together, but we never seem to get around to it. Maybe this summer. He loves kids too." The flames behind the glass jiggled and wavered and shot higher, blue at their tips. "The bad part of it is that I'm too old to have babies. That's the sorry part."

Judith wondered how Jessica had managed to create this peaceful kingdom of hers in the middle of the forest, the mountains sometimes grey or purple, sometimes rose or gold in the distance, where calm reigned, and the pleasures of solitude were real and sought after, not there by default. She remembered the gentle old man in the park in Wisdom, a Jew who had seen the worst of the world, then thought of her own house there, much like this one, come to think of it, but in which no peace reigned, and no acceptance of the way things are.

"I remain incarcerated in my awful house and in my own past. And in pain," she said to her daughter, a remark Jessica seemed not to know how to handle. "How on earth did you do this?" waving a hand to indicate the peace and warmth in the simple room, the small house, the perfect silence of the towering, somehow protective forest.

"Mom, I don't have your history," Jess said. "Your 'baggage,' as they say. No family from the time you were fifteen, two mismatched marriages. No money to speak of. All that turmoil for so many awful years. Our dad abandoning us, you with your heart broken. The awful trauma of Victor's death, as if it was your fault." She paused. "Or our fault. I think we all felt we were guilty of killing him. We were only kids, but I think especially Lucy felt guilty."

Judith chose not to follow this tack; hadn't she been over this and over it? She had talked herself blue in the face trying to help Cathy and Lucy with Victor's death. She could not go over that again; it was too terrible to remember.

But she said now to her child, "You made up your own mind about everything from the time you were a teenager, and you didn't even make any mistakes, that I know of anyway. How did you do that?"

Jessie shrugged. "I can tell you what I thought," she said, "but how or why I can't say, unless it was that I always knew — and I'm sorry to say it, Mom, but it's true — I always knew how loved I was, and I don't think Lucinda or Cathy did. I mean, Victor always favoured Lucinda, but I can see now that it was in a not-very-good way. I can't speak for Alice. I can hardly remember the sister I knew."

Judith's heart was rattling against her ribs. "I loved all my children . . . equally," she whispered, feeling the greatest liar, because it had always been this one or that over the others at any given moment, even as she knew this was also true. Jess turned her head to study her mother, but Judith didn't look up, not wanting to see Jess's expression.

"I saw when Dad left you, that investing everything in other people, unless you were Mother Teresa, was not ever going to work if you wanted to be happy. I have tried to invest in myself instead."

Judith found herself wondering how this applied to Carly and the other wounded children Jess said she had cared for. She remembered viscerally, almost unbearably so, how she had gone to work every day knowing how much her own children needed her to be at home with them, how wracked she was with guilt all through their childhoods, and then with anger because it wasn't fair that she had to choose. To invest in yourself.

"Well, I guess," she said, not realizing she was speaking aloud, "you have to find yourself first."

After a while, Jess said, "Do you know who Judith was?"

"What?"

"Judith, the biblical Judith. You're named after her. Do you know her story?"

"I suppose I once did, but — no, I don't remember who she was. Old Testament, right?"

"Yes, a very old story, but whether it's the Old Testament itself depends on whether you're Catholic, Protestant, or Jewish."

"Well, it seems I am none of the above. Is that even possible?"

"As far as I know, Jews think she is a figure in a lovely folktale, not a real historical person, although they do tell the story. Protestants put the Book of Judith in the Apocrypha — biblical writings that aren't quite accepted as the true word, I guess. And Catholics accept the story as true and put it in their version of the Bible as scripture. But Judith means 'the Jewess' — how about that?"

"Mom and Dad couldn't possibly have known that, or they wouldn't have given me the name." But later, in bed, it would occur to her that perhaps her father had chosen it, instead of Mary Ann or Elizabeth or Carol or whatever properly Protestant name he could think of, as a mark of respect for the people whose remains he had come upon at Dachau.

Across from where they sat on the sofa, they could see the shadows of the forest blooming like giant flowers. "She was a very beautiful widow," Jess said.

"That lets me out," Judith said. "Eventually I became a widow, but as for beautiful, well, not quite."

An ironic drawing out of the last words caused Jess to turn her head to study her mother's profile. "I think it's interesting how your face is changing as you slowly recover from the catastrophe, and as you age. Like a screen or a veil is dissolving, and your real face is beginning to emerge."

Judith thought of old August Jespersen, of the shapely bones of his face, and despite the wrinkled skin, the creases so deep as to be scars, all from a long life of suffering and joy — from experience, from living — of its true beauty.

"You are becoming beautiful." Jessica ducked her head, as if embarrassed to be saying this.

Judith said, "I think it just happens, if you don't despair, if instead of giving up on life, you give up the fairy tales people feed you from the time you're a child. Maybe as you start to define your own way."

But Jessica was back on the story of Judith.

"Ethan says that Jews celebrate Judith at Hanukkah, so how can they think she wasn't real? It must be her spirit they celebrate." She found her wine glass and sipped from it. "Ethan's people are Jewish, but he doesn't seem to want to declare himself as such, even though of course he is. By the way, he is the one who taught me all this. He did 'Abigail' and 'Samuel' too." She laughed in a private, tender way. "Not to forget, also 'Jessica.' Invented by Shakespeare," Jess said, reading Judith's unasked question.

"Anyway, Judith lived in Judea, in a city named Bethulia. Judea was under attack by the Assyrians under a general named Holofernes, and her city was going to be wiped out. So Judith gets all gussied up to look as beautiful and seductive as possible, then she and her maid head out in the dark of night to sneak into Holofernes's camp, and get in to see him because she is so stunning. Using her wiles, she gets him to fall for her — or maybe she doesn't have to do anything, men and beautiful women after all — and when he goes to sleep, she takes his sword, cuts off his head with two strokes, puts it into her food bag, and, not forgetting to take her maid with her, heads back to Bethulia. She shows the head to her own people's commanders, who, discovering Holofernes is dead, rejoice, but back in the Assyrian camp, making the same discovery, Holofernes's army flees in disarray. Judith has saved her city. So she is a heroine for her bravery and her initiative, I guess."

"Oh yeah, just like me," Judith said.

"You spent your adulthood saving children and teenagers."

"It was my job; I got paid to do it. I was one of a legion of people getting paid to do it. I wasn't even a manager."

"I saw you come home exhausted some days, not from hard labour, but from what you had had to do. Worse, from what you had seen. Mom, I had great admiration for you when I was a child. I was in awe of you, that you could face horrors that I couldn't imagine, to help people."

Judith could feel her face warming. "What?"

"Did I never say that? Didn't you know? We — all four of us — we were so proud of having you for a mother." She paused. "I used to think that maybe that had something to do with why Lucinda was so — I don't know — erratic? You were too much for her. She couldn't sort out her feelings. Maybe she felt she was already a failure when she was like maybe twelve?"

They both laughed, imagining this going on in little Lucy's head. Impossible.

But this was a new version of herself, one that Judith had never even in her wildest imaginings touched on. Hadn't Jack, whom she had loved with everything she had, left her because she was so inadequate? Hadn't Victor told her over and over again that she simply wouldn't do? Hadn't she plodded out day after day to do a job nobody could possibly "win" at?

"I spent so many years in the middle of a hurricane," she said. "I felt beset most of my life. I was going to say 'my adult life,' but I felt beset as a child too. Maybe — I think maybe everybody feels like that. Anyway, I am not heroic," she said, her voice gone steady and soft.

"Or we are mostly all heroic," Jessica offered.

They sat on in comfortable silence, the fire giving off a soft golden light, reminding Judith once again of her childhood and the kerosene lamps that were the only illumination aside from the stars and the moon and sometimes the northern lights, and felt a brief but deep longing for that world.

"About your grandfather," she heard herself say. "My father. I've been on a journey to find out about him. All the things none of us knew: where he came from, why he left home and, as far as any of us knew, never went back."

Jessica turned her head toward her mother, put her feet on the floor, and pulled herself up to sit straight.

"I thought you were at Cathy's."

"I was, but I found out where Dad came from, and I decided to go down there along the border and have a look for myself."

"You never said much about him."

"He is a good part of why I ran away so young. I found somebody, an old man, who knew him when he was a boy. Before he went off to the war . . ."

"He fought in World War II?"

"American infantry. He was with the unit that liberated Dachau."

"Oh no."

"Worse, that was just the end of his war. His started in Sicily — oh Jess, I can't tell you the story right now — I don't know the whole story, just the bare outlines, and I suppose it's pretty typical for a soldier then. But . . ." She paused, trying to think what else to say. "But he had a very bad war. The worst, short of losing a limb or getting his head blown off, coming home blind or crippled or whatever. I mean, he and the other soldiers must have been half mad already when they hit Dachau, and then what they saw there. What *he* saw there."

"He had to have had post-traumatic stress disorder," Jess said.

"Yes, you're right. Of course! That's what was wrong with him. Only nobody called it that then, and I guess there wasn't any help for it." She remembered Jespersen saying that her father couldn't talk about it, he didn't know how; he was afraid if he did, he would bring it all crashing down around him again. That he would go mad.

Later, in bed, Judith began to wonder if she should have told Jessica the rest of the story, about the boxcars full of bodies, and the soldiers losing discipline and shooting even those who had surrendered, about what her grandfather might have been a part of. Bemused also by the Judith story, she lay awake most of the night and rose very early, went outside into the pale sunrise filtered through the thick tree branches, and with her coat on over her nightgown, walked about the shadowed yard, even a few feet into the forest, where she stood perfectly still, hardly breathing, listening, all her antennae out, for what she didn't know, then went back in, found Carly and Jess still asleep, quietly performed a minimal cleansing and teeth-brushing, dressed, and went back outside to walk in the early morning air a little longer.

As she walked and the light came up higher through the trees, Saul Richter came into her mind, and she wondered where he had gotten his calm from, how he could live having seen what he had seen. Seen! Having lived it. She could not puzzle that one out. While her father had lost his mind.

Her neck and shoulder pain had gone overnight, but her headache persisted, although with less intensity than the day before. When she smelled, of all things — something she would never smell at Catherine's, or heaven forbid, her newly Jewish daughter Lucinda's — bacon cooking, she went back inside. The sun was up now and, oh blessed sounds, songbirds were chittering away in the trees.

"I've decided to drive back home today," she told Jessica and Carly as they sat at the table spooning in porridge — so the bacon must be for her, because she was here — and Jess gazed up at her mother, smiling, while Carly kicked her legs forward and back under the table, as if anxious to be up and gone. *Poor kid,* Judith thought. She can't settle down, she's too afraid of everything. "I hope the next time I come to visit it will be for your wedding."

She was teasing, but Jess bent her head, hiding a smile, so that Judith thought, *Well, well!*

Later, when they left the house for the day, Carly marching as businesslike as a CEO straight to Jess's SUV and getting in on the passenger side, Jess followed Judith to her car and waited while she put in her bag and purse and settled herself in the driver's seat. Then Jessica leaned in the window, brushed her mother's mouth with her own, startling Judith, warmth rushing to her face as her daughter pulled her head back and said, looking directly into Judith's eyes, "I think it is time to let your pain go, Mom. I'm thinking now that it is not private pain."

CHAPTER TEN

NORMAL LIFE

The sun rose so early now as spring advanced toward summer; all the snow was gone, even the ugly blackened crusts under hedges and against fences; the trees had a faint greenish hue; and one morning in the park she stood transfixed in the pale light, thinking she was looking at a bald eagle high in a tree, straining her eyes to make sure. Golden eagles in this country were abundant, but bald eagles were only an occasional sight, usually alone but sometimes in pairs, as they passed through on their migration to their summer grounds.

But Saul Richter, although she barely heard him, always announced his presence to her by some aura of quiet surrounding him, which she felt even though she didn't know he was nearby.

"A bald eagle, I think," she said, pointing, hearing the excitement she couldn't keep out of her voice.

"Yes?" he said. "Where?" And as she turned her body to better show him where to look, the bird lifted off, the tree branch vibrating behind him as, unfolding his wings and lifting them, he soared upward and outward, his white head shining as if it had collected all the approaching light to itself and was a beacon.

"My wife and I are leaving Wisdom," Richter said when the eagle was gone. He hadn't looked at her yet; he had simply lowered his eyes to the ground when the eagle became a black dot and vanished.

"You have been driven away!"

"My wife is ill; here, we are too far from the medical help she must have."

"Did the Mounties help you?"

"No one knows, there are no clues, it doesn't matter anyway, not really. People have said they are sorry it happened."

"No!" she said. "It does matter who did it. He should be rooted out. He should be exposed!"

"We are old people." He took his hands from where he had thrust them into the pockets of his short jacket. He sighed. "We have fought enough, I think."

"I'm very sorry, I am so very sorry," she said, meaning about the gutted rabbits, about his wife. Then, quietly, "Are you really going because of your wife's illness?"

"My wife is ill," he said. "We *are* too far from medical help."

"Are you afraid here?" She thought he would be angry at her for asking this; she thought he would deny such a thing, as all the men she grew up with would be required to do, no matter what the provocation, no matter that they *were* afraid. Instead, he shrugged.

"Wouldn't it be foolish not to be? After all that in this world has happened to Jews?"

"But here," she pointed out hesitantly, "so far only graffiti, gutted hares."

He said, no longer gentle, "Where do you think that leads?" Roughly, he pushed up the sleeve of his jacket and the cotton shirt underneath. She saw, even in the still greyish light, a faded blue tattoo. She stiffened, staring. After a minute, he pushed his sleeves back into place and turned away from her. She wanted to say things, but all of them died before she could make them into words. A breeze stirred the shrubs, picked up to rush through the high branches of the trees, setting them to swaying and sighing before dying away. She made a slight noise.

"Don't," he said, kindly enough. "I think you have enough pain. Don't add what you think is mine onto yours. Haven't you seen that I am all right?"

"I don't know how you can do it." But her tone was pleading, that he might tell her how it was done, his travails coming out of another universe than her puny ones.

"You take things too seriously, I think," he said, his tone light again. *Oh my god*, how many times had she heard that? "I do not mean to diminish the great evil. I refer to the daily afflictions and slights everyone faces."

"People like me," she said, angry now herself, "think that the problem is not us, but all the people who do not take things seriously enough. Who choose not to, because it is easier." Collecting herself, she added, "I am not sure, anyway, that there is a difference," but she was becoming confused, not sure what she meant.

"There is no answer," he told her, picking up on the question behind her confusion. "Do you think that Job found the answer?" Was he grinning?

"Do you understand him? Tell me if you do, please."

But once again he chose not to reply to her question, instead asking, "Are *you* going to stay here? I ask because you seem only to be perched here, thinking of flying this way or that way." He waved his hand, fluttering his fingers, so that she laughed a little. "Is this truly your home?"

"I don't know," she told him. "But maybe it's just possible that I'm getting closer to the answer." He said nothing. "I have resolved one thing, though. One very big thing that I came here to resolve."

"Good for you," he said. "Now I must go. We leave soon, and my wife is too weak to do the packing. Me, she directs: 'Do this, do that.' And I obey." They laughed together, as if they had been talking about the weather.

"It is so strange that . . ." she began, but he was walking away and did not look back.

She would have to tell Abbie and Sam about finding Jespersen and what he had told her. She thought of saying nothing — they didn't seem to care anyway, or else they already knew and were saving her from it.

No, they didn't know. How could they? She decided to take her time deciding if, or when, or how she would tell them. But as the next day passed, and then the next, she began to wonder about the story August Jespersen had told her he had received from Anders Andreasen, long dead now. It seemed to her very unlikely that she would ever find out anything certain about what her father's participation had actually been in the — what is the term? — *extrajudicial* killings at the liberation of Dachau, but she could at least research the official story. Hadn't she promised Jespersen that she would? That would mean another trip to Calgary, one that she didn't wish to make.

She could go on the internet, she decided, maybe even tomorrow. But then she was uncertain again, because that was certainly not the main story, horrible though it was, and wrong as it certainly was — wasn't it? — but compared to the bigger story, of which the bodies in the boxcars were only a hideous, a demonic outlier, the killing of the Germans found at Dachau perhaps bordered on the inconsequential. *Well, not to them,* she thought grimly, although she knew only too well what the answer might be to that argument.

That night, nearing midnight, she was in the kitchen sipping from a fresh mug of decaffeinated coffee as she leaned back against the counter at the sink, behind her the window that faced the blank wall of her neighbour's house. She hadn't put the light on; enough spread through the open doorway from the dining room for her to see. *Time to be going to bed,* she was thinking, when the motion-activated light on the far side of the house next door came on, she heard rock music again, and, startled, turned to look out the window. This time she saw a group of young people moving in a cluster that slowly separated itself into four or five teenagers, some girls, some boys, moving from the house down the sidewalk toward the back gate before the noise stopped, the light went out, and she heard only the creak followed by a faintly audible click as the gate was opened and then shut again.

She puzzled over this; the kids seemed young to her, fourteen, fifteen maybe; wasn't it a school night? Wasn't the man next door supposed to have been a schoolteacher in Wisdom once? She had never seen him herself, knew nothing of his comings and goings. That uneasy feeling came over her again that this situation needed looking into. Disturbed, she poured the rest of her coffee into the sink, ran water into the mug, and wandered into her bedroom, putting out the lights as she went. Maybe, just maybe, in the morning she would take a little responsibility, she would go to the Mounties.

Instead, the next morning she slept late, and after her morning coffee, putting aside her uneasiness with her sister, phoned Abbie, thinking she would find out what the local gossip was about the man who lived next door to her.

"There was no scandal that I know of. He just moved on, maybe twenty years ago. Teachers do, out here, unless they're women married to local farmers or ranchers."

"It's true I haven't even seen him," Judith admitted. "For all I know he's moved away and somebody else lives there now."

Abbie, apparently not interested, asked, "Did you hear that the Richters are moving to Regina?"

"Why?" Judith asked, not wanting to say she knew this, wanting also to hear the current gossip about them.

"I believe the move is because Mrs. Richter is sick. Cancer, I heard. It's too hard on her, all that driving to the city and back for treatment."

"It wasn't too hard until somebody gutted those hares and hung them in their trees," Judith said.

"Mmmm," Abbie said, as if she hadn't heard what Judith said. "I want you and Rick to come over for coffee on Sunday afternoon. I'm going to ask Sam and Sylvia too."

"What for?" Abbie asked, a Sunday afternoon coffee invitation apparently being new to her. "There's an engagement shower in the hall that afternoon for Linda Gaines and Brett Weiler. Brett's mother goes to our church. We have to attend."

"Come before the shower, or come after, whatever works best. I have something I want to tell you."

"Now what could that be?" Abbie asked, intrigued, or pretending she was. "Give me a hint."

"It's about Dad."

"All right," Abbie said, after a silence. "We'll come after. About four, okay?" Judith knew that tone: quiet, steady, impersonal, designed to hide whatever she was really thinking.

When she called Sam's house, Sam, not Sylvia, answered.

"Can you and Sylvia come over for coffee on Sunday, about four o'clock? Are you going to that shower first?"

"Whose shower?"

"I don't know — Brett somebody and Linda Gaines, I think it was."

"Sylvia must be going, she's on the hall committee, but I'm not planning to. I can come by myself, and then when she can get away, Sylvia will come. Why aren't you inviting us for supper?" he asked, mystified. "You city people have funny ideas."

"I didn't know about the shower and — it just turned out this way, Sam. Sure, what the heck. Stay for supper. I'll put in a roast." She was about to hang up, when he said, "Wait a minute. What's this about?"

"Does it have to be about something?"

"Yeah, with you, I think it does," but he didn't sound annoyed, more teasing.

"Well, for you and Abbie. It's about . . . it's about Dad."

Silence.

"Are you sure?"

"Of course I'm sure."

"I mean, are you sure you want to go there?"

It was her turn to be mystified. "Of course, why not?" Another silence.

"Never mind. See you Sunday."

She was climbing into bed that night when she remembered she had planned to go to the RCMP detachment in Dillon and find a way to report the strange goings-on next door without actually accusing anybody of anything or sounding hysterical or appearing to be an annoying busybody. Tomorrow, she told herself, although the next day was Saturday and she supposed she would have to drive to the next town where there was a bigger detachment to find anybody in the office. She decided that reporting the activities in the house next to hers could wait until Monday.

She had barely gotten to sleep when she heard her phone ringing on the coffee table where she had left it. At first, she thought she wouldn't answer it, but then realizing it could be somebody in trouble, any one of her four daughters, or — but there wasn't anybody else — she got up, put on the lamp in the living room, and answered her phone.

There seemed to be a lot of noise on the line, static or something, voices maybe, and music. Finally, a voice spoke, a man, "Judy?" She was a little afraid; she answered hesitantly, "Yes?"

"It's me," the man said. But Jack was — who knew where? Victor was dead. Rapidly her mind went through her daughters' husbands' voices: Not Dwight in Africa, not Ian, she didn't think it could be Levi and had never heard Ethan's voice, or even met him.

"Who?"

"Me! Gilles! It is me."

Sweat popped out on her forehead; she had to change her hold on the phone. "Gilles? Where are you? What's going on?" More background noises that were slowly identifying themselves as bar racket.

He was silent, made an odd noise, then said, "Camille died today." She realized he was crying.

Where were his kids? What was he doing in a bar? Why was he calling her? She thought she ought to be angry, but in the face of such news her anger vanished.

"I'm so sorry, Gilles. Really I am. How very hard this must be." Changing her tone, she asked as gently as she could, "Shouldn't you be with your children?" He was sobbing, trying to stifle the noise, taking in deep, shaky breaths.

"Yes, it's true. I should be — I didn't think it would be so fast — we are all in shock. We don't know what to do." She had been in Wisdom perhaps eight weeks. He had told her perhaps two months before she left Calgary. Yes, it could go this way; everyone knew that.

"Have you had any sleep?"

"Not much. It's been pretty . . . intense this last week or so. Sleep would be good."

She was trying to engage him until he could get a grip on himself. "Have you had anything to eat today?"

"What? Yes, I think so. Yes, I'm sure I did."

"I am not so sure," she said teasingly.

"Maybe not. Never mind. I just — I just needed to tell somebody else I cared for — not my family."

"I know that," she said. "I'm so glad you did."

"I should go."

"Yes," she told him, still gentle. "You must go home, Gilles. Call me again when things are more settled."

He clicked off the phone without replying. *Such an emotional man,* she couldn't help but think, remembering how her own parents tried never to show any genuine emotion, disapproved of it. But Gilles really was lost in his grief, despite the misery of his and Camille's last years when they were not together, though neither were they truly apart. And he had seen her die.

She didn't think that she should take his call as anything more than it appeared to be on its face: he, bereft and in need of another adult he trusted to listen to him, to share his anguish. Maybe he would call again when the funeral was over, but she wouldn't be holding her breath. Or, later, she might call him herself, just to see how he was doing. She was proud of how well she had handled the whole business: the shock and deep-seated pleasure at hearing his voice again, mixed with the continuing pain of his removing himself from her when she needed him most.

It was one in the morning now, and, wide awake, she decided to go back to reading the novel that was waiting by her bed. She was taking the first step to her bedroom when she was brought to a stop by the throaty roar of a big diesel engine, and was caught in blinding headlights sweeping through and past her shabbily curtained window, followed by the noise of a heavy vehicle skidding to a stop out front. She rushed to pull back the deplorable curtain, which she still hadn't gotten around to changing, to see what was going on. A three-quarter-ton truck had pulled up out front, its driver having left his door wide open, headlights blazing, the motor rumbling far too loudly for a residential street in the middle of the night. She saw a light go on in the house directly across the street, heard loud voices from the house next door, and saw a man dragging a girl half his size by her arm, nearly pulling her out of her unzipped jacket, to the still-running truck, where he jerked open the passenger door and lifted her, threw her inside. Judith was about to open her own front door and scream at him to leave the child alone before she realized she hadn't put on a dressing gown and in that glare would be as good as naked. And — further thought — he was probably the girl's father. *He'd better watch out*, she thought, furious, *or he'll have his daughter on the street*. She won't tolerate that kind of handling much longer. And what had brought her to the house next door in the first place, where something was clearly wrong?

At the sight of a child being manhandled that way, she had broken into a sweat, and when she heard a door banging shut toward the back of the house, she hurried to the kitchen at the same time as the truck out front was roaring away, and through the window above the sink saw a stream of kids pouring down the short stretch of sidewalk, disappearing from her view, followed by the noise of the gate screeching open and rattling shut, then the sound of running feet fading out down the alley. And yet, no police. She hurried back to the front window, but all was quiet, the truck gone, the neighbour's light turned off. It was the same in the back yard when she returned to the kitchen window to look. The light was out there too, the yard silent and still.

She went to the bedroom, found her dressing gown, and put it on. Pulling the belt tight, shivering, she walked slowly back into the kitchen, this time snapping on the light, trying to calm herself, thinking she would go to the Dillon RCMP detachment first thing in the morning — why hadn't she done it sooner? — when she heard a sound at her back door, a scratching, no, a light tapping, and froze. After a long moment, during which the tapping got louder, more urgent-sounding, she made sure of her cellphone in her pocket, went to the door, and opened it slowly, just a crack, ready to slam it shut again if she had to.

A young girl stood there, blood trickling down her face from a cut above her eyebrow, the flesh above her eye swollen and red.

"Please," the girl whispered. Without a word, Judith pulled the door open so the child could slide in, then shut it quickly, thudding the deadbolt into place. "I just need . . ." The girl was crying openly now, her eyes on Judith's appalled face.

"What is it? What happened to you? Is there somebody I should phone? I'll call the police," She reached into her pocket for her phone.

"No, no," the girl said, stepping toward her. "No, not the police, please. Call my mom. She'll come and get me." Every one of Judith's impulses seemed wrong; she reminded herself she wasn't a professional social worker anymore, she was a stranger selected solely for her proximity; surely delivering this child to her mother was the best thing to do.

"Did you come from next door?"

The girl shook her head silently no, but with her eyes fastened on Judith's face so that Judith knew she was lying — although she'd already known that.

"What is your name?" she asked brusquely.

"Caitlin?" the girl said.

"Caitlin who?"

"Let me call my mom, please." She reached for the phone.

After a second, reluctantly, Judith handed it over. While the child dialed, and after a moment began to speak, turning away and talking too softly for her to hear, Judith found a clean cloth, ran water onto it, and when Caitlin clicked off and returned the phone, she began to sponge the blood off the girl's face. She touched the eye gently, trying to see how bad the wound was.

"It's nothing," the girl said, pulling away. Now Judith saw that the sleeve of her jean jacket had been partly ripped away at the shoulder. "My mom's coming for me. You don't need to worry about it."

"What is going on over there?" Judith asked, trying to sound merely conversational.

"I don't know," Caitlin said. She had regained some of her teen-age-girl bravado, apparently felt she owed Judith nothing, and without taking off her wet runners or being invited, wandered into the living room, where she went to the window, standing to one side, and watched the empty street.

"I can help you, Caitlin, if you let me."

"My mom's coming," the girl repeated, not taking her eyes from the street. The child was trembling, and by the quaver in her voice, was close to breaking down.

"If you need help that your mom can't give you, you can come to me. I will help. My name is . . ."

"Mrs. Clemensen, I know." Judith saw now how small she was, how she couldn't be more than fourteen at the most. Moments passed, neither spoke, nor did the girl turn around. When in a few more minutes a large old four-door car — Judith couldn't tell the colour, maybe blue or green — came fast down the street and pulled up out front, Caitlin swung around, took three quick strides to the front door, tried to open it, couldn't, she was shaking too hard, undid the deadbolt before Judith could even get there, and without a word to her rescuer, was gone, slamming the door behind her. Judith watched her run down the short length of sidewalk to the car, someone inside had leaned over and opened the door for her, she got in, the car pulled away, and once again, all was quiet. As far as she could see across the street, not a light was on in any of the houses. She thought, *doesn't mean nobody else is watching.*

In the morning, having slept no more than three or four hours, she drove to Dillon, where she found the RCMP detachment and went in, walking as if she knew precisely what she was doing and would brook no interference, and spoke to the only Mountie she found there.

"My name is Judith Clemensen. I live next door to a house in Wisdom where something not good is going on." The Mountie, young and obviously junior, blinked rapidly and straightened his shoulders, amusing Judith, who recognized that his mother was probably younger than she was, and that, Mountie or not, the boy still in him was just a tiny bit scared of her. She began to tell him what had happened, what her suspicions were, stressing that she had never so much as seen her neighbour and had no idea about what kind of man he was.

"It's those children I'm worried about," she said. "What are they doing over there at all hours of the night? What's going on?"

The Mountie said, "We'll be looking into it, ma'am."

"Drugs — that's what I thought; maybe it's a dealer's house," Judith said, sighing. But when a thought struck her that she hadn't had before, she lifted her head and said, suddenly grim, "Human trafficking? The sex trade?" She could tell by the way he blinked that, at the very least, he already knew about the house. That she was right to have come here, but also that she should have come a lot sooner, and then that she hadn't because she was trying not to become a part of village life, trying not to see anything she didn't want to see.

Ridiculous, and look how invested she had become in the Richters. For a split second she wondered if she should ask him if he had been told about the gutted hares, thinking *That's harassment! Surely that is not just venomous, but also illegal! It's hate-mongering or something.* For the first time, it occurred to her that just possibly the perpetrator or perpetrators were not even local people. The notion frightened her; her face must have changed, because the Mountie now repeated, "We'll be looking into it." It took her a second to recognize he was referring to the goings-on at the house next door to hers.

She went on to tell him about the girl who said her name was Caitlin, and that she had claimed not to have come from her neighbour's house, although it seemed obvious she had. She described the girl's mother's car — not hard to find that one — and then told about Caitlin's bruised and swollen eye and the bleeding cut, the ripped jean jacket. She even told him about how upset she had been to see how the man with the big truck had manhandled the girl Judith had decided was his daughter.

"You're not the first to complain about . . . the noise," he said, and then snapped his mouth shut, as if he wasn't supposed to even tell her that much. He put both hands on the counter between them, leaned toward her, and spoke softly, spacing the words, as if he meant that she should read deeper information into what he was saying. "We're — looking — into — it, ma'am."

"Well, all right then," she said, deflated. She remembered the Richters and the hares. "Did anybody complain to you about the gutted hares somebody hung up in the trees of a Jewish family in Wisdom?"

"Well, I heard about it. I don't know for sure if anybody complained about it to us or not. Probably not. It was just a prank."

"It was a hate crime!" she said, more vehemently than she had intended. But he had retreated again, his face had gone blank, and she realized he was irritated and wouldn't give her any help now. She wondered if she should write the RCMP a letter about it. But she hadn't even seen them herself. And now, wasn't it more important to do something about the house next door? The Richters were gone, after all, or soon would be. Yes, she decided: the house next door.

After a minute, during which the young Mountie fiddled with some papers on the counter between them and she tried to think what to do, finally, without saying goodbye or thanking him, she went back outside.

But on the way back to her car, instead of abating, her uneasiness grew. Somebody had struck Caitlin, she felt sure, somebody had pulled on her jacket as Caitlin pulled away, hard enough that the sleeve had begun to tear away from the jacket. Somebody had tried to keep her there, and she had escaped. For a long moment, she stood on the concrete steps leading from the RCMP offices down to the sidewalk, and stared out over Dillon's main street.

A row of small houses in immaculate condition, dating back to probably the 1920s, sat smugly across the road. Shiny trucks, their boxes full of various kinds of agricultural equipment, most of which she could no longer identify, passed up and down the street as she stood watching. The stores began farther down, the usual small-town businesses: drugstore, the current version of the old five-and-dime, a hardware store, a convenience store. A block over, she knew, were the doctor's office, the library (open four days a week), a pioneer museum, a chiropractor's establishment, an optician. A door opened at the building next to where she stood, a young woman stepped back, holding it open while a daisy chain of chattering prekindergarteners emerged, followed by another young woman. A daycare, then. *Normal life*, she thought, and wondered how this peaceful scene could exist alongside wrongdoing, injustice, malice, and despair. And imagined, in a flash so quick she hardly noticed, pulling herself up into a world of flowers and fresh baking and loving families, her feet and legs struggling to kick and pull themselves up out of black, greasy muck, a layer so deep it seemed bottomless.

Knowing she could do nothing more about the house next door, and that she was now going to be cooking supper on Sunday for her family, she stopped at the larger grocery store, bought groceries, and drove back to Wisdom. Instead of taking her usual route down the back alley and parking in her shed, deciding to take a good look at the neighbour's house, she parked in front of her own house. She got out of her car, went slowly around to the passenger side, staring at the cream-coloured brick house while trying to pretend she wasn't, and opened the car's back door, where she had set her bags of groceries. All she saw, though, was the wide-open door to the attached garage, and that it was empty, not just of vehicles but of any other items. The front-room curtains were pulled back, the blinds up, and with the sun at the angle it was, she could see that the inside of the house was empty too.

She was going out for her second and last bags of groceries when she heard someone calling, "Judith. Oh Judy!" It was the aged woman across the street, Tillie. She was coming toward Judith, a heavy sweater thrown over her shoulders. "Yoo-hoo!"

"I knew your mom and dad," she said when she reached Judith. "Your mom went to school with my mother, Mercy Critchfield."

"Oh yes," Judith said, "I remember the name." For once she actually did remember it. "Were we in school together?"

"Heavens no," Tillie said. "I was long gone when you came on the scene. I would have come over sooner, but Abbie said you needed some time, and then you been gone a bit." Judith set down her load on the sidewalk. "Here, give me that," the woman said. "I'll help you get it into the house."

Each of them carried one of the remaining bags of groceries into Judith's house through the front door into the living room. Here Tillie stopped, giving a swift, intent look around but saying nothing. Judith resisted the urge to say that she knew the place still looked pretty awful. She remembered such women well enough from her childhood that she knew being deprecating about her failures as a housekeeper wouldn't earn her a pass, but instead would give Tillie the right to scold her. Better to let the woman think she was untidy and willing to live with ugly, worn-out things than give herself up to Tillie's criticism.

"Do you know the man next door?" Judith asked.

"Heavens no, not *that* man. Hardly ever even see him around. Something fishy there, I've always thought, and now we know."

"Know what?" Judith asked.

"He beat it out of here about five this morning. Saw him go, throwing things into his half-ton like a crazy fella, and then he was gone. What does that tell you?"

"I've never seen the police there," Judith said, faking dubiousness to get Tillie to give her more information.

"Oh, there's been some young undercover man around town for weeks."

"How do you know that? I mean, if he was undercover?"

"His family came from north of here. Once he said his name, Brad Fournier, everybody knew what was going on. Knew he was a Mountie. And people, parents that is, been complaining to them for a while. Bound to happen," tossing her head in the direction of the house, "that he, Harris I mean, had to go on the run."

"My gosh," Judith said. "I had no idea. What was going on over there anyway?" Immediately she knew she had made a mistake. She should have said, "But I thought he was a schoolteacher," or something clueless like that, requiring correction. Tillie clamped her mouth shut. *Which,* Judith thought, *might mean she doesn't know another thing but hopes Judith will think she does.* Hurriedly, she asked, "Can you stay for coffee?"

"Got to go. You'll hear about it soon enough." Tillie bustled out the door, not responding to Judith's thanks. *Why do the women here, like Tillie, always give me the feeling I've got some infectious disease?*

Indeed, when the next afternoon Sam, Sylvia, Abbie, and Rick arrived, the goings-on next door was the first subject of conversation.

"They're sending some men down from Regina to go over the place, I heard," Sam said. "Specialists, I guess, looking for evidence."

"But evidence of what?" Judith asked.

"Oh Judy, don't be so . . ." This from Abbie.

"How am I supposed to know if you don't tell me?"

Sylvia said, "Nobody knows *for sure*, and the kids have been told not to talk about what they know. I think — we all think it isn't just a pedophile thing. We suspect it is something bigger, linked maybe to some kind of, I don't know, mob activity, I guess. 'It is said,'" she made air quotes, "that a girl is missing."

"What kind of mob?" Judith asked, being deliberately obtuse. "Italian? Asian? Hispanic? Indigenous?" Nobody answered. "Who is missing? You did say 'missing?'" Judging by the fidgeting, they didn't like the subject one bit.

Abigail said, "Let's not talk about it. It's Sunday; it's a family gathering." She rearranged herself in her chair, putting her ankles together and arranging her feet neatly side by side, her hands folded on her lap. The smell of roasting beef wafted in from the kitchen.

"What girl?" Judith persisted. "Who? How old is she?"

Again, nobody replied, more shifting, and gazing anywhere but at Judith.

Later, in the kitchen, Sylvia would tell her the girl's name — Tonya Nichol — but it meant nothing to Judith, although she filed it away mentally, just in case.

"So," Sam said, comfortably, "you got us all together to tell us something, I think."

CHAPTER ELEVEN

TRUTH

"Yes. You know I went to Sage." Sam and Abigail nodded warily. Sylvia had a politely interested expression on her face, and Rick had turned his head to look out the window. "I went a second time. After my brain injury review in Medicine Hat. I went to Haley to look up the municipal records on our grandparents' farm, where Dad grew up." Nobody moved. "I forgot to say that I got *this*." Here she lifted the red-covered local history book from the shelf under the coffee table. "This is the history of Sage. It has a short piece in it about our family." Still nobody moved, surprising Judith a little; it occurred to her that probably they thought there wouldn't be anything new in it.

"It was signed by a man named August Jespersen. Mr. Jespersen is still alive." Abbie clasped her hands together; Sam cleared his throat; Rick was still looking out the window; although now Sylvia looked interested. "I went to see him, and he told me that when he was young, he and Dad used to tomcat around." She laughed, a choking sound; she could feel a deep burbling starting low in her gut, and stopped herself, recognizing that if she went on laughing, she would not be able to stop. Sam grinned briefly; Rick glanced at her and away again; Abbie's mouth tightened.

"They had another friend, a man named Anders Andreasen. He and Dad joined the American infantry together and went to war together. Anders is dead now, but he is the one who told his and our father's story to August Jespersen. Told it the night before he died, according to Mr. Jespersen."

"What story?" Sam asked. Now he was moving uncomfortably, as if the armchair had sprung lumps that were hurting his backside. Abbie appeared to be holding her breath, and a crease had appeared between her eyebrows.

"You know Dad had a terrible war," Judith said.

"I don't know that," Abbie said. "How do you know it? I mean, how does anybody know what anybody's war was like? Isn't all war terrible for the soldiers?"

"The 'grunts,'" Rick said, smiling vaguely, still looking out the window. The roast beef smell was getting stronger. She had to get the potatoes and other vegetables on.

"I only know what Jespersen told me," she admitted, recalling that she had yet to do anything about reading history; she vowed this time to really do so. "He said that Dad and Anders fought with the American infantry; that they started in Sicily, went on to fight in France right at the end of the war, and then went on into Germany." Again Abbie moved as if she were impatient with how long Judith was taking.

"He and Anders were with the unit that liberated Dachau on April 29, 1945. As if they hadn't already been through more than any human being should have to go through. Then they saw Dachau." Was anybody even listening to her? "You know about Dachau?" she asked, faltering, when the only reaction was from Sylvia, a soft intake of breath.

Rick said, "Who doesn't?"

Judith, intending to go on about the boxcars and whatever else she could say to them that wouldn't upset them too much, suddenly wondered if she should.

She repeated, "Dad . . . was in the unit that liberated Dachau."

At some point, Abbie had crossed her ankles. Now she uncrossed them, sat straighter, as if she were about to rise. Sam leaned forward.

"Is that roast about ready? I'm starving."

"Me too," Rick said.

"What?" Judith wanted to ask them why they didn't seem to care, or what was going on, but Abbie interrupted.

"We'll talk some more about this after supper," she declared, already rising, about to go to the kitchen. Nobody appeared ready to dispute her. Sylvia turned her head to stare first at her husband, and then at Abbie. Neither looked back.

"I can pour some more coffee if that's okay, Judith," she asked. "Or should we have wine now?"

"Let's wait with the wine," Abbie said, her gaze fixed in the direction of the kitchen, as if she were in her own house. "Unless somebody wants some now." To Judith, she said in a resigned way, "Obviously, we have to talk more. But after supper."

Annoyed, Judith said, "You sit here. I have to turn on the potatoes and the vegetables. We'll be able to eat in about twenty minutes." She hurried into the kitchen and turned on the burners under the pots of already-prepared vegetables, checked the roast, set out the plastic bag of rolls to be transferred to a bread dish when everything else was ready. Then she hurried back to the living room and sat back in her usual place. She asked her now subdued guests, "Did you know about Dachau?"

"Knew he was a soldier," was all Abbie, who was sitting again, would say. "Sam knew he came from dirt poor farmers. Of course he had to go out on his own. No mystery there." But her face was flushed, and her movements, as she shifted in her chair, were jerky.

Sam said, "Why do you go on with this? Can't you tell we don't want to talk about it?"

Sylvia said, "Sam," in a low voice.

"You know things I don't know," Judith said stubbornly. "Things I have a right to know. I can see that now. You've been acting funny ever since I first mentioned Dad's funeral, and the more I do to find out who he really was, the weirder you behave."

"Could we please talk about something else for now?" Abbie

pleaded. Before Judith could object, she went on, "After supper, Judy. Please?" There was an unexpectedly tremulous note in her voice that struck Judith into a momentarily defeated silence.

Sylvia cleared her throat. She said softly, her eyes on the floor, "I love having you back, Judith, even if we didn't know each other at all. I love that you're here, finally, filling up that empty space that it seems to me has always been there."

Touched, Judith said, "I'm so glad Sammie got you for a wife."

"Good heavens!" Abbie exclaimed. "Yes, yes, we're all glad you're back." But she sounded more irritated than joyful, and Rick made a hushing sound at her that served only to change her expression to injured.

After a moment, Sam said, apparently to Rick, "I hear Jake McCormack's finally building a new house."

"Took him long enough," Abbie said, in an abrupt shift. "Making Wendy and the kids live in that settler's shack all these years, while he's got the best machinery in the country!" This was so unlike Abbie, who in Judith's opinion tended toward mealy-mouthedness, that she realized that Abbie was rattled.

"Something's boiling over," Rick remarked. All three women leaped up and, Judith in the lead, rushed to the kitchen.

After she had rescued the potatoes and mopped the stovetop, Judith took the roast out of the oven and made the gravy while Sylvia began mashing the potatoes, and Abbie made the salad. They could hear the rumble of Rick and Sam's voices in the living room, although not what they were saying. Even anxious as she was, Judith couldn't help but wonder how Gilles — the absent, long-gone Gilles — would have fit in with them, imagining the stiffly polite conversation the three men would be having, Gilles knowing nothing about farming, Rick wary of French Canadians, and Sam needing to lead in every situation. *Well, there's always the weather*, she thought.

They finished preparing the food, transferred it to serving bowls, and put them on the table that Judith had set before they arrived.

When everything was on the table, she asked Rick to carve the roast — was Sam mildly disgruntled at this? Even Abigail had a little wine, but still, the air at the table was short of convivial, the conversation strained, tension vibrating among them.

They ate quickly, and Judith and Sylvia wasted no time clearing the dishes while Abbie cut and served the apple pie Judith had bought at the Co-op. Dinner seemed to Judith to be over in no time, but she had stopped caring by now and wanted only to say whatever had to be said and finally have this matter of their father's life and what it had done to him and especially to his children out in the open, acknowledged, and ended. She found herself wondering if she would then be able to go back to the city but, faintly shaken by this, quickly dismissed the thought.

The table cleared fully, the dishes scraped, rinsed, and piled in the kitchen waiting to be washed and put away, they all returned to the living room and sat down, the men, Sylvia, and Judith with fresh glasses of wine, only Abigail abstaining now.

"There are some things that need to be said," Abigail announced.

"Things you don't know," Sam said. "Things nobody knows." He and Abbie exchanged glances.

"Like what?" Judith asked. There was a high humming in her head.

Sylvia was silent, but lines had suddenly appeared in her face, as if she were older than Judith knew her to be. Whatever it was, she didn't know it either, but she was afraid. How long had she been waiting to hear it?

"Give me some of that wine," Abbie said, and, hiding her surprise, Judith got an empty glass, and Rick filled it and handed it to his wife. She went on, "I told you how bad Dad got after we were all gone from the farm and then Mom died. How frightening he was. Even dangerous."

"You remember Schlapp?" Sam asked, and Abbie shot him a glance Judith couldn't read. Judith nodded, although she didn't remember him other than the name and a vague recall of rumours about him.

"Do you remember that when his wife finally left him, she told everybody he had been a guard in a prison camp?"

"Concentration camp," Sylvia corrected Sam, her tone crisp, as if glad to know anything at all about whatever was going on here. "There was a difference. People didn't know whether to believe her or not, my father said. He was an unpleasant, strange man, kept to himself. Even did his business in other towns and never came into Wisdom, or hardly ever. People forgot for long periods, I think, that he was still out there all by himself. He kept these dogs too, Dad said. I'd forgotten that part. Vicious, apparently, so nobody went to his place if they could possibly help it. But," she shrugged, as if she had said too much, "I was just a little kid."

Judith interrupted, furious now. "What the hell is it you're not telling me?"

"Calm down," Abbie said, in her dismissive big-sister way, and Judith wanted to slap her. Abbie turned questioningly to Sam, who simply gazed back. After a second she turned back to Judith.

"Dad heard about Schlapp, probably in town, I guess."

"He got obsessed with the man," Sam said, rolling his empty wine glass in his palms, his mouth working.

"Around then," Abbie went on, "he got so worked up that a couple of times I had to get the Mounties to subdue him. I was getting afraid of him." Abbie sipped a little. "I was afraid for him too. I'd bring him food most days, and most days he didn't eat it; I'd take back the dishes to wash, and the food had hardly been touched. Wouldn't change his clothes either when I brought clean ones and wanted to take the dirty ones back to the farm to wash them. Like he was suspicious of me." Abbie's face was flushed, her long neck mottled; she turned her head away as if to escape telling the next part. Sam made a noise, but Abbie interrupted. "It was my fault. I knew he should be taken away for treatment or something, the Mounties kept saying I would have to, Sammie said so too, but I just wasn't quite ready. I'm to blame."

"You are not to blame," Sam said. "Not any more than I am. But he was our father, no matter what. I guess we . . ." His voice trailed away.

"Judy," Abbie said, as if she feared Judith had stopped listening, "one night he put on his army uniform — I didn't even know he still had a uniform — I think Mom must have kept it, because I can't see that Dad would have. Or he could have bought it somewhere too. Or picked it up at an Army and Navy store across the border."

"I think it was only his jacket," Sam said. "Took his .22."

"I hid the shotgun ages before, thank goodness." Abbie again. "But he got pretty fierce when he thought I was taking his .22, so I had to leave it. When the Mounties came those times, we searched every-where for it so they could take it, but we couldn't find it, so I had to promise them I'd get it from him, and I was trying to figure out how, but . . ."

"He went to the Schlapp place in that old fencing truck. Remember? We used to use it for picking rock too. Anyway, he drove to Schlapp's place in it and . . . he shot him."

"What?" Judith stood up, then sat down again, hard. Sylvia gasped, looking from Abbie to Sam. Sam went on.

"Shot him a couple of times. His chest, his head. Out in his yard, on his way to the corrals, right at the gate. Corral was full of cattle. Musta spooked them," he added meditatively. "It's a wonder they didn't break the corral gate or something."

Abbie took over. "The dogs were locked in a shed. Don't know who did that, Dad or Schlapp."

"Then he went home, back to our old farm where he still lived. A few hours later the Mounties found him sitting at the kitchen table, still in his uniform, rifle on the table, staring into space."

"But how . . ." Judith was dumbfounded. "How did anybody know? Or how did they know it was Dad? Are you sure?"

"Schlapp was shipping cattle that day," Sam said. "The trucker found him almost right away, I guess. That would be why the dogs were locked up," he added, as if this last had just occurred to him.

"And the neighbours had seen that old truck of his turning up the road to Schlapp's — nobody else on that road, no neighbours ever went there — and coming back again. Wondered what was up, they said. I guess everybody knew Dad had gone . . . funny. You know how it is. Knew it was Dad's truck."

Judith could think of nothing to say; she sat, mouth open, staring at them while chills ran down her back at the same time as sweat pooled between her breasts and dampened her palms.

Sylvia let out only a long, whispering *Ohhhh*.

"That happened when I was gone away to school. Nobody ever told me." She turned to Sam. "Not even when I got engaged to you!"

Abbie said, "The Mounties took him away, and from jail they took him for psychiatric testing."

Sam shrugged, morose now. "He was — what do you call it — umm, catatonic, sort of? For a long time he never left the locked ward at the psychiatric hospital. The one to the north," he added, before Judith could ask.

"I never knew any of that," Sylvia said to her husband. Sam didn't look at her. "It was all hushed up," she said. "Typical," she laughed angrily.

"Nobody missed Schlapp," Abbie said. "There was no problem there, once the oldest son came back and sold the place and went away again. People said the son told the police his old man had it coming to him. And don't forget, Dad had been respected — up until he lost it, anyway. Everybody knew he had . . . troubles. Nobody blamed him. But Schlapp . . ." She shook her head, mouth pursed, her cheeks flushed. "His . . . daughters," she muttered, staring at her lap.

"Yeah," Sam said. "The whole thing happened so fast it was over before anybody really noticed."

Abbie said, "Before you ask why we didn't tell you, it had been some years since we'd heard from you. We were worried about what it would do to you."

"Other than a Christmas card," Sam said, angry now. "We didn't know how stable you were." He spit *stable*, as though to punish her.

"You were wrong!" Judith cried, twisting her torso away from them, covering her face, then putting down her hands. Was this always what they wanted? That she should pay for what she had done? It took all her self-control not to wail.

Abbie said, more gently, "Judy, you didn't even come to Mom's funeral! After that, why would we think you cared about Dad?"

"I didn't hate him," she said quietly, aware she sounded like a child. She was shaking, gripping her hands together to get them to stop.

Sylvia said softly, "Take it easy, Judy." To Sam, she said, more briskly, "I think that's enough."

Ignoring his wife, Sam said, "This is the story. Dad never went to trial. There was a hearing, and a judge listened to the experts and found him unfit to stand trial. So he was committed to the psychiatric hospital. He was there for . . ."

"He is still there," Abbie interrupted, her voice for the first time loud.

"What?" Judith whispered. "Still there?"

"Yes," Abbie said. "Our father is still alive, still under sentencing to stay there until he gets cured or dies." Was there a hint of triumph in her tone? Later, Judith would think there had been.

"But he is . . . ninety now?" She fell against the back of the sofa. Her heart was pounding so hard in her ears, she was having trouble hearing. "What?" she said again.

"Eighty-nine," Sam said. "Look, Judy. He's kind of . . . I mean . . ." His anger at her seemed to have dissipated.

"He is lost in dementia," Abbie said. "He has been for, I don't know, a lot of years."

"We don't go to see him anymore. Haven't for a long time. He doesn't know us." Sam spread out his hands, palms up, helplessly, so unlike him. Judith remembered that their dad had loved Sam, that Sam had loved him.

"He's in a special facility for the few people from that era in his situation. We can tell you how to get there if you want to try to, but it's a waste of time. He won't know you. It will just break your heart," Abbie said. Tears had begun running silently down her cheeks. She lowered her head and put her hands over her face, took long gasps, a strangled sound, her shoulders shaking. Rick stirred, about to go to her, but Sylvia got to her first, crouched beside her, and put her arm around Abbie's shoulders, murmuring into her ear.

"You should have told me," Judith said, although she too was no longer angry. "I had a right to know."

Sam said, "When you ran away, you lost your rights." Sylvia had gone back to her chair, and now she put a hand on Sam's arm, as if to hold him back.

Judith shook her head no. "I can't lose my rights to my own parents."

Sylvia said, briskly, "It's no use quarrelling about that. We should get back to the point here."

"We?" Abbie said. Sylvia made an exasperated gesture and turned her head away from her sister-in-law.

"What's the point?" Sam asked his wife. "Can you tell me that?" But Judith was regaining her senses now; Abbie had stopped crying and was wiping her face with her palms.

"I wanted to know — a long time ago — I always needed to know why Dad was the way he was. Why he cried out in the night and frightened us all so badly. Why he hurt Mom. What was wrong with him. And I thought he was dead. How could you not tell me he wasn't dead?" This last a wail she couldn't suppress. She swallowed down the next one and the one after that, reminding herself she'd thought he had been dead for years, although she didn't really know when he'd died and couldn't think about it, she realized now, because she felt so guilty.

But wait a minute: Abigail had written her a note or two or three of them in which she had said things like, *with Dad being gone*, and *after*

Dad departed. Of course, Judith had thought she was being kind, trying to let her know gently that he had died. But she hadn't ever said there was a funeral. She was sure of that. Although the fact that she could no longer be sure of anything hit her now, and she was terrified and would have gotten up and run away, but Sylvia was speaking, quietly, so gently that the sound of her voice calmed Judith.

"But it was so simple, if only people had known: his post-traumatic stress disorder from his war service. Nobody had a name for it. Maybe 'shell-shocked,' I don't know. Lack of moral fibre or something like that, they called it in the First World War." Sylvia was intervening as if to lower the tension, or maybe she was still stuck on the fact of Henry Clemensen being alive and incarcerated. The others ignored her, as if she hadn't spoken.

"He killed a man," Judith said. "Our own father, and instead of jail, he went to a hospital for the insane," as if these facts were in dispute.

"Where he got worse instead of better," Sam said.

"Those new drugs kept him quiet though," Abbie interjected. "No more rages or screaming craziness, no more violence — but there was never a cure." She looked away. "If he did get better, they would just have sent him to jail."

"Did you know about Dachau, that he had been there?" Judith asked again. Abbie and Sam shook their heads no.

"Only that he was a returned soldier," Abbie said.

"The war has been over for what? Seventy years or so?" Sam said. Again, that gesture of incomprehension, of helplessness. "He should have gotten better. Shouldn't he?" He looked at his two sisters as if they would know the answer.

They sat in silence for a long time, Judith thinking she would go see him immediately. She would see her father. Ask him to forgive her. No, she would...

She got up and went into the kitchen, where she ran hot water into the sink and began to wash the dishes. She could hear the voices of the others, low, in the living room, but no one came out to help her. She bent over the sink, her hands immersed in the soapy water, stifling the noise that was trying to come up from deep in her gut.

She heard the front door open and then shut. Then someone was standing in the doorway into the kitchen. Sylvia.

"Is everyone gone?"

"Yes." She seemed awkward to Judith, her usual grace vanished. "I came in my own car. Sam came separately. I'll drive myself home soon." Judith began to scrub the roasting pan. "I can stay all night if you would rather not be alone."

"I'm okay. You don't need to stay with me." She scrubbed harder. Flecks of burned meat were stuck hard to the bottom of the roasting pan. She would need a sharp knife to get them off.

"You've had a terrible shock."

"I have been betrayed," she said, scrubbing harder.

"They honestly thought they were doing the best thing for everybody." Judith kept scrubbing, her fingertips beginning to sting from their pressure against the metal scraping pad and it against the pan. "I didn't know either, Judy. I know I'm not in the same situation as you are, but still ..."

"I suppose I'll get over it in time."

"Yes, you will," Sylvia said.

"I suppose you're right about that. I suppose *they* feel betrayed by me." She could hear Sylvia changing her position, although not moving from the doorway.

"It could be that they were punishing you for disappearing in the first place. For finding it so easy to just come back."

Judith wanted to scream at Sylvia about all the wrongs she had suffered at their hands, of the cruelty of such an act, a blow against her that she did not deserve. But she held on against it, scrubbing harder. Her fingertips were stinging.

"I did what I thought I had to do. I was a child." That she had not been a child for the last fifty years wasn't something she would say.

"I suppose you'll go see your father now."

"I have to get over the shock first. I have to know how I feel." It occurred to her that through all of this her head had not ached at all, that what she felt now was exhaustion. "I think I would rather be alone, Sylvia," she said. "I appreciate your kindness, I really do, but I think I will take a tranquillizer and go to bed."

Sylvia waited a moment, then said, "Yes, of course, all right."

When she was gone, Judith abandoned the roasting pan in the now cold dishwater, rinsed the blood off her fingers, and holding a tissue around them, changed into her nightclothes. But bed was no longer inviting, despite her fatigue, and she sat in the armchair that Sam favoured, in her living room, thinking she would read for a while and then go to bed. But she found herself reading the same paragraph over and over again and still not taking it in, so that after a few minutes, she put the book aside and sat staring into space.

At ten o'clock, her cellphone rang. Thinking it was probably Abbie, she wasn't going to answer it, until it occurred to her that if she didn't, Abbie might make Rick drive back into town to make sure she was all right.

"Hello, *ma chère amie*." It was Gilles.

"I'm so glad to hear from you." Indeed, at the sound of his voice, relief began to sweep through her, and she was afraid she might start crying. Then, remembering his trouble, she asked, "How are you? How is everything?" She could tell by the quality of stillness behind his voice and the softness of his breathing that he was in his bedroom, and alone.

"We bury Camille tomorrow," he said. "I am better now, thanks. I'm just back from prayers. Everyone has gone to bed so that we can be strong for tomorrow. You did say to call."

"I have had my own travails," she told him. As easily as if she were talking about the weather, words spilled out of her. "It seems my father is still alive and is locked away in a psychiatric hospital. They say he has severe dementia."

"How could you not know he was still alive?" he said wonderingly, after a startled pause.

"I think . . ." she hesitated. "No, I think that is a story for another time." But something flashed through her mind then that she couldn't quite grasp: Those notes from Abbie? What else would she think but that he was dead. "Are you getting any sleep?"

"I have a pill to take for tonight only. The doctor was very firm about that. You must tell me about this, Judith, when you are ready."

"I will," she said, then, "Good for the doctor." They were speaking to each other as if they were still lovers. "I am so sorry about Camille. I know how much you loved her."

"I loved you too," he said. "I don't think I knew that. But Camille, she . . . never went away, not out of my head or my heart. Sometimes it happens that way. Even when we couldn't get along."

"I think as long as there was Camille, there was no real hope for us," she said, but her tone was gentle, wishing only to acknowledge the truth behind the way things had gone with them. "Are you all right with that?" She had begun to wonder if it was not Camille he loved but the home she represented: the village, the parents and the grandparents, the very grass and trees, and ponds and rivers of their childhood, as she had never stopped missing the sky and the fields of hers.

"She said to me before she died that I would be all right. But I can't talk about that." A deep breath. "I just wanted to talk to you."

"I am glad you did." It seemed there was nothing else to say, but they stayed on the line for a moment longer, listening to each other's breathing before Gilles said, "I suppose we should both get some sleep now."

"Good night."

"Good night."

She went to bed then, and in her inexplicable but profound exhaustion, fell like a stone into the deepest of sleeps.

CHAPTER TWELVE

SMALL THINGS

In her dream, she was walking with her mother by the stream in the park where she had stood and talked with Saul Richter. But the park had become their own farm, the pasture west of the house where they liked to go in the evening after the work was done, before dark came down. They walked side by side, her mother still young, slender to the point of thinness, and with a faint sprinkling of freckles across the fine, pale skin of her face and on her neck and arms where the sleeves of her housedress ended. Judith longed for her mother to grasp her hand and hold it as they walked, but her mother never did, and did not now. Only when they were toddlers and needed to be led and held upright so they wouldn't trip over roots or stones or get their legs tangled in the tall grass.

Tiny white flowers like little stars bloomed delicately at the tips of the grasses; the only sound was their whispering and rustling. The light was fading now, the sky to the west turning pink and orange, and as the sun disappeared, a rich, deep blue, the stars gleaming pinpricks in its fabric. Her mother walked on, the sound of her skirt moving through the grass indistinguishable from that of the grass moving in the light breeze, Judith trying to keep up, tripping, righting herself, rushing on, the grass getting taller and thicker, holding her back.

But her mother kept walking toward the hills behind which all the light had slid, Judith running behind her, calling, but her mother didn't turn back, not even to wave goodbye, until she melded into the hill's consuming darkness.

On waking, the dream still fresh in her mind, Judith thought, *I hated my mother too*, and was astonished and ashamed. Eventually she thought that, while this was true, it was truer that she had loved her mother with every particle of her being, and had longed for her love every second of her life.

The next day, when Abbie phoned, Judith didn't answer. Sam didn't call, but that didn't surprise her. She knew, too, that Sylvia would not berate Sam or Abbie for what they had kept from Judith and herself, an act that she knew Judith felt was a crime against her. She did not know if Sylvia thought it was a crime against Judith or not. Trying to weigh the moral questions was too hard. She was beginning to think that there was no such thing as moral equivalency, that each act stood by itself. But what sense did that make? There had to be a standard, didn't there?

She kept telling herself that she must go at once to see her father, but made no move to pack or fill her car with gas, or even try to ask precisely how to find him. She spent the morning housecleaning too vigorously, as if her life depended on removing every speck of dirt, but when each room shone, still not going. She went to the park, thinking fresh air would calm her, because she wasn't calm, although she had been telling herself she was, but was instead in a state of high agitation that she couldn't control. *I have to go see Dad*, she repeated to herself. *I have to go right away; what if he dies before I get there?* But still she didn't go, and could not say why she didn't. She kept imagining the long, intimate conversation they would have, how they would declare their love for each other, how they would forgive each other. And then she laughed at herself, and thought that she was the one who had lost her mind. *Why, oh why did Abbie let me think he was dead?*

Early on the second morning, she went back to the park, and walking alone through the cool shadows among the trees, she asked herself again, *Why don't I go?* and answered, *Fear*—that he wouldn't know her, that he would accuse or berate her or turn away from her. *All I want is to see him again. I want to ask his forgiveness*, she thought, then wondered if what she really wanted was for him to ask her for forgiveness.

As she let herself into her house, the phone was ringing.

"Two things," Catherine announced. "First, the mediator issued his judgement, and your settlement has arrived. It is ten thousand dollars. Second, Ian and I are divorcing. I've moved out of the condo, left it to him—he was the one who wanted to live like that. Well, maybe I did a little bit. But I'd rather start over again, and he wants to keep going, not lose his foothold on . . . whatever it is he thinks he has a foothold on."

"Oh my dear, I'm so sorry."

"I'll be fine, Mom," she said brusquely. "I am fine."

"Where are you staying then? With a girlfriend?"

"I've bought a small place closer to my office. Pretty close to where your condo used to be, in fact. Do you want me to mail you the cheque?"

"I'm . . . stunned," Judith said. "I just spent the last couple of days . . ." But this was no way to tell her, especially not when Catherine was in crisis herself. It occurred to her to wonder how Catherine had made the move so quickly and realized that she had to have already found the new place when Judith had last visited her. "No, I'll come and get the cheque. I want to see how you're doing. I'm not going to take no for an answer, so give me the address and phone number. I'm coming right now." She could go see her father after Calgary; first things first.

"Gee, Mom," Catherine said in a thin, high voice. "You don't need to. I'm okay."

"I know you're strong, but I am your mother, and this is not some-thing to get through all by yourself. I'll be there by evening." It was only seven in the morning. Easy-peasy, and she felt pleased with her-self until she remembered she didn't know where exactly her father was or even the name of the place. Would Abbie be up? Of course she would be up. But she made herself a pot of coffee first and put bread into the toaster, like an idiot burning her fingers, and had to stop, force herself to take some deep breaths, force herself to think as if she were planning a day at work instead of once more merely stumbling from calamity to catastrophe and back again.

She was remembering Catherine and Ian's wedding, held in a private room at one of the city's best restaurants, a judge presiding, the guests all successful, ambitious young professionals except for the parents, who didn't quite rise to the same level, standing around looking badly dressed and ill at ease. The way that all emotion was fashionably muted at Catherine's wasn't a bit better than the fake joy at Lucinda's first one, all those skinny, sickly-looking girls with smudged eye make-up, chipped purple nail polish, and wreaths of wilting flowers on their heads that Lucinda must have made them wear. She could barely remember Alice and Dwight's wedding. Small and cheap, no alcohol, and boring mainstream music. Hadn't it been religious music? Oh yes, she sighed. Exhorting everybody to love Jesus and then everything would be fine. She laughed, though, when she remembered there was still Jessica: there might after all be a less-than-perfect, glitch-ridden, authentically happy wedding celebration. Then she sobered, panic rushing through her: Dad! She had to get there fast! The panic draining away as quickly as it had come. She had waited fifty years; she could wait a couple more days.

No wonder she couldn't remember his funeral. Abbie had implied he was dead, so naturally she'd thought they had had the funeral. She must have started thinking he was dead about the time when Catherine was still a pre-schooler, Victor had begun his steady raging, making them all walk on tiptoe all the time, and then, at the same time she had to go to court over that sixteen-year-old, Teresa-something, whose dad was that political bigwig — they were trying to rescue her from his sexual assaults, and he was fighting back with all the money in the world, claiming she was a liar and mentally ill, just trying to

save his own reputation and powerful enough to get away with it —
too many people afraid of him — and Judith couldn't stop thinking
about the injustice, and about that poor little daughter of his. She was
just not rational; she was just in a mental fog — no, not a fog, it was
a typhoon, and she was living in the middle of it. That her father was
dead, that he had had a funeral or been cremated without a ceremony
— she couldn't deal with that — that she would never see him again
and it was her own fault. It was better not to think about it. No wonder
she had only the vaguest notion of when this had all happened. She
was a long way from ready to dig into that research.

But they knew she thought he was dead; hadn't they just made a
big production of announcing to her that he wasn't? They had let her
think he was — no, Sam had been surprised when he saw that she
thought he was dead. He must have talked to Abbie about it; maybe he
had it out with her. All these years, he must have thought Judith was
just a terrible daughter, a bad person, one who didn't even care about
her own father. And yet he didn't tell her, he just left it alone until
Sunday afternoon when they had their family gathering. He knew she
thought their father was dead, and he must have half known or maybe
fully known why she thought that. Abbie's little trick.

Abbie had deliberately let her think that. And then acted angry
when Judith said she'd been back for the funeral when she knew she
couldn't have been because there was no funeral. Was Abbie the crazy one here and not her, Judith? Or was she angry because Judith had
come back and she knew she would find out that she hadn't been told
the truth? Not at all, not once — all these years, her sister had kept
the truth from Judith. Abbie wanted him forgotten; she wanted the
scandal forgotten; she wanted her dignity and her respect in the community. Mrs. Pillar-of-the-Community. She must have dropped hints
now and then, at just the right moment and place, that both her parents were dead, or made some oblique comments that led people to
think Henry Clemensen was long dead too, as their mother Eunice

was. If people around town had expressed sympathy to Sam, he would have thought they were talking about the murder and incarceration. Nobody would say "dead" to him. They would say, "Sorry about your dad." And Sam would grunt and mutter and change the subject. That's how Abbie got away with it.

But then Judith thought, *But I never asked about him, not once. I could have written to Abbie or Sam; I could have tried writing to Dad, and I didn't.* Her face was hot with shame; how much easier to lay all the blame at her sister's door.

But on the phone now with Abbie, Judith simply said, "I'm going to see Dad. I need you to tell me where he is."

Abbie said only, "I'm leaving soon for town to buy groceries. I'll bring you an address and a map."

When an hour later she arrived, despite everything, Judith had the coffee ready and the cups and cream and sugar set out on the kitchen table. When Abbie was seated, the map on the table in front of her, she said, "You deliberately let me believe that Dad was dead."

Instead of going still and looking guilty, as Judith had expected, Abbie flared up.

"I did not!" Her eyes were burning, and she leaned toward Judith so that she half wondered if she should move back, out of range.

"Of course you did," Judith said. How many times had she dealt with lying parents, lying kids? You don't back down, and you do not show fear. Although sometimes she had had to bring a police officer with her. "If you hadn't done that, I might have made my peace with him. But you were too busy punishing me!"

Abbie's face had gone white. She got clumsily to her feet, shaking so hard that she held onto the table edge with both hands so as not to fall.

"Don't be silly!" she said. "Everything is about you." She fell back into her chair.

"Oh stop it, Abbie," Judith said. "You know I'm right. It was your own little project. Get Judy, make her pay for her crimes."

"It's not true," Abbie said. "It isn't true."

"Drink your coffee," she said, the way Sam, when they'd been reunited just a few weeks earlier, had made her drink her hot coffee, and she had burned her mouth. "Tell me what I want to know." She swallowed the invectives piling up in her mouth. She didn't know where this might lead and preferred to wait — weeks, months, years if she had to, as Abbie, purposely, had let her wait for thirty years.

It took Abbie a minute of moving her mouth before she began to speak in a low voice, keeping her eyes fixed on the table, her hands still visibly quivering.

"At first he was in that big psychiatric hospital, the one for the northern half of the province. But then there was this move to 'normalize' as many long-term patients as possible, get them out of the big hospitals. No more locking them up and throwing away the key. They sent some to live either with their families, or in their own homes, or halfway houses, or whatever. But Dad couldn't be sent home or anywhere else. He . . . he had committed a crime. But by then, with the drugs, he was calm and easy to manage, and when the government opened this new little 'farm' for people like Dad who would never be able to go home but who didn't respond to — I don't know — psychiatric therapy, I guess, they had to make a place for them, until one by one they all died off." She lifted her head, looked past Judith, studying the door, as if she had forgotten she was talking to anyone.

"The anti-psychotic drugs — well, I don't know. I guess opinions are mixed about what they do to people, but I can tell you that Dad got quieter and was able to move out of a locked ward, finally, and — I don't know, he just seemed better to me. Not that I saw that much of him. Visited maybe twice a year, then only once a year. His mind was gone; he didn't know us; it was too upsetting to see him, harder to make myself drive all that way. Sammie couldn't stand it at all. He hardly ever went, and I guess he never did tell Sylvia. There was that Schlapp thing too, after all."

Schlapp thing? What a way to refer to the fact that their father had murdered a man. She would have said something, but of course this was Abbie's inability to admit their own father had killed a man in cold blood. Even if the victim was a bad man, possibly an evil one.

· It occurred to her then that the authorities would have looked into both men to find out how true their stories were. Schlapp's wife must have given the true details of his "career" in the concentration camps to the police, and they would have checked, somehow, and found she was telling the truth: Schlapp, a killer, sneaking into the country by lying about who he was. That would be partly why their father was allowed the asylum instead of some terrible prison hospital: because he was a soldier who had gone mad from what he had been through. Certainly, nobody but the justice system was asking for justice for Schlapp. So her dad was found unfit to stand trial and sent to the psychiatric hospital's locked ward.

She wondered what had happened to Schlapp's body. Had he been buried in Wisdom's cemetery? Cremated maybe? His ashes thrown to the winds? She hoped not the latter, thinking of the numbers on Richter's arm; better to seal Schlapp's ashes in concrete and sink them to the bottom of the sea.

"What happened to Schlapp?"

"He was *dead*," Abbie said.

"But somebody must have taken his body."

"I would be the last to know," Abbie said angrily, as if Schlapp had killed their father and not the other way around. "What does it matter?"

Judith said, "I'm not sure it does. But it might."

"I suppose you could ask his wife, but she hated him. And, of course, she's dead now too."

"Was Dad one of the ones they moved somewhere else?"

"Yes. The government put some of them on a farm out in the countryside not far from a small, shallow lake. Lots of grass and trees and birds. They turned them into farmers." Judith noticed she didn't say "prisoners" instead of "farmers." "Well actually, I guess a lot of them had been farmers before they got sick. But some couldn't be trusted on the machinery, so they looked after the vegetable garden — it's enormous, the institution has a small business selling whatever produce they don't need — or else they took care of flower beds and trimmed bushes, maybe cut the lawns with manual lawnmowers, painted walls, and so on."

"And Dad?"

"He weeded and watered, picked the peas, pulled the carrots, that kind of thing. Never used the machinery. He was just too dulled by the drugs."

"Was he — would you say he was maybe happy? I mean, is he?"

Abbie shrugged. "He calmed down, and that was an improvement over his confusion and huge swings in his emotions. If there is any big change or he runs out of clothes or gets sick — I mean, more than just a cold or flu — or something, they phone me or Sammie."

It was impossible to imagine what such a life could be like for the one who suffered it. Wait, she reminded herself. He could have been executed, maybe would have been if he had killed Schlapp right after the war was over instead of after the death penalty was gone from Canadian law. But surely it would have been clear he was a madman, and she wondered about the dementia Abbie was talking about. Was there some way to tell which was which?

A flush was creeping up Abbie's neck and into her cheeks, and for the first time she met Judith's eyes. "Judith, if you're going to see him, I mean — I wouldn't recommend it. He won't know you; you won't be able to understand a word he says; he might not be able to speak at all." Her tone grew more agitated. "You're best not to go," she said, turning her head away again. "He's not Dad anymore."

"I'm leaving right away to see Catherine — about the mediation settlement." She chose not to say anything about the divorce. "Then I'm going to see Dad. No matter what you say."

How old Abbie looked now; it seemed rising from her chair was hard for her. Arthritis, or a guilty conscience. *How does she reconcile what she did — although she pretends she didn't do it — with that churchgoing, righteous, good person she believes she is?* At the door, Abbie stopped, looked over her shoulder partially as if to look at Judith, then didn't, and without speaking, opened the door and went out, closing it quietly behind her.

Catherine was waiting for her when Judith arrived, a lasagna she said she'd bought in a deli reheating in the oven. At first Judith couldn't tell if she looked better or worse than when she was waiting around their flashy condo for Ian to come home, finally gave up her scrutiny, and asked. "And don't say you're fine," she added, which made Catherine laugh.

"Well, I'm sorry, but I sort of am fine," Cathy said. "But also at the same time, I admit it, maybe not so fine too."

They ate at the table in the tiny kitchen, and afterwards took their wine glasses into the somewhat larger living room, where they sat one at each end of the new red sofa and put up their feet on the scarred, once-handsome wooden chest Catherine was using for a coffee table. A couple of paintings leaned against a wall, and behind the single chair, Judith could see the corner of an open cardboard box with something that looked like a duvet spilling out of it. The floor lamp beside her provided the only light in the room except for that from the glass balcony doors. A lamp sat on the floor, its cord curled around its base.

"Is this condo temporary? And what about the divorce? Have you started it yet? Really, sweetheart, are you all right?"

Catherine sighed, got up, and pulled the blinds that covered the balcony doors, and at once the room became cozy.

"This is as permanent as anything is these days. It's handy to downtown, the building isn't jam-packed with people, and I can go to a movie or a concert without even taking out my car." She sat again on the opposite end of the couch and curled her legs under her. "As for the divorce, you know Ian: He will go for as much as he can get, and I don't feel like fighting him. He could never leave well enough alone. He always has to win."

"You're handling your own divorce?"

"I've hired a lawyer from my office. An older man. He won't let Ian walk all over him — that boys' club stuff, you know. I could tell he didn't like Ian when they met at Christmas parties."

"Don't be too darn accommodating," Judith said. "He should pay for what he has done to you," by which she meant not only her daughter's broken heart, but the way she, although already so demanding of herself, in trying to meet Ian's determination that only the best would do, had turned herself into somebody it was often hard to like, and was far from the child Judith felt she had raised, far from the real Cathy. Cathy was holding her wine glass in both hands and looking down into it, wearing an expression so childlike in its hurt that Judith moved to her, put her arms around her, and held her tightly. "I'm so sorry," she whispered. "It will be all right, it will be fine," at which tough, smart, impatiently ambitious Cathy began to sob into her mother's shoulder, so hard that her ribs shuddered.

"First — divorce — in — the — family — that's me," she said gasping, pulling back, meaning among her and her sisters. Judith thought of Lucinda, but said nothing. Catherine blew her nose, wiped her eyes, and drew in a long breath, holding it, expelling it slowly. "As everybody says, thank god there are no children." She laughed, and started to cry again, although less hard this time.

"There's still time for children," Judith assured her. "You're just past thirty." Again, Catherine stopped crying, and Judith said, "Once you're through this bad part, I want you to start having a little fun. Go to Australia or Iceland or Spain and stay a month if it makes you happy. You've been working too hard, ever since high school."

"I know," Cathy said. "I don't know why, I mean, I just . . . thought

I had to. *You were trying to shake off my weakness; you were trying to show Victor your worth*, Judith thought, but knew better than to say either out loud.

"Yeah," she said. "And I thought I had to run away from home at fifteen. When you're a kid, you don't know why you do anything. You think you do, but you don't."

"Anyway, I'm not getting married again," Catherine said, and Judith had to bite her tongue to keep from saying, *Sure you are. I bet in eighteen months you'll be married again.*

At breakfast the following morning, Catherine handed Judith the cheque from the mediation process, asking, "What are you going to do with it?"

"I guess I'm going to Israel for the birth of Lucinda's baby. That was the only reason I wanted the money. Not that I really want to go to Israel, but . . ." She shrugged. "Why don't you come with me?"

"I think I'd rather go to Maui, thanks. I've been talking about it with a girlfriend from work. We're even thinking about renting a condo and staying for a whole month." She put their dishes in the sink and went to the closet. "I probably can't get away that long right now, with the divorce. I have to be here to keep a close eye on Ian, I think. But for two weeks anyway."

She was stepping into her high heels at the door, slipping on her jacket, when Judith realized she hadn't told her about her grandfather. As Catherine took one last glance in the gilt-framed mirror by the door, Judith recognized with a jolt that it had come from her own condo and had been Cathy's father's choice. Catherine was reaching for her briefcase.

"See you at dinner," and she was gone, closing the door softly behind her.

Judith thought of skipping the research she had in mind and going straight to see her father. What did all that war stuff matter now? But something stubborn inside took hold of her, as if a second person were lodged in her gut, and she readied herself and left the condo.

On the CTrain up to the university, she was surrounded by students hanging on with one hand and gazing into their phones, or pecking away at them, or talking into them, or with ear buds stuck in their ears, nodding to music only they could hear. But they were pleasant, polite kids, and one of them had given Judith her seat; when they were all getting off at the university stop, they made way for her as if she were their mother. She thought, then, walking down the platform in their midst, that maybe the world wasn't going to hell in that handbasket after all. She thought of Abbie, too, and knew that she would never admit what she had done. But she knew that she had done it and, further, that it was no small thing.

A young library assistant went into the stacks to find the only two books available on the subject of Dachau, or at least partly on it, and brought them back to her. She found a comfortable chair, sat down, and began paging through first one book and then the other. One of them, stuck on what were apparently the officially accepted facts about liberation day at Dachau — April 29, 1945, the date now carved permanently into her brain — she put aside after a half hour. So, she thought, Jespersen, or Andreasen, was telling the truth, both about the actions of the young soldiers who'd arrived there, and the atrocities they had found. And what happened that day at Dachau with the young soldiers shouldn't have happened, no question about that. And it seemed that, ever since, the military had done its best to avoid mentioning anything about it beyond numbers of prisoners rescued and so on, so that the unit's name wouldn't be blackened and no young soldiers who had fought so bravely would wind up in military prison. She had now seen the first of the photos of the ecstatic prisoners behind the electrified fence, and she was surprised that many wore caps and that their striped prison costumes were not always ragged and filthy. It took some reading before she understood that these were not the Jewish prisoners, but the standard prisoners of war who occupied most of the large camp. But juxtaposed to these photos were photos of piles of naked corpses.

The second book showed more photos of corpses thrown into high, tangled heaps, as if human bodies were refuse like anything else — old tires, kitchen garbage, rotten buildings — bulldozed into piles in order to burn them. She read on: Nearly thirty-two thousand prisoners in Dachau on Liberation Day, and only about three thousand of them Jews. Those grinning, shouting prisoners hanging on to the fence in their striped prisoners' garb and caps included Léon Blum, who already had been the prime minister of France and immediately after the war would become its president — he was a Jew! Was he too famous or important to kill? — and a number of other famous people. There were also ordinary German criminals who'd been moved there from regular jails, and Germans who had refused to become Nazis, or were caught defying them or, guilty of nothing, had been denounced by neighbours who hated them or who merely wanted to be on the right side of the Nazis. There were also gypsies, homosexuals, many communists who had had the pleasure of being the first prisoners in the camp back in 1933 when Heinrich Himmler had established it, newspapermen who hadn't been supportive enough of the Third Reich, others who were designated "enemies of the Reich," people there by accident or by mistake, having been caught up in sweeps of others; there were even about one thousand Catholic priests. Dachau, it turned out, wasn't meant to be an extermination camp —*Then why all the bodies?* Judith asked the author indignantly — it was a "sorting point," the writer claimed. But as the war went on, it most assuredly did become a killing camp for Jews and others, definitely, although not for all the thousands of prisoners housed separately from the Jews.

But things had apparently gotten awfully messed up as the Allies approached, fighting their way through France and into Germany where resistance had finally softened, then south toward Munich. It would seem that the German army had gone frantic, the main objective in the few days before the Americans arrived having been to get rid of the evidence, all those piles of bodies, as well as to dig up the mass burial sites and burn the bodies, to empty the concentration camps of Jews and burn the crematories and the evidences of the agonies the Jews, and for the most part the Jews alone, had suffered in the camps. At Dachau, she read, there was even a hospital building that housed, in cleanliness and with good care, wounded, recuperating German soldiers, not SS men, but they were turned out from their beds on that day, every one of them, regardless of their condition, by the Americans. Not a tear shed for them — they who had not shed a tear for the most abject prisoners of all or for the murdered.

Information was coming at her too fast, it was piling up, Dachau was at last becoming real.

There was also a training camp for German soldiers where, she learned, among other notorious Nazis, Adolf Eichmann had trained to begin his careful death-dealing work, which would end in his execution by hanging in Israel in 1962 for war crimes. Upwards of one hundred prisoners were dying per day when the Allies arrived, a number that had escalated rapidly as the Nazis ran out of food for their prisoners, medical care, and coal to burn the bodies, not only to get rid of the evidence, but also to stop epidemics of cholera and typhus.

So, in advance of the arrival of the Allies, the Nazis had marched off hundreds of prisoners to other camps to the east, many, many dying along the way; they had taken away loads of the bodies and burned them wherever they were dumped. They had marched their own guilty guards and commanders out of there so as not to be caught when the Allies arrived.

At last she came to the part that Jespersen had told her about, the part that was unclear to her, and that, now that she thought of it, she hadn't fully believed, surely it couldn't be true — the boxcars full of bodies. But Jespersen's story was true: having run out of coal, in order to hide their unspeakable crimes, the Nazis had sent bodies by train to Dachau. Her father would have come upon that: the long line of boxcars full of corpses. She would read in other books, later that day, that there "weren't more than five hundred" bodies, or some other lesser number, as if to mitigate guilt, or even to dampen down a story that was too horrible to believe, or that the old soldiers telling the story hadn't themselves seen. Or had, and couldn't believe their eyes. It seemed to her, looking at the photos of bodies spilling from the cars, that no one could ever know the precise number and yet there it was, the precise, official number: 2,310.

On the way to the cafeteria in the student building, she had to sprint for a shadowed spot between two buildings so as not to be seen vomiting. She wanted to think something profound about what she had seen and read, but couldn't. The dirt was still the dirt, the rough block of stone against which she had placed her palms to support herself was still familiar stone, as were the cool shadows in which she hid. Even her vomitus smelled no different than the vomitus from her concussion. Freed of her nausea now, her head began thumping painfully. She stood still for a moment, taking deep breaths which reduced the thumping to a more distant, steadier pain. Students, between classes, had begun to walk by in groups, chatting brightly, not many feet from where she stood.

She found the cafeteria, first went into the bathroom, rinsed her mouth and her face, drank a few mouthfuls of water from a fountain she found in a corner, and, still feeling shaky, sat down with a cup of coffee. In the chatter and colour in the cafeteria, the miasma of death that had engulfed her was diminishing. Thousands if not millions of others had struggled over this knowledge just as she was, tomes had been written about it by sufferers, survivors, and cool historians alike, and she wondered if any of them had understood how such a thing could happen. That it had happened over seventy years ago now shamed her, because for all her adulthood she had done her best to avoid knowing more than the bare outlines of it, she had not wanted to know more, had thought she wouldn't be able to bear knowing what other people seemed to be able to handle, and now found that in a not-so-distant way, all along it had been her story too. Not as a Jew, a survivor, or a relative of those murdered there, perhaps found in those very boxcars, but that the mere sight of the Nazi crimes had destroyed her father, and thus damaged her family and, down to the second generation, herself. Possibly even the third, thinking of Lucinda. Although in comparison, their suffering was nothing.

Thinking of the hares in the Richters' trees that had driven them out of Wisdom to the safety to be found in numbers in a city, she was ashamed that when she heard about it from Saul Richter himself, she had done nothing other than commiserate, when she should have raised hell about it, should have kept going no matter what until the perpetrator was caught and punished. It was a hate crime, after all. It was criminal; it was disgusting. And, she thought, this isn't over yet, and then she thought of her haunted father killing 'Old Schlapp' as the people of the village referred to him when they thought of him at all, which was almost never, not even when his wife left him and told people who he really was. Nobody investigated him until he turned up dead, when he should have been in prison all along.

After a while she got up, leaving her barely touched coffee, and went outside, where she called a taxi and asked to be taken to the Military Museums, a place where in all her years in Calgary she had never been, believing that the war was mere history, best forgotten.

At the library in the Military Museums, she began to read more specifically about the travails of the American 157th Infantry Regiment's 45th Infantry Division and the Third Battalion, called Thunderbird and commanded by Felix Sparks, at first a captain and by the time they reached France, a lieutenant colonel. This was the infantry unit to which her father and Anders Andreasen had belonged, and the unit that arrived at Dachau first. Once the logistics — *Just the facts, ma'am*, she thought — were clear in her head, she called another taxi to take her back to Catherine's condo, where she set up her laptop on the coffee table, and, in hopes of finding some personal reminiscences about that day from the soldiers who had been there, and who were not anti-Semites, kept researching, hoping that she might even come across her father's name.

She began calling up the surprisingly large amount of material online. These were mostly "I was there" accounts, and although they differed in details from what she had already read — no Germans were killed, fifty were killed, three hundred were killed — they agreed that a large number of German soldiers found in and around the camp, whether guards or serving other purposes, had been lined up by the American soldiers along the brick wall of the coal yard shed. Their commanding officer had set up a machine gun manned by a soldier to guard them, then went off to reconnoitre the nearby area.

But the soldier — nobody seemed to know why — began firing. At the sound of the machine gun, she read, the commanding officer came running back, and when the soldier crouched at the gun wouldn't stop firing, the officer had to resort to kicking him over to force him to stop. One way or another, it seemed all of the prisoners were killed. How many "all" was varied from account to account, but she came across the same photo a couple of times, which showed a long line of piled up, uniformed bodies that she felt sure could not have been faked, and exactly three soldiers standing among them, two of them holding their hands in the air. She hadn't the heart to try to count the bodies in the pile.

What did not vary in the accounts was that I Company, the one that had to have been her father's, had entered not through the main gate, but instead where the railway entered the camp because, as Jespersen had said, their commander was afraid the main gate, with its unspeakable slogan above it, *Arbeit Macht Frei* or "Work Brings Freedom," was booby-trapped. What did not vary was that when the men of that company saw the boxcars with the bodies piled in them, they variously vomited, began to scream, or temporarily lost their minds, and some — many? a few? —went after German guards or soldiers and killed them with their pistols and could not be stopped until their commander, Lieutenant Colonel Felix Sparks, fired his pistol in the air. Such was the degree of their rage and horror that later that day, or maybe the next day, Company I was withdrawn and replaced by Company C. Whether it was true, as some accounts said, that this replacement was due to the emotional state of the soldiers of Company I or was simply a logistical move, there was no way for her to know.

She found that Sparks had died in the United States "with his boots on" at about ninety-three years. She wondered if after Dachau he had screamed in the night and sometimes, in his agonized thrashing, blackened his wife's eyes or her chest. She wondered what would make the difference in a man that he remained calm in such a situation, and what would make him lose all self-control, enough so as to kill in a directed yet random way. Which kind was her father? Which kind was she?

It was, that very day — a fact never to be forgotten — the division's 511th day of combat. From the time they had landed in Sicily, they had had 2,540 officer casualties and 60,023 casualties in the ranks.

She kept reading while the confused repetition of facts or non-facts flattened, barely reached her, until she no longer remembered why she was doing this, or what she had hoped to settle. She had stumbled on this material, that was all; her search was to find out why her father screamed in the night, why he had finally lost his mind. She thought now that she knew.

But still, in some ways it was maddening to her that his name hadn't been mentioned in any of the soldiers' stories online, nor was he in any pictures. A phantom, her father. *My phantom, not-dead father.*

CHAPTER THIRTEEN

HENRY'S FARM

She buzzed the intercom fastened to one of the posts supporting the finely worked wrought-iron gate, which seemed more an adornment than a barrier. She had called ahead to say she was coming, and now repeated that she was Henry Clemensen's daughter, Judith Clemensen-Horvat. Almost immediately, the gates silently opened. She drove down a lane lined with tall poplars and, here and there, groups of lilac and cotoneaster bushes, and surely those were honeysuckle, for perhaps half a kilometre, until she saw a low white stucco building with a grey roof and short wings jutting out on each side from the main doors. She noticed then that the grounds were not quite fully circled by a high, dense caragana hedge, set well enough back so as not to seem, she supposed, a prison fence. As instructed, she parked her car in the lot in front of the building.

When she stepped onto the asphalt, she could hear a tractor in the near distance, although she couldn't see it, and smelled that unmistakable spring-in-the-country smell: last fall's now-rotting leaves and damp old grass, new grass reaching up through the sod, sap beginning to circulate and ooze, the fresh loamy soil, even, or especially, the new-washed spring air. A couple of men in worn jeans and loose work shirts were turning the earth of a long flower bed against the building. They looked up when they heard her car arrive, but went back to their work immediately. They were like a Millet painting, *The Gleaners* maybe.

She thought of the workmen's slow, meditative quality, as if this work had gone on for many years and would go on just so for many more. She preferred not to think that they were probably drugged to the gills, which accounted for their slowness.

She went into the building through double oak doors replete with fancy wooden scrollwork but nonetheless heavy and solid. She would bet not even a medieval battering ram could break them down. The foyer had another buzzer system and double glass doors, but when she pushed one of them, it opened like any glass door in a supermarket or a hospital. The building was cool and quiet inside, though well lit, but she moved tentatively, turning right as the female voice on the intercom had told her to do. A young woman in a blue-flowered yellow dress stepped out of a doorway ahead of her.

"Mrs. Clemensen-Horvat?" Judith didn't know why she had used the double name. Oh yes she did: To sound like someone to be reckoned with, *giving herself airs*, her mother would have said, because Clemensen was her maiden name and, as Victor was long dead and before that gone from her life, neither was she truly Mrs. Horvat.

"Mrs. Donaldson. I'm manager here," the woman said, extending her hand. She ushered Judith into her small, cluttered office, and once she was seated, remarked, "Henry hasn't had anyone visit him in . . ." running her finger down a page of the large book opened on her desk before her, "almost two years! But then, most of our elderly people have no one left out there," tossing her head to indicate the world beyond the stylish gate, and the fence Judith hadn't seen that, probably, was hidden in behind the high caragana hedges. "We have become their family."

"I'm the middle child," Judith said. "I left home very young, before . . . all that happened had happened." She could feel her mouth quivering, and hurried on. "I never knew he was here. Nobody told me. I thought he was dead. For most of my adult life I thought my father was dead." Mrs. Donaldson studied her, her face still, but Judith recognized a softening in the politely professional expression.

"That must have been ... unnerving," she said quietly, as if "shocking" were too strong a word.

"I have to see him."

"I hate to do this, but as we have never seen you here before, I think I should ask for some ID." She was brisk, not looking at Judith, who fumbled in her purse, found her driver's licence with its routinely unflattering photo of her, and showed it to Mrs. Donaldson. "Thank you." She made a note on the page before her. "As it happens, Dr. Moscovitch is here today on his monthly visit — our chief psychiatrist. I think perhaps you should talk with him before you see your father. It could be a difficult visit." She raised her eyes from the ledger to meet Judith's. Difficult? For a second, Judith thought she might cry.

"I know he is far gone into dementia. I know he won't know me. I know he won't say anything sensible. I . . ."

"I'll see if Dr. Moscovitch is free." She went out, leaving the door open. In a few moments, during which time Judith didn't move, she came back. "Come this way." Judith followed her a short way down the hall to another open door. This room was larger, had a thin, sage-coloured rug on the floor, a couple of muted landscapes with pale frames on the walls, two upholstered, dark green, comfortable-looking chairs across from the desk, and a long, vertical window to one side of it. A short, trim man with grey hair stood behind the desk, his hand out to greet her. He was wearing a plain white shirt, open at the throat, the sleeves rolled, and khaki-coloured cotton pants.

When they were both seated and Mrs. Donaldson had gone, closing the door behind her, he said, "I am told — much to my surprise, I must say — that you didn't know your father was still alive?"

"Yes," she said. "It's the usual long story. I won't bore you with it, but the whole business," by which she meant the murder, the brief incarceration, the years in the mental hospital, "was kept from me. My sister seems to have believed it was better I didn't know." She wanted to say that keeping it from her was *pure maliciousness on the part of my sister*, but managed not to.

He gazed at her with an interested, sympathetic expression. He said, "Or maybe she was trying to save you from the pain she and your brother had to have suffered." He smiled at her, raising his groomed white eyebrows as if in inquiry. When she was silent, he continued.

"Actually, this isn't the first time I have heard that. Families were ashamed; they thought it was best if the children didn't know there was psychiatric illness in the family, thinking that if the children didn't know, they wouldn't have to worry about whether one day they too might become ill. Or they wouldn't have to feel the shame, I suppose. I haven't made a study of it, although I'm sure there is literature."

"May I see him now?" She was embarrassed at being so abrupt, but it didn't appear to bother him. He put both elbows on his desk, not looking at her, toying with an expensive-looking fountain pen.

"Yes, of course. It wouldn't make any difference in his condition now, I don't believe, although the human mind is full of wonders." He shook his head slowly, as if he couldn't believe what he had seen in his long career. Judith knew, also, that he was considering her, wondering what to tell her and what to hold back.

"He is a very old man now," he said. She nodded impatiently. "He is unwell. In fact, we were considering sending him to the hospital in town, where they can give him better care now than we can."

"How unwell?"

"He is near death," he said, his voice gentle. "His systems are failing him; they are worn out with age. You came pretty much at the last possible moment." The noise of the tractor was growing louder; the gauzy white curtain at the window stirred.

"Do my brother and sister know? I mean, so that they can come?" He nodded. "I need to see him," she said, half rising, beginning to lose her self-control, anxious not to show it, but the drive to see him now overwhelming her need for dignity.

"I would be remiss if I didn't caution you that he is beyond communication. Or so I believe." He gave her a look that seemed to say again, *But one never knows.* A stab of fear hit her in her gut, and she struggled to hide it. Then she was standing, shifting uneasily, trying to hold her hands steady, clasping them, then letting them fall by her sides.

"Will you — stay with me?" Heat was rising in her face.

"Yes," he said, coming around from behind his desk, taking her arm in a courtly manner, his touch at once surprising and comforting. Together they walked a short distance down the hall, past the main entrance to another room, where, just as they reached it, the door opened and a woman in a pink dress with darker pink geometric patterns on it was exiting.

"Nancy," the doctor said. "This is Henry's other daughter." He looked questioningly at Judith.

"Judith," she said. Nancy was carrying a small tray with an array of tiny medicine cups on it.

"It is so good you have come, Judith." Her smile contained both sympathy and something stronger, as if she too was invested in her patient's situation.

"Have you called my sister and my brother?" She had already asked this question, she remembered, but the doctor had merely nodded; she wanted assurances. "I didn't know he was ill, or that his situation was so serious. This is a coincidence that I came right now. I don't want them to think I kept anything from them." Even in her confusion and fear, the irony didn't escape her.

"Mrs. Donaldson called your sister last night," Nancy said. "It seems unlikely that either of them will come, although they did leave instructions to call — again. She told us you were coming, but I, at least, had no idea you would arrive today." She lowered her head and walked slowly away, studying the small cards laid out beside the medicine cups on her tray.

"Come," the doctor said. "This is one of our hospital rooms," he whispered. "Henry has his own room down the other hall, but here we can keep a closer eye on him."

Someone lay on the partially raised bed, so impossibly white that she had trouble at first separating the face, the head, from the bleached white of the sheets. The doctor lowered his arm from hers; she took a few steps to stand beside her father's chest so that she could look directly into his face. She stared at him until she found hints in the skeletal form lying before her of the father of her childhood. How unexpectedly smooth his face, all lines and wrinkles melted, how large his nose seemed now, how delicately white the thin covering of hair over his pale scalp. But the aura of electric vigour that was at the same time menace was gone.

She said, "Dad? Daddy?" She noticed in some corner of her mind that was not engaged, that watcher-self again, that her knees felt weak enough to fail her. She put both hands, palms down, on the cool sheets at the edge of the bed to steady herself. After a moment, she lifted her right hand, touched his cheek with her fingertips, then bent and kissed his forehead. "Dad?" she whispered.

He opened his eyes; she knew at once that he wasn't seeing her; they were dark, they were deeper than pools, they were — blue, she told herself, they were blue. But in them there was no longer any echo of colour.

"It's me, Judy, come to see you." His lips moved, but his eyes seemed fixed on inner space. "I'm sorry I didn't come before, but I didn't know where you were. I am so glad to find you at last."

He had moved his gaze to her face, seeming to study her, but in the gaze was only darkness. She looked inquiringly over her shoulder to the doctor who had remained at the foot of the bed. He nodded, though barely perceptibly, and soundlessly left the room. She found she didn't mind his absence.

"Sammie is running the farm," she told her father. "He is doing very well. You would be proud." It occurred to her that the movements he was making with his lips might mean he was thirsty. She found a cotton swab resting in a glass on the bedside cabinet, moistened it in his water glass, and rubbed its damp end gently across his lips. He opened his mouth reflexively, like an infant, and she pushed the wet swab inside, rolled it carefully against his tongue and the roof of his mouth, removed it, and set it back in its plastic glass. She remained standing by his head, holding her face not far from his, suppressing each memory that came rising up, wanting to stick to the essence: My father. This is my father.

Distantly, she heard the sound of the tractor moving away again and caught a hint of diesel fumes wafting through the open window. A meadowlark called, its cry purity itself, not so much embroidering the air as inscribing it with clear sound, its music resonant to her of her once-and-now-beloved prairie childhood.

As if in answer to the yellow-breasted bird's inquiry, a voice said, into the suddenly silent air, "I had three children."

Did he say that? Could he have said that? She listened to the echo of the words, found that the voice was wrong, she didn't know this voice, yet there was no one else in the room. Hope surged: she had questions to ask him, answers she wanted, she wanted to talk with him, she wanted — but hope died as quickly as it had risen.

After a minute had passed, during which her heart beat faster, then quieted, she said, "Yes, Abigail and Samuel. I am Judith." The name echoed in the large, plain room with its high white ceiling: *Judith. Judith. Judith.* The curtains from the single window across from his bed rippled, and this time she smelled, faintly, sage and grasses.

But he had no more words, it seemed. She bent to kiss his face again, whispering to him things that she knew made no sense even if he could understand, although she knew he couldn't. After a moment, she noticed a wooden chair pushed against the wall by the window. She went to the chair and sat down. Not long after, the nurse in the pink dress, Nancy, came back. She was carrying a teacup on a saucer; steam rose from it, and the tea's fragrance, lemon and ginger, wafted toward her.

She handed Judith the cup and saucer, went to the bed, clasped her father's thin wrist, took his pulse, listened with her stethoscope to his heart, smiled at Judith, and was about to go away again.

"Wait," Judith said. "Please." Nancy turned to her, questioningly. "I don't know what to do," she said.

Nancy said, "His time here is nearly over. A few hours, perhaps. Stay if you wish, or go if you prefer."

"I need a bathroom," she said, the need abruptly urgent, and rose quickly, slopping the tea into the saucer, which she set roughly on the floor, going to the door where Nancy pointed down the hall and said, "On your right."

Sometime later, Mrs. Donaldson in her bright yellow-and-blue dress came into the bathroom where Judith leaned against one of the sinks, her back to it and to the mirror above it, so she wouldn't have to see herself.

"Oh, there you are," Mrs. Donaldson said. "Dr. Moscovitch says that he is available if you would like to talk to him." Judith shook her head no too quickly. Then, puzzled, she asked, "I feel I ought to stay? But I feel I have no right to be here, now. After so very many years. After I ran away, a long time ago."

"You are the only one here," Mrs. Donaldson said. "You're his daughter, aren't you? Of course you have every right to be here. You represent his family — your family. *They* are not here." But Judith thought Mrs. Donaldson was wrong, that she didn't understand. Nonetheless, she went back to her father's room and sat in the chair again. Someone had taken away the cup and saucer and wiped the floor where she had spilled tea.

She sat quietly for an hour or so, staring into space, or looking at her knees, or across the room to the door, still open. Curious, it occurred to her that her father wasn't connected to any beeping machines; there were no glowing electronic monitors by his bed, no machinery at all. Nancy came in and went out, and came in again, each time smiling at her, checking her father's respirations and pulse, and listening to his heart. Now and then, when Nancy wasn't there, Judith would rise, go to his bedside, and put her hand carefully, gently, against his cheek or on his forehead. Then she would sit again. Once, she cupped her hands on each side of his throat, then dropped them and went back to the chair and sat again.

The next time Nancy came in, Judith said, "I'm going out for just a minute."

She never was able to recall how long she had walked the grounds, but would guess, and would tell Sammie and Abbie, that it was for maybe ten minutes, although sometimes she thought it had been longer. She only came back in when she noticed Mrs. Donaldson, easy to spot in her colourful dress, standing in the front entryway holding open one of the doors, beckoning her. Judith hurried back across the lawn to her, already knowing what she would be told. She had no idea how she felt.

"He simply slipped away," Mrs. Donaldson said. "Just now, just this minute." She put her arm around Judith's shoulders as they walked into the building and the short distance to his room. Nancy was there, straightening her father's bedsheets around him and smoothing the pillows.

"I am so glad you were here," she told Judith, and to her surprise, at some distant level, Judith knew her own uncertainty had gone; she was glad too, although she suspected that the combination of not knowing for so many years that he was alive, and then to be with him up to the moment of his death but not at it, would haunt her — that and Abbie's pathetic villainy — that she would be no more free of this than her father had been of the boxcars full of bodies. But then she thought that there was no comparison, and the murdered hares hanging outside the Richter's kitchen window flew past her. For the first time — or was it? — the idea rushing into her mind and out again in less than a millisecond, that maybe somebody had come from outside the community, from a city somewhere, to deliver the warning to the Jews. Even as it flashed past her, she saw its plausibility.

Her father's face was hardly different than it had been when she had left the room, however long ago that had been, but now she saw that his skin and whatever flesh was left beneath it had relaxed and the wrinkles and creases that had to have been there before had reappeared. For the first time, she knew this was her father; in death, he looked at last like himself, and she made a noise so full of emotion she frightened herself and sweat broke out all over her body. But, in another flash, that selfness of his she had seen had vanished, and lying before her was the corpse of the man who had been her father.

She stayed with him a few minutes more, trying just to breathe. Nancy returned.

"We have a quiet room where you can be alone for a while. The staff is getting papers in order, and perhaps you want to call your family?" Obediently, Judith followed her out the door and down the hall to an empty lounge with an armchair, a table with a wooden chair at it, and a coffee machine and cups on a stand in the corner. It puzzled her immensely that things hadn't ended.

After a while, Mrs. Donaldson came into the room where Judith was sitting quietly, waiting not just for the papers she was to sign but for her father's few belongings to be given to her so that she could take them back home with her. This latter disturbed her terribly; more, she realized, than the fact of his death. She wondered if she should be crying, but didn't.

"And, Mrs. Clemensen-Horvat —"

"Just Clemensen," Judith interjected.

"Our staff and residents will have a small service here for your father, maybe in a week or so. I hope that is all right with you."

"Of course," Judith said. "I'm sorry I won't be able to come back for it." She hadn't thought that her dad had friends here or, at least, people who had known him and worked with him for many years. That for many years this had been his home, not his prison, not some never-never land where he was waiting out an interval, a sojourner, him — Henry Clemensen — until he could go back to his life. She saw him standing with the men in the flowerbed, a spade in his hands, talking with them as they turned the earth, and a bottomless pit opened beneath her — she had to put out a hand to keep from dropping into it, because in that instant she saw what had been lost: his life, her life, their life together.

Mrs. Donaldson said, "Are you all right? This is such a hard time ..." Judith thought she must have made a noise.

"Yes," she said. "Maybe my brother and sister will come to his memorial service." And after a second, "Maybe I will too."

"The funeral home is here to take your father's remains to their establishment in town. The director gave me his card so that you can meet with him in the morning about your wishes. Is that all right?" Judith nodded.

"Yes, thank you," she said, accepting the card and putting it carefully into her purse.

When she had calmed herself sufficiently, she phoned Abigail, who sounded unmoved but said she would tell Sam and call her back. A few minutes later, her cellphone rang. Abigail and Sam had decided, provided Judith was in agreement, that she should escort his remains to the funeral home in the nearby small city, where she would have him cremated. Judith didn't need to stay, as the funeral director would eventually send them the ashes and they could decide then what to do with them, and whether they would or would not have a memorial service for him at Abigail's church, which had once been his and their mother's. At this last, Abbie's voice broke, before she recovered.

"I think this must be very hard for you," Abbie said, her voice losing some of its stiffness. "I'm sorry for that. We didn't mean to put you in this position — it just happened." Hearing this, Judith knew once and for all that Abbie would never admit to what she had done, that she would never apologize, never ask forgiveness. And if she wouldn't admit to it, she would never explain why, either. But Judith hadn't the energy for recriminations.

"I'm glad I was here." She knew then that there would be no service in or near Wisdom, no stirring up the old shame, no loss of face for Sam, but especially not for Abbie.

After she hung up, Judith toyed with the idea of waiting for the urn containing his ashes in order to bring him home herself, but didn't know how long that would be — days perhaps, she guessed — and eventually decided not to wait. But it was late afternoon now, too late to start the long drive home, and anyway, she had to make arrangements with the funeral company before she could leave. She would have to stay overnight in a motel. Schlapp came into her mind, the man her father had killed, which had brought her to this moment. Not a soul had mourned him, and again, briefly, she wondered what had become of his remains, for — Oh bizarre circumstance, he had been a guard in concentration camps, had assisted in the torture and murder of Jews, maybe even at Dachau — he was not a convicted murderer, while her father was incarcerated for life. That was why they were taking so long with the paperwork! Her father was a prisoner here! Maybe the state wanted her father's remains, too, as it had his life. And who had buried Schlapp? Or cremated him? The repercussions of this thought sickened her.

She knew what she would insist Abbie and Sammy do: come here for the service, the only one there would be; she would keep his ashes, and the three of them would bury them on Sam's place that was the home farm, the one their father and mother had established and worked for so many years. She would not allow Abbie and Sam to scatter his remains to the wind as if he had never been born, had never lived on earth.

Mrs. Donaldson came into the room and set papers on the table, indicating Judith should read and sign them. She carried a large brown paper bag, folded over double at its top, the folds held together with a large paper clip. She set it beside the armchair Judith had been sitting in without indicating what it was. Judith signed the few papers, and while Mrs. Donaldson was saying goodbye, a middle-aged man wearing an orderly's clothing slipped into the room and set a second bag down beside the first.

"From the laundry room," he said softly, and went out again.

Nancy put her head in the door, "The men from the funeral home have come and gone," addressing Judith. For a second, Judith didn't know what she meant, but of course, they had taken away her father's remains.

Once in her motel room, she couldn't settle, turned the television on, turned it off again, drank some water, considered going out to find a restaurant, but didn't go. She ran a bath, thinking the hot water would relax her, but once in the tub, she found that even though she was immersed in it, she couldn't feel the water. Puzzled, she looked down and saw, or thought she saw, an amorphous silver-grey space an inch or two wide between her forearm and the water. Her first reaction was to deny having seen it, and yet she might have been sitting in a tub of air for all she felt against her body. How very odd this was, not quite scary, but, besides baffling, annoying: She needed the sensation of heat and the physical relaxation it would bring. She asked herself, *If I accept that this barrier is real, then what is it?* And after some thought, answered herself: *I have been so very stressed, so very shocked, that my soul or else my self has taken itself right out of my physical body.*

Her clever social-worker self announced, too, that she probably shouldn't be alone at such a time, and she thought of phoning Catherine or Jessica but didn't because they were too far away to help her, and Sam and Abigail wouldn't be coming. How is it that when you most need people they aren't there? Somehow, she must be to blame for this. She should have asked somebody to come with her, but it hadn't even occurred to her. Because she had wanted to see Dad alone. *I thought I had the right to see him alone.*

Later, she opened the two paper bags. The one the orderly had brought contained a pair of faded blue pajamas, a couple of freshly laundered, worn shirts, two pairs of socks, some underwear, and one pair of heavy denim pants, very worn. She wondered if she should even bother to bring them home, but knew Abigail was bound to question her about his belongings, and as none of these clothes were prison-issue, she didn't think; Abbie and Sam might have provided them, so she refolded the top of the bag and set it on the floor beside her suitcase.

The second paper bag contained his shaving equipment, a comb, a hairbrush, a fresh bar of soap, toothpaste and toothbrush, some shampoo, two small, crusted tubes, one of antibiotic salve, the other lip balm — items he must have had for years. In the bottom of the bag was a rectangular box about three inches by five inches, covered in age-soiled red silk with tiny Chinese-looking, bright blue flowers woven into the fabric. A tarnished brass-coloured metal clasp was glued to the front of the box to hold the lid shut. The box was a cheap trinket from a five-and-dime store probably, Kresge's or Woolworth's maybe, stores long gone. Something stirred in her when she saw it: It had been her mother's, although she had no idea who had given it to her. Maybe her father when he was a young man and they were about to be married. Both of them the poorest of the poor. That they might have been in love all those years ago seemed a whimsical, touching notion. She wondered how the little box had ended here, in her father's few possessions, and thought that Abbie had sent it with him, or brought it herself, once he was settled.

She took it out of the bag and set it on the bed table in the circle of warm light from the lamp, unfastened the clasp, and lifted the lid. The interior was lined with clean red satin, although it gave off a faint musty odour. Lying on the bottom was a round brass coin or a medal fixed to a wrinkled corded ribbon whose original colour had been blue. She would have to clean the medal to see what it said, but it had to be his, probably an I-was-there remembrance from his World War II service. She doubted that it was a medal given for bravery — although, why not? — only because it was so unassuming. Maybe he had brought it with him himself to the farm; maybe somewhere in the clouded recesses of his brain he knew that he had been a soldier, that maybe the most significant part of his life had been the years he had fought in the haze and stench and murderous clamour of the war in Europe, the comrades he had suffered with, and, when they had the chance, drank and 'tomcatted' with. And the killings. The boxcars of bodies. She straightened the medal on its ribbon and closed the lid carefully, pressing down the flimsy catch and pressing it in place. Afterwards, it was the small brass medal that stayed with her, this single reward of his. This memorial.

Eventually, though, without turning off the bedside lamp or checking the lock on the door, she fell asleep. When she woke again it was after midnight. Her face was wet, her pillow damp, and her chest ached as though she had been crying for a long time. The stuffy, thick air of the motel room had cleared; the small room was imbued with a warmth so strong she could almost see it. She sat up, and as she was trying to get her bearings, the atmosphere around her began to crackle as if suffused with delicate electricity, the light from the bedside lamp, never bright, dimmed, and brightened again, and she felt a presence with her in the room.

Many years later, when she was very old, she would finally tell her daughters about this. "No choirs of angels sang, no voice spoke, but I knew it was him, and he was . . . joyful."

PART III

JERUSALEM

CHAPTER FOURTEEN

STRUCK IN THE HEART

As her plane from Heathrow circled Ben Gurion Airport, and she looked out her window at Israel sunk below in inscrutable blackness, she was too tired to be excited any more, and had given up, too, on being nervous about what awaited her.

When Catherine said that she wouldn't go with her mother to visit Lucinda, Judith, angry though she was with Abigail, thought that she should ask her. No use asking Sam, and anyway, if they wanted to go, Sylvia would take care of such a trip. But her sister had never gone anywhere; even Judith had been to Europe twice, and while she knew Abbie would think going to, say, France, a ridiculous notion, she was a lifelong Christian, so surely there would be no question about Jerusalem.

If Judith had told anyone what Abbie had done to her, that person would have said, "So you never spoke to her again," and this reaction had been her first. But with fifty years of as-good-as silence behind them, she didn't think she could go back to that, no matter how grievous her wound. Or, simply, were their motivations, both of them in their separate strikes against each other, so complex and confused that neither knew the appropriate behaviour? Thinking this, when she called Abbie to ask her if she wanted to go to Jerusalem with her in two months, and before she could, Abbie asked her to Sunday supper, Judith, surprising herself, said yes.

They were in Abbie's kitchen when Judith asked her. Abbie was setting the table. Her sister's assured movements halted, she lifted her head, her cheeks flushing pink, and breathed out softly, "The Holy City!" Her head quirked at an odd angle, she continued to stare at something Judith couldn't see before she went back to setting knives, forks, and spoons by plates. She said nothing more, finishing with the utensils, wiping her hands on her apron busily, turning with too-rapid, jerky movements to the stove where pots hissed steam.

"I need to talk to Rick."

"Of course, but don't take too long, because you'll have to get a passport and we should make our reservations at the same time and . . ."

Abbie was opening the oven door, pulling the roast forward, taking off the heavy lid, making a racket as if to shut out her sister's voice, and Judith had the sudden intuition that Abbie wasn't just exercising wifely protocol in asking Rick first, but that she really did not want to go to Jerusalem. Indeed, less than a week later, she phoned to say she wouldn't be coming with her. Judith said, "I thought seeing the Holy City was the dream of your life."

"Not my life. Mom's life maybe, but not mine."

There was a long silence during which Judith tried to imagine their mother getting on a plane and flying to Israel and almost laughed at the picture, it being so alien to everything she remembered about her mother.

"But I just don't get it," she said. "I mean, I thought you would jump at the chance to be a pilgrim, to see the place where Jesus was resurrected . . ." Not that she fully believed any of this herself, but still, maybe when she actually traversed the true *Via Dolorosa* and all the rest of it — Jesus's tomb, Mary's grave — she would be moved, she would become a full believer. She even halfway hoped this would happen. "Won't you think about it some more?"

"Stop it, Judy. I'm not going, and that's that."

But in the few weeks that followed, before Judith drove once more to Calgary, stayed overnight in Cathy's empty apartment — she was in Maui with her best friend — parked her car at the airport, and boarded her plane for Heathrow, she couldn't stop thinking about Abbie's refusal. Surely it wasn't money. Abbie and Rick were obsessively frugal and probably had quite a lot of cash stored away. *For what?* she wondered. *For the Apocalypse?* No, it wasn't the cost. Was it that, after a lifetime of piety, constant prayer, and churchgoing, when confronted with the reality of the Holy City, she was afraid in some other way? Not that the plane would crash, not that she would be mugged, or be made sick by strange food, or catch a strange disease. Or, it being Israel after all, of bombs.

Maybe Abbie thought that in Jerusalem she would be found out. *She knows she's a sinner just like everybody else.* Trying to keep her place in her church, trying to be sure the community respected her, enough to make them forget that her father, the murderer, the crazy man, had ever been a part of the church, had ever lived in the community.

Judith tried to put herself into Abbie's head, to imagine the Holy City as it would appear to her: A celestial city, glowing softly in rays of light coming directly from heaven, the crumbling stones of antiquity made only of sponge like a set for a television show, a stand-in for the Heavenly City that all her life preachers had glorified, and into which she prayed she would one day be admitted. A fierce light behind it all, too dazzling to look at; so powerful it would melt flesh and bones: the Light of God.

Did she have some absurd idea that going to Jerusalem would be the same thing as going, too early, to her death? Leaving behind grass and trees, running streams and birdsong, and great moss- or lichen-covered rocks so beautiful they broke the heart? Leaving behind her husband and her children and — truly — the only home a human was strong enough to bear? She was afraid of . . . of what? Salvation? It reminded Judith of Jung, who wanted with every ounce of his being to go to Rome, but who fainted when he tried to get on the train to go there, and couldn't. The Rome that was the ground of all he had spent his life seeking to know. But this was fanciful where Abbie was concerned.

It seemed to Judith now that the myth of salvation had kept her family from flying apart, until, eventually, the family flew apart anyway. She was gone, Sammie got married, their mother died, their father went crazy, while Abbie alone hung on and hung on and — she was still hanging on. Now, just maybe, Judith thought, Abbie was wondering if she had made a mistake; was afraid that in the Holy City she would find, not the Jesus she sought, but the final end to the religious belief that since her childhood had held her together.

The plane was descending now, the roar filling the cabin, and then, with a long sizzling whine, they were on the ground, leaning forward as the plane seemed to accelerate when it touched the runway, leaning back as it braked and decelerated. She had forgotten how thrilling flying could be, and in this exquisite moment, she forgot Abbie, forgot her family's travails, even realized she hadn't had a headache for a couple of days.

But, she thought, as they taxied and the runway lights whipped past and she caught a glimpse of the brightly lit terminal ahead — her first view of Israel — *Don't we all try our best; don't we all sometimes succeed and sometimes fail, and don't we all try to be good, whatever being good might be?* Not for the first time she thought how people had no idea what being good was, short of the self-abnegation of a Mother Teresa. What about all those people she had seen on television declaring tearfully, "I'm a good person!" even while any fool could see that they were liars who cared nothing for the needs of others. What could they possibly mean? Goodness — it baffled her, too. Kindness, now that was another, more workable thing. Kindness she understood, and the young couple who'd taken her in when she ran away and wound up in Calgary came into her mind.

Then she was gathering her things, rising to stand in the crowded aisle, walking off the plane and down hallway after hallway through the strange terminal in the midst of the crowd of travellers. Maybe it's a good thing Abbie didn't come if it frightened her so much, no matter what the reason.

No, she had Abbie's motivation all wrong. She would have stopped dead right there in the wide hall had she not been carried on the crush of people anxious to get through customs and out of the terminal. It wasn't about Abbie's faith or lack of it, or her fears, or her attempt to save Judith from suffering. Preventing her from knowing their father was alive wasn't to punish her for running away from the family, hurting their parents, or leaving Abbie with the responsibility, or to deal almost alone, with what their father finally did that got him sent away.

No. *It was her revenge, because I got away and she didn't.* Judith was the brat, the problem, the bad one, but she had the guts to go, and Abbie didn't. And even more surprising, her anger at her sister dissolved now in a wave of pity, followed quickly by a cold dismissiveness. If only Abbie knew, she thought, how hard Judith's life had been. How much easier it would have been to have stayed, married a farmer like she did, had a family, rarely left the countryside. Or how much she'd wanted to come back, but she'd needed them to ask her to come back, and they never did. What could she have thought but that she must have done the right thing to leave if she was not loved. She thought then how tormented Abbie must be under that pious exterior; how impossible it was that she and Judith could ever really be friends again. No wonder she hadn't wanted to come with Judith to Israel.

Finally through customs, her bags collected, she went out into the wide hall where the lights were too bright, the noises too loud, blurring into a senseless growl. Something kept dinging, although she couldn't tell what it was. A man in a black suit and white shirt unbuttoned at the neck stood before her. How long had he been there?

On her drive from the airport to Jerusalem with her son-in-law Levi, a bomb went off in the far distance, although Levi assured her it was thunder. No thunder she had ever heard sounded like that, she told herself, but she was so jetlagged and exhausted that, despite the sound and the jolt of something that wasn't exactly fear, she fell asleep anyway, and then dozed in and out of a state of groggy awareness, then slept more deeply. She dreamed of Lucy coming home, thin and pale, telling her, "I have left Thomas," and bursting into sobs, clinging to her mother, Judith waiting out the tears before she asked, "Why did you leave him?"

"Our house wasn't ever home," she said. "And anyway, I have the flu." But as was so often the case with Lucy, this was only partly the truth; half of it was a pathetic lie.

Blood everywhere, the sheets soaked, a trail on the floor leading into the bathroom, where she found a corpse-like Lucinda crumpled against the side of the tub, mouth open in a silent Edvard Munch scream, raising her hands to her mother, blood dripping from them. Judith could hear herself screaming.

"Judith, Judith." Levi was driving one-handed, patting her knee to wake her. "You were having a bad dream!" She was about to tell him what she had been dreaming when she realized she could never do that. Levi must never know about Lucy's abortion, unless Lucinda had already told him.

"I don't remember," she said. "I think I was trying to scream, but I couldn't get the sound out."

"You are overtired," he told her. "And coming to Israel, it can be dangerous, I think people believe that, anyway. You are just maybe overwrought."

"I am very tired," Judith agreed, and slept the rest of the way through the darkened countryside, into the ancient city of Jerusalem, waking only at Levi shaking her shoulder in the driveway of his and Lucinda's home. Already he had her suitcases out of the car and had set them on the front steps. He waited while Judith fumbled with her seatbelt and blearily extricated herself from the vehicle. Her first thought was how warm the air was, how it had a quality that wasn't in the air in Wisdom and certainly not in that of Calgary, although if asked, she would have been able to say only that it was the faint smell of a different kind of distance — maybe it was desert instead of the clean, gripping air of the mountains.

Levi was offering her his arm when a light over the door clicked on, the door opened, and a bulky figure stood in it. As her eyes adjusted, Judith saw that it was Lucinda in her full glory, in the late stage of her pregnancy.

"Mom!" Judith dropped Levi's arm and hurried, less quickly than she might have, she was so stiff, up the steps, where mother and daughter embraced, both crying, and then Levi, making murmuring noises, was ushering them into the house and into a small sitting room, where Judith was guided to a wide sofa and Lucinda sat across from her on a firmer chair with a straight back. Judith noticed that the room was appointed as any room in Canada would be, nothing strange here. In the hall, Levi was closing the front door; she heard two locks snap shut, and then he was thumping down the hall with the suitcases, one of them full of gifts.

Lucy was coming into full focus now. Still, Judith couldn't quite find the little girl in her, the recalcitrant teenager, the troubled young woman. She had the same dark hair and pale skin and sensual mouth, held herself the same way, and walked, with allowances made for her pregnancy, in the same way Lucy had always walked. But something had changed in her, or was missing. Some darkness in her eyes, some edginess in her movements, as if she could never be expected to stay in one place. Maybe it was only that she was too heavy, too tired, her pregnancy too advanced, for the old Lucy to have room to exist anymore.

Judith said, in her bewilderment, joy, and fear, "You should be in bed, dear! You didn't need to wait up for me!"

Levi — Judith noticed for the first time what a very handsome man he was — had returned to sit on the chair's arm beside Lucy, where he put his arm around her shoulders, and Lucy, sniffing and brushing away tears, leaned her head against his ribs. Something hard and frightened settled down with a satisfying 'thunk' in Judith's chest before it vanished.

As she lay in the comfortable bed in the darkness of the guest room, the house silent, no sound coming from outside although she was in a city the size of Calgary, she thought about that boom she had heard and the flash of white light; it seemed as though she might have dreamt it.

I am in Jerusalem, she told herself. And, trying it out, *I am in the Holy City*, and finding this far stranger, could hardly believe it either.

"But I didn't come to be a tourist," Judith protested over dinner the next evening. Sunk in jet lag, she had slept through breakfast and lunch.

"Now," Levi announced. "It is settled. You cannot come all this way and not even go to the Old City, and that is that." But he was grinning at her as he said it.

Judith said only, "Give me a day or two, will you, Levi? I'm still not quite myself, I want to spend time with Lucy — and besides, who will be here for Lucy if she goes into labour?"

He said only, seeming distracted, "It is taken care of," giving an airy wave to dismiss the concern.

It had grown dark outside; even in broad daylight, though, little of the outdoors could be seen through the wide-slatted window-coverings. How peaceful it was inside this small house. After they had eaten and Levi had cleared the table and sent his wife and mother-in-law to the sitting room, he came in only to announce that he had work to do (he was an accountant at a large factory that made — she didn't know what) and would be upstairs in his study. When the sound of his feet on the stairs had died away, Judith said, "I have so many questions."

"Yes? You can see I am happy. Although I will be glad to have this over with," Lucinda said, pointing down to her bulk. They talked about the course of her pregnancy, which had been normal, no surprises, and Lucy assured her that she had been watched very closely by her doctor as she was old to be having a first baby. At last, seeming tired, or subject to some emotion Judith thought might have been about the years of quarrels and absences and Judith's too-frequent anger with her, Lucy seemed to settle into herself, sitting motionless. At last, she lifted her eyes to her mother.

"I know you want to know how somebody like me could become a Jew."

"You mean, Protestant?" Judith asked, puzzled.

"I mean, disturbed," Lucy answered, a wry smile appearing.

"Not 'disturbed'!" Judith said, alarmed. "Never 'disturbed'!"

"Oh, come on, Mom. We both know I did a lot of crazy things when I was growing up. And then, marrying Thomas — that crazy wedding."

"What was that all about?" Judith allowed herself to ask, but Lucy only shrugged and looked away, and instead of answering, said, "I will have to show you some of my poems." Judith was too startled to say anything about "my poems," but at least half of her was thinking, What now? "Oh yes," Lucy said, smiling. "In New York I was dating a poet, we hung out with a bunch of poets and went to readings. Sometimes I was just . . . struck in the heart by what I heard. I wanted to try writing poetry." She had even made a fist and tapped her chest over her heart, lifting her chin and looking away from her mother.

"Anyway, Jonathan helped me a bit with my poems, but then he wouldn't anymore." She laughed, looking away. "I would have lines — now and then, not always — that would slow him right down, just for a second, and then he would put the page down and walk away. I would be hurt, until I figured out that he was jealous. Eventually, we broke up, and then I met Levi!"

"And you have kept up writing poetry?"

"Oh, yes. It is here that I have become a poet. A real one." What a tone was in her voice, one Judith had never heard from her before, although she had heard it in Jessica's voice when she was talking about adopting Carly.

"I can't understand this," Judith said, finally, touching her forehead with bunched fingertips.

"Israel," Lucy said.

"You mean, because it is so different — this life you lead?"

"No, not exactly. Because it truly is a — if not a holy place, it is . . . it is . . . full of Spirit," but she was frowning, staring at her knees, as if trying to think how to explain this. "Spirit is everywhere here."

"I don't know what you mean," Judith said, keeping her voice gentle, as if Lucy were a wild animal, easily startled.

"Is Calgary full of Spirit?" Lucy asked. "Is Wisdom?"

"Not that I've noticed," Judith said. "But tell me — what are we talking about? What does 'full of Spirit' mean?"

"The night I first arrived here, on my first visit before we were married," Lucy said, "Levi was late meeting me because there had been an accident on the freeway, and he couldn't get through for quite a while. I was so tired that I was — my nerves were screaming — I was wound up like a top. I thought I wouldn't sleep for a week even though I was so tired. Like a small child gets sometimes, you know?" Judith nodded, her eyes fixed on her daughter's face.

"Finally, I went to bed in Levi's mother and father's house. I was rigid between the sheets, my heart was hammering: *beat-beat-beat-beat*," she kept the rhythm with her hand. "My breath was too fast, I couldn't slow it down. I lay there listening to every sound. I was lying on my back, and stiff, so stiff, and I couldn't relax." She paused, looked across the softly lit room past her mother, her voice changing, growing softer, lighter. "I thought, I will never sleep again. It seemed so very far away, I could hardly remember how one sleeps.

"Then a hand came down on me. I mean, I couldn't see it; I don't know what it was, but it seemed to me to be a hand, and it started down at my toes and moved gently and slowly up my body, and behind it, and as it went" — now she was gesturing, showing the flattened hand, palm down, moving up her body — "all the muscles, so taut they were" — she frowned and clenched her jaw to demonstrate — "so very taut, and as the hand passed over them, they loosened and relaxed, muscle after muscle" — slowing her speech — "all the way up my body." She was smiling to herself. "The next thing I knew it was morning, or rather, like for you, it was noon, and I was wide awake, and not a touch of jet lag. How could I live anywhere else after that? I knew I was where I had always needed to be, where I belonged."

It was not so much that her face glowed, or that a beam of light had descended on her, or that a choir of angels had begun to sing, as it was a steadiness had settled in Lucinda's face, that seemed, in Judith's gaze, to come from inside her daughter, moving slowly outward to inhabit her skin, her flesh beneath it, her bones, her eyes. It was as if Judith was finally, for the first time, seeing Lucinda.

The next morning after breakfast Judith asked her daughter, "But what has this to do with Judaism?" She meant the spirit that Lucy claimed was everywhere; she meant the hand that had calmed and relaxed her. "Is this Judaism?"

"I don't know what it was," Lucy said. "I have no idea."

"But you are now a Jew, am I right?"

"No, no," Lucy said. She had collapsed onto a kitchen chair, the one without armrests that Levi had sat in at breakfast before he left for work, and closing her eyes, blew out air softly. Then she was up again, pacing, one hand against her lower back.

"It's complicated. You can't just decide you'll be a Jew. You have to — sort of — apply. You go to a rabbi — I had to go to him three times before he accepted me — and then you have to study and learn, take courses, and answer questions and do ceremonies — I can't tell you it all."

Judith couldn't believe that a woman who had run as hard as she had away from formal religion should give birth to not one but two daughters who fell into what she thought of as the 'clutches' of formal religious practice: *Lucinda here in Israel, and Alice in* — she corrected herself — *at-the-moment-not-so-far-off Africa.* She felt a faint thrill at this thought, she who had barely travelled and never to exotic places, wasn't she now more than halfway to Tanzania? Clearly their fathers and I failed them, although that puzzled her too, because surely to want God wasn't a failing. But to *choose* to be a Jew: it frightened her, thinking of Saul Richter, a very real man she knew, who had suffered more than, all her life, she could face even just to hear about, because he was a Jew. What was it Lucinda wanted? She could not understand.

When Alice had heard she would be in Israel, she had tried to convince Judith to go on to Tanzania to visit her and Dwight. In some peculiar way, this had seemed unthinkable to Judith. She could adjust to only one new culture and climate and way of life at a time, she told Alice. She was not young, Alice would have to remember that. Things were harder on her now, especially since the concussion, than they would have been only ten years ago. That had a tendency to silence any one of her daughters. Alice had said, in a distant way, as if she were thinking about something else, "I don't know how much longer we'll be here," which Judith had taken to mean that they might be sent on to another community as they once had, years ago, or even to another African country, although, come to think of it, hadn't she mentioned Bolivia once? Surely they were too young to retire.

"So are you now, officially, formally . . ." She paused, not wanting to ask the usually but not always rhetorical question she had heard asked more than once in her life: *What is a Jew?* And for which it seemed no single answer existed.

"I am working toward the goal, but it takes a long time; so far I have agreed to live by the Seven Laws of Noah."

"Which are?"

"Thou shalt not kill, that sort of thing, nothing scary." Lucinda was laughing. "Nothing that a Christian doesn't believe too. We — I mean, they, or us — just handle it differently. It's where you start. I'm not a full practitioner or adherent of Judaism yet, but I intend to be.

"And Daniel was conceived when I was not — I am not yet — a Jew so when he is thirteen, he will have to go through the steps to officially — ouch!"

"What? What?" She was on her feet, reaching for Lucy.

"Nothing, a twinge."

"I think it will be soon."

"I do too. I'm glad Levi will be home at noon. He is trying to stay near me."

Late that night Judith went with Levi and Lucy to the hospital, where in reasonably short order for a first baby — mid-morning of the next day — Lucy gave birth to a healthy little boy. Judith remembered that although Jacob, Alice's oldest, had been born in Calgary, she had made it to the hospital too late for the birth, and so little Daniel, or he who would in eight days be Daniel, was the only one of her grandchildren whose birth she had been a part of. And when she thought, first, that he would be her special grandchild, she remembered with something like an internal wail, that he would be in Israel and, as with Alice's three boys in Africa, she wouldn't even know him. Then she remembered, too, that she had deprived her mother of her grandchildren, and that her children had had as good as no grandparents at all, having rarely seen Jack's parents and Victor's being deceased.

It seemed to her in a moment of reverie halfway between sleep and waking, as she and Levi waited in the lounge while the nurses moved Lucy to her own room and bathed her and took care of her before they could see her and hug and kiss her, although Levi had been with her through the birth, that a pall of unacknowledged pain lay over modern families, at least in North America: that continuity was lost, that families no longer knew each other, that in the rush to modernity the greater value of familial love and support had been frayed and damaged almost beyond repair. That nobody had a real family anymore.

Not for the first time, she regretted in her deepest self her long-ago desertion of her parents and siblings. And yet . . .

Levi, smiling sleepily to himself, sat beside her and when he heard her sigh, he roused himself to ask unexpectedly, "Are you upset that she will convert? That her son will be a Jew?"

"Never upset," Judith said. "Not at all, don't even think of it. I might be upset if you were more . . . fanatical about your religion. If your religion oppressed her so she couldn't do anything she wanted to do. But a Jew? No. And to see her so content. Lucy hasn't much history of contentment."

Levi grinned at that. "So I found out," he said. "But now, she is fine." After a moment, he added, "We understand she is fragile." Judith's understanding was that this would be all she would know about Levi and her daughter. "I will show you her poems," he said, his voice changing, becoming lighter with something that sounded like delight. "She is published in some prestigious places. What a talent your daughter has. My wife." He said the last phrase softly, filled with a tender awe.

Lucinda and the baby had been home from the hospital three days when Levi announced that today Rivka was coming over with the children, bringing a woman hired to care for Lucy and Daniel, and that Judith was going to tour this very day the Old City at last.

She was surprised when, after some time driving through the city, Levi arrived at what he told her was the Damascus Gate, where he turned her over to a professional guide he had hired to take her around.

"He will take you through the Christian sector," Levi explained. "We Jews do not believe that the Saviour has come, so you see . . ." He threw out his hands apologetically. "I have found someone my family has known a long time, and he is absolutely to be trusted. He will keep you safe." This last worried Judith just a little. Surely anywhere one could trust one's professional guide; surely there should be a police and army presence that would keep everyone safe. But this was Israel, and she knew nothing and had no choice but to put her faith in Levi, who said that he would be waiting in this very place in the late afternoon to take her back to the house.

Her guide was a middle-aged man dressed in jeans and a shirt open at the throat.

"My name is Alex," he said. "And yes, I am born here, although my parents were Russians." He was short and blocky and wore a straw hat over curly blond hair. He took excessive care for her: that she was seeing what she wanted to see, or what he thought she would want to see, a woman from a Christian country, that she wasn't too tired and needed to sit.

"The sun is always too hot at this time of the year. This is a desert country," he told her. "Even here in Jerusalem in the cooler mountains, it is still too hot!" He kept her walking in the shade as far as possible, and handed her a bottle of cold water to carry with her. She followed him up hill and down dale, as she told her other daughters on her return to Canada, stumbling up and down stone stairs, entering the bowels of the stony earth, into caverns far below the cobbled or cutstone streets, where lamps lit the darkness and the crowds moved slowly, whispering, or else in utter silence, some crossing themselves. She remembered there being a lot of kneeling, and the longer she walked down avenues and winding lanes, and climbed and descended, and stared gravely at blocks of stone that were said to be sarcophagi or else places where important things had happened — she even leaned over the railing to stare into the Garden of Gethsemane with its ancient gnarled olive trees, that, to be frank, she thought impressively ugly — the more faintly ridiculous the whole business began to seem. And yet she walked and nodded and asked questions and obeyed her guide, and stared in wonder at walls and towers and turrets and the shining dome of the Golden Mosque, Al-Aqsa, the third holiest site to the followers of Islam, and where once the Great Temple of the Jews had been. How confusing things were: Christian beliefs juxtaposed to

Jewish beliefs, side by side and intermingled with Muslim beliefs. She would never straighten it all out.

Alex took her, also, to the women's side of the Wailing Wall. Beyond the crowd of praying, bowing women, rows deep, some in what looked like religious dress but most dressed as she was, the closest almost nose to the wall, and all the crevices into which messages were to be pressed bulging, overflowing with small, folded slips of paper, she could hear laughter and the gayest singing. It was coming from the other side of the wall that separated the women's side from the men's side. The men could dance and sing, she thought, why couldn't the women? But she was a Christian and had no right to say a word, although she did think of Lucinda, if briefly. Her own mother's voice in her head: *She made her bed, let her lie in it.* And yet, she had seen for herself: Lucinda had never seemed so much herself, so calm, so satisfied.

Which thought sobered her immensely, and she took the slip of paper and the pencil Alex had given her and wrote a note to God thanking him for bringing her most troubled daughter to happiness at last. Then she struggled to find a crevasse that would accept it, stuffing it in, pressing it as hard as she could with her fingertips so it would stay. When she saw all the folded, crumbled slips of paper lying in the stone dust and rubble at the bottom of the wall, she wanted to cry.

Afterwards, although she hid these thoughts completely from her daughter's new family, she would think of only two things: How utterly confused she was about where she had been, what she had seen, what was where, which stood for whatever it stood for. But more importantly, how completely disbelieving she found herself that any of the sites shown to her were the actual historic sites where the principal events of the Jesus, Joseph, and Mary story she had been taught as a child took place. And worse, that the principal events of that story had actually taken place at all, and that all that childhood teaching had been about only a myth; that if it had happened at all, it had happened in another realm, not on this earth.

When the day was finished, her guide took her again to the same gate where he had met her hours earlier, where Levi was waiting for her. On the slow drive home through heavy traffic — *this too is Jerusalem*, she dared to think — she remembered having asked her guide, "But, how do you know with such certainty that these events did take place here?" He had replied with a brusque and dismissive question: "If not here, then where?" She had been trying not to offend, but her guide had been irate at her questioning what was for him the simple truth.

This utter disbelief that had descended upon her, this stubborn emotional equanimity of hers in the face of the awed, transporting piety of most of the other visitors who surrounded her at every site, took her completely by surprise and greatly puzzled her. She could not credit it, nor could she explain it to herself; she hadn't felt disdain, nor was she repulsed, and she continued to be extremely interested; she simply believed none of it. It was archeology to her now, that was all. And, she supposed, sociology, and mythology and ...

What about Lucinda and her claim that 'here Spirit is everywhere?' She had no answer to that one, having not experienced such a thing herself.

Unless, she suddenly thought, maybe this complete and final disbelief that felt like a cleansing, not so much of her as of the very stones themselves — although her new absolute disbelief remained indisputable — was itself a manifestation of Lucinda's 'Spirit that is everywhere.' This erasing of the foundation of her family's world, even of that of the community in which she was raised, was so blasphemous to her that she was vaguely frightened. Maybe she was as guilty as any of the devout pilgrims she had walked with today of having led too narrow a life, of being too willing to accept indoctrination. *But wasn't I the one who walked away?*

Afterwards, she would retain only the memory of the shine of gold, of patches of rocks worn smooth from the hands or lips of pilgrims, the stone remainders of ancient temples or of Roman pillars, walkways, walls, and steps, the olive trees distorted by their vast age, of stumbling on the worn cobblestones, seeing the faces of the tourists, religious pilgrims or not, and the varied costumes, signifying she wasn't sure what, worn by local people. And, especially, the dark silhouettes of cypress trees reaching through the warm beige stone of the city toward the blazing blue sky.

The gift that had been given to her was to be free of the fairy tales in which she'd been raised, so that she could at last go to her own experiences and ideas in order to build a system in which she didn't have to strain to believe, but knew, brick by brick, to be true. And in which she might remain herself.

About Judaism and its beliefs, she would do her best to think nothing: she knew too little about the subject, and Judaism was so old that she could not even think about it as true or not true. Levi and his family were good people, they were excellent people; they had taken on her daughter when she, Judith, had given up on her; she would die before she would offend them. That was the third thing, after her confusion, and the descent of a final, cleansing disbelief in the Christian myth. When she returned, exhausted from the long day of trudging about, climbing stairs and descending them, she expressed her intense gratitude to Levi, Lucinda, and his family over and over again, wanting them to recognize her sincerity. In fact, she *was* grateful; she was sincere. Levi said, carefully, as Lucinda had already explained to Judith in one of their intimate talks, "We are not a devout family. If we were, I would not have been able to marry Lucinda. My family would have disowned me. But we make compromises with our systems of belief; we support each other. And always, we remain Jews: we remain Israelis."

There was one more thing she wished to do. She sat with Levi on the deck of his house a day after her visit to the Old City, while in the coolness of the house Lucinda nursed tiny, beautiful, already black-haired Daniel.

"I would like to go to Yad Vashem."

"You're sure? It is — difficult."

"It is the Holocaust Memorial. I feel I cannot leave Israel without paying my respects." She didn't think she would tell Levi that her Canadian father had been one of the American soldiers who had liberated Dachau, and that, in part, what he had seen there had not only destroyed him but had changed his entire family into something it wouldn't otherwise have been. Instead, she said, "I am prepared — as well as a non-Jew can be, I believe. In the small town I came from, there was an elderly Jewish couple. I didn't know the wife, but the husband and I chatted a few times. It turns out he had been in the camps." She indicated the inside of her forearm.

"Ahhh," Levi said. He was silent, thinking what to say to her, she knew it.

"I suppose, although I didn't think of it then, that he and his wife are part of what brought me here. I would have come for Lucinda," she put in quickly, "but they added a strong reason."

The Holocaust History Museum was housed in one of the most dramatic buildings she had ever been in. Part stone, in the interior mostly slabs of bare grey concrete, it was designed to embody a sense of foreboding, a heavy, dark mass, to convey the feeling of what it was to be a prisoner labouring under the weight of constant and most terrible fear and hopelessness, although the latter was contradicted in places by the building's soaring lines.

She walked slowly through gallery after gallery documenting in large photographs and artefacts — a battered Zyklon B can, for example, was the one she would remember most clearly — in chronological order, the history of the event called the Holocaust. How it began slowly, bit by bit; how it grew worse and worse; how it reached its peak of depravity, cruelty, utter senselessness, to its closure, if there could ever be any kind of closure for those who were there, in the camps, and for those who survived thinking forever of those who did not. It was clear to her now why it was said that the Holocaust was different from other mass extinctions through history. She saw this was true. *This* Holocaust would live on forever in infamy because of its meticulously planned and carefully carried out murders; because of its truly insane industrialization of genocide. And there was something bigger and darker behind that, which she felt all day as she walked, and that had come roaring out of a time and a darkness long before history.

Horror after horror, so that sometimes she had to look away, as much in disbelief that such things had happened on this same earth that she walked on as in revulsion and pity. But the photo whose contents would never leave her again was of a Catholic priest looking over his shoulder to stare at what as far as she could remember was a group of Nazi soldiers mercilessly beating some Jews. The priest was tall and thin, he was wearing a long, black cassock.

But what she could not forget was the priest's face. It was not the melancholy, pitying face of depictions of Mary, or even of those of Jesus on the cross, suffering and sorrowing over humanity. His look was beyond one of horror or shock or even fear. It was as if — how she struggled to find words to tell herself what his face had turned into — it was as if, in the extremity of his sudden knowledge, his shocked soul, stripped of sentiment, prevarication, denial, or mere pity, had risen up to become his face. His face was thus grotesque, warped, twisted out of shape, no longer quite human, or was the full and virtually unique expression of outraged humanity. It was a face that had seen a vision of hell.

Judith recognized it; it was a photo she had seen before and failed to understand but had been horrified by even then, whenever she had last seen it. Maybe when she had been studying those photos at the university library or in the books at the Military Museums back in Calgary. She thought now that despite all his piety, his years of study, his belief system, and his practice of it, he sees how inadequate it is in the face of the real thing, which clearly had been until this moment beyond his capacity to imagine. Or perhaps his desire to imagine. Of the suffering shown in picture after picture, she was speechless.

Not until she was back in Lucinda and Levi's house did she try to relate her experience of Yad Vashem to what she had found out about her father and his experience at Dachau in 1945. And then it occurred to her that Saul Richter might have been in one of the photos, and thought of the disembowelled hares hanging in the trees of the only Jews in town. Filled with revulsion, her immediate reaction had been to think that the perpetrator had to be, quite simply, stupid, ignorant of the implications of what he or they had done, and only accidentally invoking echoes of the camps. Now she saw the intentional symbolism, and that the act was loaded with threat.

She didn't want to tell Lucinda about any of what she had seen at Yad Vashem, and told her only when she asked, "It was endlessly interesting — and too terrible for words. The research part of it, documenting the families, the library and so on, they were especially notable." Lucinda didn't inquire any further. Nor did she say much to Levi about her experience other than to lower her head when he asked, and mutter clichés. Seeing her inability to speak about it to him, he busied himself with a newspaper.

The bris was held in the home of Levi's parents, Abira and Yosef, because it was bigger and better appointed. On the eighth day from the baby's birth, when the guests had gathered, the ceremony of the removal of the baby's foreskin took place, the rabbi serious and careful, Lucinda looking away at the vital moment, the baby making a short cry and then — that was that. The naming ritual took place; the baby was declared to be named Daniel, and then the celebration began.

Here Judith met more people than whose names she would ever be able to remember, and after the ceremony was over, little Daniel was passed around and cooed at and exclaimed over. Judith, by this time, found herself in so heightened a state of receptiveness that she drank two glasses of wine, at the same time hardly noticing she had, while also hoping that the wine might deaden her too-intense feelings. Lucinda sat in an armchair, in the excitement finally rising and moving around freely to laugh and crow and hug the people who entered the living room after having passed by the soon-groaning table where the gifts for the baby were piled.

Another long table was covered with plates, trays, pans, and baskets of food, although helpful relatives she couldn't have named pointed out that what she thought was chicken was instead tofu in a sauce, that dairy and meats would never, in a religious home, be served at the same table, and that in this family all compromised so as to make it possible for all members to be included. Levi and Lucinda didn't keep a kosher kitchen — here, Judith gave up. Possibly Abira and Josef did, but she wasn't going to ask. One of the guests had even brought a Yemini delicacy, compressed layers of phyllo pastry cut into cubes and served with slices of hard-boiled egg, reminding her again that she was in the Middle East, of all the extraordinary places, and that although she had seen people she thought were Arabs everywhere, she had not spoken to or met one, other than the shopkeepers who had called to her as she passed by in the alleyways and from the shops of the Old City.

When she had pointed this out to Levi's mother, Abira said that nowadays some of the young Israelis were taking lessons in Arabic. "It is good," she said. "It used to be you wouldn't do that." And later she said, "When you come next time, we will take you to a kibbutz. Yosef was raised in one."

On the plane home, once the confusion and noise and colour of her Jerusalem experience was behind her, she would think more about what she had learned there about human capabilities for doing evil to others than she would about Lucinda and the grandson who had been named Daniel. It was not that she had failed to know the world was full of horrors — she had looked after neglected, abandoned, abused children and young people for most of forty years. More than once she had thought she couldn't go on in that work because she had seen more than anyone should have to see of what could happen to the innocents and the helpless.

After a while, her thoughts began to shift to the fact that not only was Mr. Richter still alive but was leading a steady, quiet life with his wife and seemed to have overcome his torments somehow: By rising above them? By placing his faith somewhere else? By helping her even though he knew nothing of her, only intuited somehow that she had needed help? And even in the face of all that had happened to the Jewish people through history, even through the Holocaust, anti-Semitism was still alive and well and living in places like Wisdom, Saskatchewan.

Nearly twenty hours later, she disembarked in Calgary, dazed with exhaustion and also relieved to be back on safe territory. Coming out of customs, she looked about for Catherine, and, not seeing her anywhere, was about to phone her on her cell when she heard a male voice calling her name. Turning, she saw it was Gilles, rushing across the crowded hall toward her.

"I couldn't reach you in Wisdom, and your cellphone was always turned off, so I called Catherine. I said she didn't need to leave work, that I would pick you up."

They hugged perfunctorily, Gilles kissing her cheek. In the car, speeding down the Deerfoot Trail, she asked him how he was doing. Months had passed since Camille's death, during which time his phone calls had grown farther apart and finally stopped altogether. She had thought about it and decided she would let him go, a decision she found less painful than she had thought it would be. She supposed she would spend the rest of her life alone. Men did not want old women; not even old men wanted them.

"What is this about, Gilles?" she asked him finally. "I've been through a lot these last few months, I haven't spoken to you since maybe June, and I sure don't have the energy for nonsense." She was grateful that he didn't ask her what she meant by nonsense.

He said, "I have been dating," and laughed out loud. He was thinner, as always, needed a shave, and his hair was longer, freeing some of its waviness. She would not tell him he looked good.

"And?"

"There are lots of fifty-year-old divorcées out there, I found out. I was amazed. I dated a few of them. Nothing much, nothing happened. One of them still phones me." He laughed again. "Samantha, Ardis, and Jane."

"Nice names," Judith said, but she was fighting to keep her eyes open.

"I might have settled down with any of them. They were all good women. Good enough. As good as I am." He had paused between each sentence, as if puzzled.

"Was it that you didn't love any of them?"

"I could have loved them, in time, I think." But he still sounded puzzled.

"Love is not love which alters when it alteration finds . . ." Judith yawned, continued. "It is the star to every wand'ring bark . . ."

"Oh yes," he said, laughing a little. "Quote Shakespeare at me." After a moment, he said, "Maybe you're right," but he didn't sound convinced. She knew they were both remembering Camille.

"And you?" he asked. "What kind of a trip did you have? Israel! My, my!"

"It was fascinating," she said. "Absolutely fascinating and wonderful. And Lucinda is all right. She is the best I've ever seen her." Gilles had been with her through the Thomas thing and the wedding in New York to Levi that Judith hadn't gone to. "And the baby! Daniel is his name. He is adorable."

"Unlike most babies," Gilles teased her. But she was sound asleep,

waking only to enter Catherine's condo. Gilles carried up her suitcases, lighter now that the gifts she had brought with her to Israel were
left behind, set them in the hall, kissed her again, first on one cheek
and then the other, said he would call her in a couple of days when she
woke up as he had much to talk about with her, and left her, closing
the door quietly behind him.

LATE FALL

The pain in Judith's neck, shoulders, and down her arm, at its worst, also in her back, had dissipated bit by bit over the preceding months, until she could no longer remember the last time she had been bothered. She still had headaches now and then, but they were milder, and she had learned what not to do in order to avert them, or at least to minimize them.

"I don't go tobogganing, downhill skiing, or wrestle, or play basketball," she told Alice when she asked. "Otherwise, I'm fine."

"Considering how bad the concussion was, not even a year ago now, I think it's a wonder you've recovered so well. It takes some people a couple of years, and some never fully recover." But Alice had lost weight, her long blue lace dress was loose at the waist, and they had had to use dress tape to glue the fabric to her skin so the neckline wouldn't gape open. She kept glancing across to Dwight, who was in conversation with his oldest son Jacob, who had come with his wife Janine and baby Amos — another boy, as if the universe was trying to make up for Judith's all-female family, and who was Judith's first great-grandchild, his skin almost as ebony as his stunning mother's.

If Alice had lost weight, Dwight was thinner and was bald from chemo. His prostate cancer had spread, and things were not looking good, or so Judith suspected, although both Alice and Dwight spoke firmly of the time when Dwight would be "through this" and they could make plans for their retirement in Canada. Only the middle boy, Joshua, had elected, for the time being anyway, to stay on in Africa. Judith wondered where Jeremy, Alice and Dwight's youngest, had gotten to, but spotted him leaning against the far wall of the hall, chatting up one of the bridesmaids, a pretty blonde girl who taught with Jessica named Donna-Lee Chomyn or Chornin or something like that. She wondered what Jeremy knew about chatting up girls, given his religious upbringing in Tanzania.

"Ah well, the language of love is universal," she said out loud, without meaning to. Seeing where her eyes were going, Alice laughed.

"He does like girls, that one. I'd be happy for a wedding — in due course, I mean," glancing back to Dwight.

They were in the community hall in Parmeter, the village whose name she could never remember. The wedding was over; it had been several hours earlier in the big white church a block away, a United Church minister presiding. The church had been packed; most of the attendees were strangers to Judith, but besides Jessica's own family and their spouses or partners, there was all of Ethan's large clan too; the remainder of the guests consisted of friends of Jessica's and Ethan's, both separately and together, and of course, all the teachers from the school another block away, where both Ethan and Jessica taught.

She began to count off those who had not come: Victor, who was dead; Lucinda, Levi, and Daniel, because the baby was too young for such a long trip; Alice and Dwight's middle son, Joshua, who, truth be told, seemed to be giving his parents some kind of trouble. Judith had tried and failed to find Skye Shot in the Head, with whom she had lost touch some time in her twenties and was told she had long ago moved to Vancouver, and that when the land claims settlement had come through for his own reserve, William Bear, by then armed with a degree in business, had gone back to help with the planning and work the financial settlement had engendered: besides the selection of land, new facilities for the reserve community. Judith had wanted in some helpless way to try to make up for her neglect of these good people in all the years after she had left their home, and, failing, had thought how much she would have to atone for if she ever made it to the other side and wasn't just snuffed out as irredeemable at the instant of her death. Which implied, she realized, that she suspected there was an entity who, or that, decided.

She enumerated who had come: Abigail and Rick and their son and daughter and their spouses; Samuel and Sylvia, although not their children, all too busy in the big cities they, so far anyway, had ended up in: Montreal, Tokyo, San Francisco; Alice and Jessica's father Jack and his current wife, Marilyn, a beauty in a cream-coloured suit trimmed with beading as if she were the mother of the bride — Judith wore a draped, pomegranate-coloured silk dress with long sleeves to hide her newly flabby arms; Catherine and her new beau, Will, another lawyer but from the smaller, less demanding firm Catherine had moved to since her divorce, who looked too much like Ian for Judith's taste; of course Alice and Dwight and their other two sons. Judith hadn't seen Jack in nearly twenty years and was pleased to note that she didn't feel much of anything when she had had to shake his hand and meet Marilyn, who turned out to be a considerable bit older than she looked at first glance. And her hair was dyed, although expensively so.

Judging by the fragrances wafting from the kitchen, dinner was about to be served. Any minute now Jessica and Ethan would arrive from the official picture-taking, ready to settle in at the head table where she sat with Gilles next to Jessica's place; Jack and Marilyn sat on Ethan's far side next to his parents so Judith and Jack wouldn't have to talk to each other. People had stopped milling about or walking back and forth from the bar and were settling in at the tables. On the stage behind the head table, the band's instruments were set up and waiting for the musicians to arrive for the dance that would begin after the dinner.

Ethan's friends had helped the women carry in the three-tiered, white wedding cake with the tiny bride and groom on top. It was draped with icing-bunting decorated with pale pink icing roses and was quite beautiful, although Judith worried that it was too heavy for the small table where it had been set to be admired while waiting for the cake-cutting later on. Others, Judith didn't know who, had decorated the hall with pink lanterns and strings of tiny white lights; flights of pink and white balloons were tied to every table, and a large number were held above the dance floor in an enormous net. It was, she thought — *old cynical me!* — a veritable fairyland, which made her smile to herself, thinking about the rituals designed to keep them all safe.

Jessica had insisted that Judith and Catherine come with her while she chose her wedding dress. Judith liked a slender silk one with a long straight coat and stiff pearl-studded collar, but Jessica said she wasn't tall enough for it. She vetoed Catherine's draped and bustled choice too, as "much too elegant for a woman like me." She didn't explain what "a woman like me" meant, and neither Cathy nor Judith asked her. Alice had been at the cancer clinic with Dwight and wasn't able to go with them, but both she and Lucinda in faraway Jerusalem received instant photos of the choices on their phones and texted their opinions of each dress and cheered the final choice. Jessica shook her head no to half a dozen dresses that had unusual trim or styling, or that she judged too revealing — too tight, or bared her shoulders and arms completely.

In the end, she chose a white ballgown-style dress with, rather than sequins, pearls, or rhinestones artfully sprinkled over it, white velvet dots the size of nickels, called "flocking," on the chiffon overskirt, the bodice, and the shawl collar, all of this over a plain white silk dress.

"A sort of Daisy Mae dress," Cathy said — Judith was surprised her youngest knew who Daisy Mae was — and she and her half-sister nearly died laughing at the comparison. But Jessica still stuck with her pretty, although conventional, choice. And it did, in some odd way Judith couldn't put her finger on, suit her, or it brought out some "Jessica essence" that made the dress just right on her. Judith still hoarded a little of the glow of happiness that had suffused them all that day.

A noise at the entrance, a bustling about, announced Jessica and Ethan squeezing in the door, Jessica using her free hand to try to flatten the dress's full skirt to make room for Ethan — brown-haired, tall, slender, and sort of gently homely-looking, with a smile that warmed the room — to enter at the same time as she did. They were holding hands; they were both laughing; even from the far end of the hall, Judith saw that their eyes were full of light. Everyone stood and clapped, and some called good wishes, unintelligible in the general racket, and a clinking of spoons against water glasses began, with Judith, lost herself in their ritual, thinking disapprovingly it was too soon for that. People were taking photos with their phones, and children, halted only for a second by the wondrous sight, were now running about noisily, screaming and calling to each other and gleefully popping balloons if people didn't lift them out of their reach.

Students from the high school began to serve the roast beef — girls in white blouses and black skirts and boys in white shirts and black pants. The noise level was deafening: laughter everywhere in the room, mingling with the clinking of glasses and people chattering loudly. Then there were toasts: Jack, father of the bride, did not disgrace himself. The best man, Ethan's friend, stumbled, skipped to the end, but once his glass was raised, everyone agreed he'd given a totally fantastic speech. The family politely ignored Marilyn, who drank an awful lot of wine, Judith noticed, and was nastily pleased and then ashamed, and thought that she would later make a point of talking to the woman, and then the band arrived and were beginning to play as the last of the dishes were carried by the same high school girls and boys back to the kitchen to be washed, and the dining tables pushed to the sides to open the dance floor.

Eventually it was time for Jessica and Ethan's sets of parents to take over the floor for a couple of embarrassed rounds. Judith barely noticed she was dancing with Jack, both of them looking over the other's shoulder with fake smiles pasted on their faces, and as soon as possible they switched partners so that she danced with Ethan's father, John, and then that was over too, and the dance began properly, and most decorum slowly vanished, to be replaced by a large, noisy party. And Judith had been right: much earlier, when the cake was to be cut, some of the men had tried to move it and the small table had partially collapsed, sending the cake sliding floorward, to be caught by a groomsman whose tuxedo jacket now had a shiny, sticky streak all down one arm and over half of his chest. "A drycleaner will get that out in a second," a bosomy older woman informed him, as everyone crowded around him to help and the bridesmaids worked to repair the ruined patch of the cake, and everyone else exclaimed at first in horror and then laughed and then ate the cake, or saved it to put under their pillows so as to dream of the love to come.

Hours later, the hall emptied and mostly cleaned — the high school kids again, those not too stoned to figure out how to clean, and also all the adult males who stacked the chairs and took down the tables to stack them too, after the women had removed the paper tablecloths, scrunching them and stuffing them into giant garbage bags. Apparently, Jessica had organized a committee to finish the cleanup the next morning, as she and Ethan were leaving at once for Calgary and a honeymoon in Mexico.

At last Judith and Gilles could leave, but they had chosen to stay in Jessica's house for the night, perhaps even to help with the cleaning the next morning. Everyone else either lived nearby, was staying in the town's only motel, or was heading back to their homes in Calgary. Thank God, Judith said to Gilles, that it had neither rained, snowed, or hailed, nor was there an avalanche, a flood, a whirlwind, or a firestorm. And not more than half the guests had drunk too much. The other half was driving home the first half. And wasn't that yellow dress the Holmes girl wore just the loveliest thing you ever saw? And couldn't that tall Barnes boy dance? What a pleasure to watch him!

Something seemed to have happened to the motion-sensor yard light, because it didn't go on when Gilles drove the car into Jessica's yard. He left the headlights on until Judith went inside and turned on the lights in the house. Then he followed her in. The back of the car was full of wedding presents people had brought to the dance, but they would just have to stay out there for the night; Gilles was too tired to cart them in, and, as everyone knew, Jessica and Ethan had left, so there would be no *chivaree*, and the presents were safe and so were they from the pot-banging and the loud singing of probably indecent songs and from having to invite in the drunken people who were assailing them for one last drink.

When they were ensconced at last in Jessica and Ethan's queen-size bed in the heart of the cabin, Judith said, "I can't remember being so happy."

Gilles held her, kissing her forehead. "Not even at our wedding?" They had married in late September at city hall, a judge they had never seen before and never would again presiding grumpily, as if he thought this was all a big waste of his valuable time. For all they knew, it was. And Judith had bought herself a teal blue, light wool suit, very stylish and expensive, with matching shoes, and had carried a bouquet of hard-to-find lilies of the valley, and Adrianna had taken her lunch hour to be her witness while Gilles brought his oldest son, Christian, who happened to be in town that weekend. Otherwise, it was just the two of them, including when they went to lunch afterwards, and then back home to the condo they had bought together. They made a handsome couple, though neither was without misgivings, and said so, and worried about how things would be in a year, or two years, but, knowing as they did that anything could happen and there was no predicting the future, decided to give it a go anyway.

"Not even at our wedding," she said. "I thought maybe four months ago that the world had ended, that it *should* end, that we didn't deserve it. All we humans do is despoil it and kill and maim each other."

"Sometimes you can't see the light for all the dark," he said, yawning. She leaned over and kissed his forehead and thought, *I guess this is love*, and was glad.

Outside, the wind had picked up; it was four in the morning; before long there was a pattering on the roof, and the wind moving through the trees grew louder, heaving the heavy branches about and causing them to whistle, drone, creak, and thump. It was only late October; surely there wasn't a storm already.

"Winter is coming," Gilles said, but nearly asleep, Judith heard his voice as if it had come into the room on the wind.

For some reason, she suddenly remembered the girl, Tonya Nichol, the one people said was missing from Wisdom. Everyone was mystified and spoke of her in near whispers, as if to speak aloud about what had happened to her would awaken evil. Abbie had told her only that, yes, she was a real girl, fifteen or sixteen, exceptionally pretty and a natural blonde, whose parents farmed on the high plateau north of town, poor people but decent. She had been gone perhaps six months, no one knew for sure, much less where she had gone. "Some say she is dead," Abbie said. Then, unusual for her, "I think so myself." But she refused to say why she thought this. Judith thought it more likely that she was chained to a bed in a putrid basement in a house in some ordinary neighbourhood in Calgary or Vancouver, by now an addict — softened up so she could go into high-end prostitution — and Harris, whoever he was, paid off for catching her and bringing her to her captors.

Her mind wandered to Saul Richter and his wife, Ada, who had had to leave Wisdom, and then on it meandered, though, it seemed, purposefully, to Dachau and the horrors there, whose tentacles had reached into every corner of the known world, even to gutted hares in Wisdom.

She fell asleep and dreamed that heavy black beetles were crawling onto her forearms and delving inside her skin, turning into black, beetle-size discs as they slipped inside to form blackish, disfiguring lumps under her skin. She tried to stop them, found that stopping them wasn't within her power. But on the outside of her left arm, just above the wrist, she managed to grasp one before the skin sealed over it and pulled on it, refusing to let go as she wrested it upward, the flesh around it swollen, pale and damp, and the disc, as she pulled it out, losing its shape, fading to a harmless light pink. How triumphant she felt that she had removed one of them, and knew that the upturned flesh would sink, and the scar where the disc had been would eventually heal over. The rest of the discs, though, remained buried in her flesh, faintly visible as grey lumps marring the smoothness of her arms.

She woke, horrified enough to pull herself into a sitting position beside the slumbering Gilles, drew a deep breath, took her bearings, calming herself, and slid back down under the covers, closing her eyes and vowing not to think of it again. She would be an old woman, Gilles long dead, when she began that final assessment of her life, before she would feel she really understood the dream.

But before long she was asleep again, and in this dream everything in Jessica's house was made of large, creamy white flowers of a kind she had never seen before; Judith was riding in a carriage made of them, travelling slowly down an avenue lined so thickly with them it was as if she were passing between high banks of delicately glinting snow. And she, gowned in white flowers, going to what destination she did not know.

The End

ACKNOWLEDGEMENTS

I think of *Leaving Wisdom* as the novel in what has turned out to be my series of novels about the rural agricultural people of the southern Great Plains of Canada, in particular the women of that world (excepting *The Gates of the Sun*), although — who knows — there might be time for one more in my writing life. My first and greatest thank you has to be to the Butala family, into which I married in 1976 and by so doing was brought into a world about which I knew virtually nothing other than what I had learned, as a small child, about nature. The larger area and its people, both farmers and ranchers, whether they meant to or not, taught me about that agricultural world and its stresses and pleasures as well as how it has evolved from the days of the first settlers. I thank all of them too. Thanks also to my Israeli friends, who gave me a glimpse of that fascinating world, not only when I visited them in Tel Aviv. Thanks to Coteau Books (RIP) and to my peerless editor there, Dave Margoshes, who worked with a manuscript in many ways different from this book. Thanks to the wonderful people at Thistledown who brought my manuscript to life at last as *Leaving Wisdom*: to Elizabeth Philips, who gave me half its name, and to Naomi Lewis, who edited it with such care and intelligence, and who helped me keep track of facts about Judaism and to

249

my diligent copy editor Bobbi Mitchell. My agent, Marilyn Biderman, has been a lifeline. I couldn't keep going without the support of my two remaining sisters, Cynthia and Deanna, and that of my son, Sean Hoy, his wife Carol, and my grown grandchildren, Declan and Maeve. Peter Butala and my parents, Archie and Amy Le Blanc, remain potent figures in my life and in my writing.

SHARON BUTALA is the author of twenty-one books of fiction and nonfiction, numerous essays and articles, some poetry and five produced plays. She published her first novel in 1984, *Country of the Heart*, which was nominated for the Books in Canada First Novel Award, followed closely by a collection of short stories, *Queen of the Headaches* (shortlisted for the Governor General's Award). Sharon's books have been on the Canadian bestseller lists, including her memoir, *The Perfection of the Morning*, which reached #1 in July 1994. Her work has been nominated for, and received, numerous awards. Most recently, her story collection *Season of Fury and Wonder* was nominated for the Rogers Trust Fiction Prize and won the City of Calgary's W.O. Mitchell Book Prize for 2020. She is an Officer of the Order of Canada. She lives in Calgary.